9-22

THE INKWELL CHRONICLES

CHRONICLES

The Ink of Elspet

J. D. PEABODY

Nashville, Tennessee

ISBNs: 978-1-5460-0198-0 (hardcover), 978-1-5460-0200-0 (ebook)

WorthyKids
Hachette Book Group
1290 Avenue of the Americas
New York, NY 10104

Library of Congress Cataloging-in-Publication Data
Names: Peabody, J. D., author.
Title: The inkwell chronicles : the ink of Elspet / J.D. Peabody.
Description: New York, NY : WorthyKids, [2022] | Audience: Ages 8–12. |
    Summary: When eleven-year-old Everett and his little sister Bea discover
    a curious pen, its enchanted ink leads them to a magical world, where
    they must find and protect the last Inkwell and save their missing
    father, but to do so, Everett must tap into the most magical power of
    all—his courage.
Identifiers: LCCN 2022000999 | ISBN 9781546001980 (hardcover)
Subjects: CYAC: Magic—Fiction. | Brothers and sisters—Fiction. | Missing
    persons—Fiction. | Fantasy. | LCGFT: Fantasy fiction.
Classification: LCC PZ7.1.P39 In 2022 | DDC [Fic]—dc23
LC record available at https://lccn.loc.gov/2022000999

Cover illustration by Kristina Kister
Map illustration by Jensine Eckwall
Calamus Scroll illustration, facing page, by Addison Peabody
Designed by Georgina Chidlow-Irvin and Bart Dawson

Printed and bound in the United States of America
LSC-C
Printing 1, 2022

To Isaac, Addison, and Annika,
who continue to bring joy and play into my life.
You inspired these pages, even as you outpaced them.
So glad I'm your dad.

OSGOOD // DaVINCI

CALAMUS SCROLL

No. 157303   OXFORD

Fig.1.

For the transcription of written messages

The Day It All Changed

"Are you out there?"

The voice came from inside the old trunk.

A frantic pounding accompanied it.

"Ev! Ev, are you there? I can't hear you counting."

It was Everett Drake's little sister, Bea. He had locked her in the trunk, daring her to escape in less than a minute.

"Ev! Answer me!"

He didn't even hear her.

The soggy London sky seeped rain like water from a sponge, spilling dreariness down the windowpanes and giving Everett an excuse to stay inside the vicarage, reading.

Vicarages are built to house ministers and their families. This one was especially drab, save for the turret some builder added as an afterthought. It was a bit like dressing up an ugly dog in a colorful sweater, and the effect was not entirely convincing.

Still, the room at the top of the turret was just castle-like enough for all Everett and Bea's imagined escapades, and just enough removed from the rest of the residence to discourage the housekeeper, Mrs. Crimp, from monitoring their activities. Avoiding her attention was always preferable.

This particular day, Everett sprawled out on the floor upstairs, chin resting in his hands, engrossed in one of his favorite comic books, *Max Courageous: Into Tomorrow*. The daring adventurer Maximillian Courageous (or MC, as Everett liked to call him) was piloting his ship through the galaxy to escape—

The trunk lid flew open, and Bea burst forth, hands above her head, cheeks flushed with exertion, and hair a defiant mess. "Was that a record?" She lowered her arms and eyed her brother with suspicion. "You weren't even counting, were you?"

Ever since finding a biography of Harry Houdini at the library, Bea had been determined to learn the skills of an escape artist. Ambitious as that may be for an eight year old, she kept asking Everett to tie her shoes together or trap her in her room or lock her in the old trunk. (There was a nice way to cheat when breaking out of the trunk, because she was too smart to purposely trap herself anywhere. But her brother didn't need to know how she did it.) She had developed her very own Rules of Escape, number one of which was to make your brother play his part.

Despite her glowering, Everett didn't look up. "Sorry. You didn't give me enough time." He tried to sound apologetic. "I'm pretty sure that was your fastest yet."

All in all, it had begun as a typical day in the vicarage.

Some people might imagine growing up next door to a church would be a dreadful bore, that having a vicar for a father sounds like the opposite of fun. But Everett and Bea's father was the Reverend Marcus Drake, and he was anything but dull.

Marcus was the creator of the Max Courageous comics. His lifelike illustrations brought the stories vividly to life.

It's fair to say comic books are an unlikely hobby for a clergyman. Yet Marcus saw it as a calling. He hoped his stories would inspire young people, especially his own children.

"You can have greater influence than you know," he would often tell Everett and Bea. "Doing the right thing takes real bravery and integrity. Your actions matter more than any superhero's."

Everett found that hard to believe. He didn't feel very strong, let alone brave. He couldn't picture himself making any difference in the world, the way his father had, fighting Nazis during the war and doing church work ever since.

"I wish I could show you what I see," Marcus told him, "because you're a remarkable boy, Everett. You're interested in the world. And it's far more meaningful to be interestED than to try to be interestING."

Everett wasn't quite sure what he meant by that. He longed to be clever like MC, to do important things and live out great stories. Which is why he often retreated to the turret to lose himself in his comic books.

This afternoon, however, Bea had her own plans for her brother, and reading was not on the agenda. She stood in the trunk preparing to give him a scolding even MC would fear, but just as she opened her mouth, their father's voice boomed up the stairs. "Everett! Bea! Come down and say goodbye."

Bea hopped out of the trunk, slammed the lid shut, and raced toward the stairs. "Beat you to the bottom!"

Everett followed more slowly, sensing that familiar, hollow churning in his stomach. It happened whenever their father took a trip.

He hated feeling like such a baby. He was eleven. A boy his age should be able to go to bed without being tucked in by his father.

Perhaps he'd feel differently if he had a mother at home, but he didn't. She had died giving birth to Bea. A long time ago. Everett barely remembered her. All he could picture of her was a yellow dress and her warm, smiling eyes.

Eyes completely unlike the housekeeper's, who would be scrutinizing his every move for an entire week.

The Drake family shared the vicarage with Isadora Crimp. Not by choice—the spiteful woman came with the house. Mrs. Crimp (or, The Cramps, as the children referred to her behind her back) looked as unfortunate as her name, with a pinched hook of a nose and gray-streaked hair swept up into the most severe knot atop her head.

"You, boy," she screeched each time she spoke to Everett. It was always "You, boy—step aside!" Or "You, boy—stop that incessant noise!" Everett was convinced she didn't even know his real name.

Isadora's husband, Reginald Crimp, had been a previous vicar of St. Francis. Not the holiest of men, Reginald ran off with a great deal of the church's money, leaving Isadora and the congregation in a quandary.

After much deliberation, the church elders voted three to two to keep her on as caretaker for the vicarage. Without any prospects of her own, she had no choice but to accept their charity, and she resented it mightily.

She made that very clear the day the Drake family moved in. "I am not here to supervise your offspring, Reverend," she stated flatly.

Everett decided she must have a different understanding of "not supervising," because the old buzzard circled them constantly, watching for any sign of weakness. One day, he tracked mud into the living room and she rapped him across the shins with a broom handle. "You, boy—scrub that mess clean or I will tell the vicar."

Everett preempted her report and told his father himself.

Marcus frowned as he listened. "I'm sorry, son."

Everett bent down and gingerly touched his lower legs. "Why does she have to be so mean?"

"She's had a rough go of things."

"That's no excuse."

"And I promise I'll speak with her," said Marcus. "But she's not your enemy, all right?"

While that may have been true, sharing a common adversary with Bea made Everett fiercely protective of his little sister. The turret became their safe haven since The Cramps had bad knees and disliked negotiating the stairs.

But at present, Marcus stood in the entryway, looking very official in his black suit and white clerical collar, with the same straight posture as his army days. The silver rims of his glasses accentuated the flecks of silver sprinkled through his dark hair.

His face lit up when he saw his daughter scrambling down the stairs. Placing his briefcase on the floor, he opened his arms wide just as Bea launched herself at him from the third step.

Bea squeezed him with all her might. "Why do you have to go clear to Scotland?"

Marcus set her down, kissing the top of her head. "If I could stay with you forever, I would. But every once in a while, I have to conduct a secret mission."

"Does it have to do with MC?"

Marcus raised his finger to his lips. "Shh. You didn't hear it from me." He gave her a knowing wink, then turned, searching for Everett. "There you are! Come on down, son." Marcus checked his watch. "I don't want to miss my train."

Everett shuffled his way to the bottom of the stairs. "Can't we stay with someone else?"

Marcus placed both hands on his shoulders. "Listen, Ev.

You're the man of the house while I'm gone. I'm counting on you to look after your sister, all right? Now let's join hands for the blessing."

After saying a brief prayer, he drew Everett and Bea close for one last hug.

Everett didn't lift his arms to return the embrace. The thought of a whole week in the care of The Cramps filled him with resentment. He shook himself free.

Marcus picked up his briefcase and travel bag. "I love you two," he said. "See you soon." With that, he stepped outside and into the waiting cab.

Bea followed him to the porch and waved madly until the car was out of sight.

Everett chose to remain inside—a choice that haunted him for a very long time.

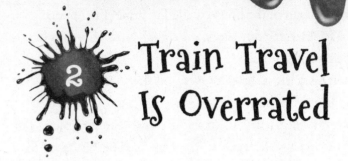

Train Travel Is Overrated

One week later, the *Night Scotsman Express* streaked across the sleeping English countryside, playing an endless drum roll as it thundered back down the tracks toward London.

Marcus sat in the dining car. Grateful as he was for the end of tea rationing, his cup sat untouched on the table. He glanced from the window back to his wristwatch for the hundredth time. Five thirty-two. He could hardly wait to be home with his children.

The train left Aberdeen hours ago, with no hint of a threat, but the uneasiness would not let him sleep.

Seasoned ministers tend to be good judges of character, and no one rang any alarm bells for Marcus on this trip. The train was full of weary business travelers, families, and haggard soldiers (including a handful of rambunctious American servicemen)—all paying attention to everything except the middle-aged clergyman. One amusing benefit of being a vicar was that whenever he wore his collar, strangers avoided eye contact.

This far into the journey, everyone was settled in and trying to catch whatever sleep possible. Yes, Marcus was sure it would be safe. And since he couldn't sleep, he might as well get some work done.

He grabbed his briefcase and made his way back toward the rear of the train, where he could be guaranteed a measure of privacy in his sleeping berth.

The last compartment before the sleeper car had no passengers, only a conductor standing in front of him, his large girth wedged between seats like a cork in a bottle. "Turning in, Reverend?"

The man's mouth was entirely hidden by an enormous red-and-silver mustache, but his eyes made it clear there was a smile under there somewhere.

"For a bit," Marcus said, rubbing the back of his neck. "It's been a long day. And night."

The conductor nodded knowingly and tipped his hat, revealing a mop of unruly red-and-gray curls. "Indeed it has. Rest assured I'll do what I can to prevent any disturbances for the remainder of our trip."

Marcus thanked him, and the conductor slid open the door at the end of the aisle. The sleeper car was dim and hushed. Individual berths lined both sides of the aisle, swathed in curtains that swayed with the motion of the train. Marcus was grateful he wasn't hoping to sleep, because some rather dramatic snores reverberated from the bunk below his. He clambered into his spot and pulled the curtain tightly closed.

Finally. No one would find him here. Switching on the light above his bunk, he unlocked his briefcase, pulling out rolled-up papers. Closing the case again, he unfurled the documents across it.

They were storyboards—frames for the next *Max Courageous* comic book. The images were so lifelike, and those colors! Unbelievably vivid. He knew pride was a sin, yet Marcus couldn't help but be impressed. Hard to believe these words and illustrations emerged from his pen.

He retrieved it from his jacket pocket. Marcus bit his lip, hesitating. He had been warned about the risks of using it in unsecured public spaces—places where others might take notice. But surely there was no harm here, hidden in a private compartment of a moving train.

He unscrewed the cap and started to write. It only produced a dry, scratching sound. The pen needed refilling.

Reaching back into the briefcase, he carefully withdrew a glass container as big as a milk bottle, filled with a bluish black ink. Marcus held it up. Like a liquid kaleidoscope, the appearance of this Ink changed as you rotated it. Maybe the vibration of the train was playing tricks on him, but the bottle itself seemed to pulsate. Marcus thought of the people who had entrusted it to him and their fears of being caught. He hoped they were safe.

Removing the stopper, he dipped the fountain pen in to refill it. Just as the tip reached the bottle, the train lurched around a bend, knocking the Ink over and spilling some of the mysterious liquid.

Muttering a few rather unvicarlike curses, Marcus whisked out his handkerchief to absorb as much as possible. What a waste. He wished he had not been in such a rush to start working.

Searching for somewhere to stow the soaked handkerchief, he removed his glasses case from his pocket and tucked the wet rag inside. The case was waterproof and airtight, so at least it wouldn't stain his jacket.

With a fresh sheet of paper atop the briefcase, he soon became absorbed in his drawing and forgot the spill entirely.

Two things happened as he worked—one beautiful and one inevitable.

The beautiful was obvious: Lines streamed at a furious rate from the tip of the pen, propelling themselves outward in all directions. Images practically drew themselves across the page as fast as Marcus could move his hand.

Every color flowed at once from the same source— delicious reds and brilliant aquas and rich purples. Each hue knew exactly where to land on the page. It was magical, except the ideas all came from his own mind. Whenever he held the pen, Marcus practically became Max Courageous, each scene as clear as if he were living it himself.

The pen called forth all the best in Marcus's imagination and made it even better. No, it was as if the Ink made the story what it was meant to be all along, as if it released some Creative Something deep inside of him that had been locked away for a very long time. It was Marcus in print—gloriously, wonderfully in print. That was the beautiful part.

The inevitable part was the aroma released when the bottle was opened. To be sure, the average nose would never detect even the slightest of odors. But the fresh Ink emitted a powerful identifying scent that floated far and wide. And certain individuals, such as the tall military officer sitting in the first-class coach with his eyes closed, could smell it as clearly as a hound picks up the scent of a fox.

When the tiniest atoms of Ink wafted their way toward the front of the train, he breathed them in. His eyes flew open, scanning the car for what caused the offensive stench. With one gloved hand, he suppressed a cough.

Rising to his full height in the aisle, the man cut an imposing figure in his uniform. His dark hair formed an oil slick above his colorless face.

And then there were his eyes. Upon smelling the Ink, his irises and pupils turned to liquid. They melted from symmetrical circles into shapeless black puddles swirling freely around his eyeballs.

He stood for a moment between the seats, cracking his neck from side to side.

Then he went hunting for the source of the Stink.

Moving deliberately with the trace of a limp, he gained speed as he went. All his senses confirmed he was close. His breathing grew shallow and labored. His eyes stung. His throat grew tight. But his instincts had been right to catch this train. The Stink was on board.

He entered the last car before the sleeping compartment. Empty. Barreling down the aisle, he reached to open the door at the far end.

A massive electrical shock crackled through the air, causing his hand to recoil involuntarily and tingeing the air with a sharp, burning odor. The man shook out his fingers. He had not anticipated that, and the pools in his eyes boiled with rage as the sensation brought back distant memories.

Bending closer, he examined the door. Lodged in the handle, almost invisible to the naked eye, was a small copper-colored filament, no thicker than a human hair.

"Your ticket cannae get you into that car, laddie."

The man spun about to find himself face-to-face with the conductor standing like a barricade in the aisle behind him. Both men's eyes registered surprise.

"You!" seethed the officer. He tilted his chin down, puffed out his cheeks, then like an aerosol can, blew a cloud of steam directly in the conductor's face.

"Save your nasty breath. You of all people should know the Mind Murk doesn't affect me," said the conductor, waving away the steam and stepping closer. "Or has it been so long, you've forgotten?"

Furious, the officer swung a fist with superhuman force that undoubtedly would have caved in the conductor's jaw.

But with remarkable speed for his size, the conductor stepped to one side, grabbed the man's arm, and used the forward motion of the punch to propel him to the far end of the car.

"Still posing as a soldier boy?"

"It's Commander."

"That's a new rank. Your own invention?"

The man snarled. "You can't stand between me and that Stink! I have legions at my disposal now!"

"Maybe. But not on my train."

The conductor removed a fountain pen from the chest pocket of his jacket and drew with it in the air as if he were waving a wand. "Remember this?"

The pen arced through the empty space and a giant glowing shield of blue light that spanned the width of the aisle took shape. The conductor moved the length of the empty car, pushing the shield toward the other man.

Rather than fight, the Commander abruptly turned and vanished into the next coach. He knew what he needed to do. The possibility of revenge against an old enemy only strengthened his resolve.

The conductor clicked his pen, and the blue shield evaporated in a puff of smoke. He retrieved the strand of copper from the door handle and made his way to Marcus's berth.

Jotting a quick note as he went, he slipped it silently under the curtain.

Marcus read and reread the chilling words: "Blotter on board! Make preparations."

He shoved the drawings in the briefcase, his hands shaking. Clearly, he had underestimated the danger of using this Ink in public.

Meanwhile, the Commander—whom the conductor referred to as a *blotter*—made his way through car after car, his left foot dragging ever so slightly as he headed toward the front of the train.

Normally, he relied on Mind Murk to conceal his true identity. This time he didn't care. Anything blocking his path was promptly crushed or kicked aside. An elderly man made the mistake of taking too long to find his seat, and the blotter roughly heaved him out of his way without losing stride, leaving him unconscious on the floor.

When he reached the front end of the lead passenger car, the door was locked. The blotter forced it open to a blast of cold morning air. Sleepy travelers blinked in irritation, then stunned disbelief.

Ahead was the coal tender, with a ladder up the face of it. The blotter jumped, climbing up over the side. He walked across the top of the coal, ignoring the sooty smoke billowing at him from the steam engine.

The *Night Scotsman* was clacking steadily nearer to

London's Harrow & Wealdstone station. The engineer studied the signal lights along the track to ensure he approached at the appropriate speed.

Engrossed in his duties, he didn't notice the Commander's hand until it gripped his neck, rendering him unconscious. The blotter rolled the engineer's body to the floor and took his seat. He shoved the throttle all the way forward.

The train accelerated, screaming at top speed. With no more effort than it takes to bend a pipe cleaner, the Commander twisted the handle out of shape to such a degree that no one would be able to reverse what he had done.

The locomotive was now hurtling out of control toward the busy station at the beginning of a workday.

And two other passenger trains were still boarding at the platform.

Satisfied, the blotter turned to leave. A pair of batlike wings stretched out from where they had been concealed between his shoulder blades. He flapped them once, stepped out of the engine, and shot into the air to watch from above as the train hurtled onward.

It would be the worst railroad crash Britain had ever seen.

An Angel on Platform Six

"Can you hear me, sir?"

The voice sounded distant and muffled. Marcus opened his eyes to see the concerned face of an American Air Force nurse.

She looked slightly blurry, and he realized his glasses were filthy. What was going on? Why was his head throbbing? And why was he on a gurney?

"There's been an accident. Do you know where you are?"

Marcus tried to shake the haze from his brain. "I would have said London, but you're American."

She laughed, relieved to get a response. "London's right. I'm stationed at the American Air Force hospital. We're the nearest medical facility."

She held his face still, looking into first one eye, then the other. "Can you tell me what day it is?"

Marcus scanned his memory. "Tuesday. No, Wednesday, October 8, 1952."

The nurse took a tube of lipstick and used it to draw a

large *X* on his forehead. "Sorry, it's all I have to write with. This will tell doctors which patients have been seen. Don't wipe it off. I'll be back to check on you soon."

And with that she was gone.

Lying on the stretcher, Marcus suddenly found the entire day rushing back—the train, the horrific jolt sending him airborne, the unbearable screech of metal scraping against metal.

His briefcase! He felt around on the gurney, but there was nothing. He pulled himself up to a sitting position, only to nearly pass out with the effort. He collapsed back down. Catching his breath, he rolled to the side and looked toward the train.

What he saw was a heap of twisted black metal, piled up behind an engine, which was perched on its nose and leaning precariously over a sideways passenger car of another train. The platform looked like a war zone, with dozens of wounded and dazed passengers in makeshift triage. Wreckage was everywhere.

Luggage and belongings were piled near the ticketing office. And there, among the debris, he saw it. One side was slightly dented, but the briefcase appeared intact. He had to get to it.

Mustering every ounce of strength, Marcus rolled himself off the gurney and onto the wooden platform. He might be too dizzy to walk the fifty feet to his briefcase, but he could crawl.

Which he did—one agonizing board at a time. It must have made for a bizarre sight—a vicar in tattered clothes, inching his way on hands and knees. Yet with the chaos all around, once again Marcus found himself invisible.

When he reached the briefcase, he held his breath as he opened it up. Good: The bottle was still there. But not the pen!

Sick with worry, he rifled back and forth through everything before remembering he had put it in his pocket. He patted his jacket and, to his great relief, felt the pen tucked inside.

Pushing the briefcase in front of him, Marcus crawled back toward his stretcher. With his eyes down, he ran into a man's legs standing squarely in his way. Dreading who it might be, he looked up to see the ample form of the conductor, hands on his hips.

"Not much of a nap for you on the train, was it?" Reaching down, the conductor gently helped him to his feet. Keeping an arm around him for support, he moved the vicar toward the gurney.

"Is all of this my fault?" Marcus missed a step and stumbled.

"Save your energy." The conductor spoke in an intense whisper. "The only one to blame for this is the blotter. He derailed the train. We've got to get you out of here."

A cry pierced the air, coming from an upended train car that was about to topple to the ground. People were still trapped inside.

Concern clouded the conductor's face as he looked from Marcus to the train. "I have to go help them. Hide the Ink before he finds you."

"But how could he—"

"You're marked. He can smell it on your hands!"

With that, the train conductor darted away, and Marcus lay back down. He reached his hand into his pocket and pulled out the pen, trying to force his clouded brain to imagine a way of hiding it on the platform. There were no obvious choices. What if someone discovered the hiding spot before he could return for it?

Just then a woman's voice loudly exclaimed, "Oh, no! No, no, no!"

Craning to the left, Marcus saw the nurse from earlier, standing beside an injured passenger and looking in exasperation at her empty tube of lipstick.

She noticed the pen in Marcus's hand. "I'm going to need that." She walked over and snatched it from his grasp. "Wow. This looks expensive."

Marcus clutched her arm to beg for it back when over her shoulder he spotted the intimidating form of the blotter, now disguised as a medic. It had to be him—those eyes were inhuman. And the strange way he was sniffing at injured passengers was not normal behavior. The conductor wasn't going to be able to help. The nurse was now the only hope Marcus had.

"I don't think I'll make it." Beads of sweat formed on his skin.

"Sure you will, Reverend."

"No! Listen to me. I need you to promise me something."

He willed himself to remain conscious and pulled the nurse close, so the blotter couldn't hear. "Promise me! Deliver that pen to my children."

With trembling fingers, he spun the combination lock on his briefcase and pushed it toward her. "Lock it in here. Only my children—no one else. Especially not the housekeeper. The address is on the tag."

Sensing his urgency, the nurse nodded. "I promise. But you're going to be fine."

"Tell my children—" Marcus blacked out and slumped back on the gurney.

The nurse checked for his pulse, which was still there. She picked up the briefcase, put the pen behind her ear, and headed back to work.

Moments later, the Commander-turned-medic came alongside the unconscious clergyman. He made a show of checking for a pulse himself, which brought Marcus's stained fingers close to his face. The blotter's pupils became stormy with recognition, and the Stink burned his nasal passages. Having found his target, he turned his head and retched.

It was the most potent stench he had ever encountered, driving him nearly mad. With a gloved hand, he searched the man's pockets but found no pen—just a glasses case with a rag soaked in the detestable liquid. And a photograph of the man with what were presumably his children. The blotter returned the glasses case but slipped the picture in his own pocket for future reference.

How had a clergyman come into possession of such a lethal concentration of Stink? Who in Aberdeen was his source? And where was the infernal writing instrument he had used?

Answers were needed, but not here. There would be a thorough interrogation when this man regained consciousness. Stealing a bedsheet from a nearby patient, the blotter draped it over the vicar as if he were dead.

The nurse looked up and noticed the medic with the distinctive gait wheeling the gurney quickly down the platform. She recognized the torn jacket sleeve of the vicar's uncovered arm hanging down at the side of the gurney. A wave of disbelief and deep sadness for the reverend's family swept over her.

She consoled herself with the thought that at least she would be able to tell his children their father had helped save lives in the simple act of sharing his pen. Her eyes teared up as she looked at it in her hand. With renewed determination, she removed the pen's cap and looked for the next forehead in need of a miracle.

Unwelcome News

4

Everett and Bea were upstairs when the doorbell rang. Living in a vicarage, you begin to know by instinct when someone arrives with bad news. And both children had that sinking feeling that this particular chime meant trouble. They scrambled to the top of the stairs to see who was there.

Mrs. Crimp answered the door. Two somber-faced policemen stood on the porch. One cleared his throat, as if what he had to share was stuck there. "Excuse me, ma'am. I'm Officer Stanley. Are you Mrs. Drake?"

"Certainly not. I oversee the premises."

The officer became flustered. "I see. I see." He looked at his partner for rescue, which never came.

Mrs. Crimp crossed her arms, drumming her bony fingers on her elbow. "I am a busy woman, sir. Please state your business."

"It's just that there's news about Reverend Drake. May we come in?"

"No need to intrude further," Mrs. Crimp barked. "Anything you have to say can be said right here."

At that point Bea went tearing down the stairs into the entryway, with Everett close behind. If this concerned their father, they were not going to hear it secondhand from her.

"What about my daddy?" Bea demanded, pushing past Mrs. Crimp through the front door.

Officer Stanley got down on one knee, removing his hat. His voice cracked as he spoke. "I'm afraid there's bad news, dear."

He hesitated, concern in his eyes. "Your father was in a terrible railway accident early this morning."

Everett joined them outside, his heart pounding. "Is he hurt?"

The officer lowered his gaze. "There's a chance he could still be alive somewhere in the wreckage, but . . ." His voice trailed off.

The world stopped revolving in that moment. The police officer's pained expression would be forever etched in the children's memories, the shadows on the porch frozen in time. Everett felt as if his strength had seeped out of every pore in his body. He could hardly breathe.

For a long moment, no one spoke.

"Are you here to remove the children?"

They all turned, not quite able to grasp what Mrs. Crimp was suggesting.

There was the faintest hint of a cruel smile on her thin

lips. "I'm not their mother. With their father presumed dead, these urchins are now the responsibility of the state."

If there hadn't been two policemen standing in front of him, Everett would have rushed to push her off the porch. Instead, he just spat, "You mean old cow!" and stomped into the yard, his cheeks a bright shade of red. His worst nightmare was coming true. He walked in a tight, furious circle around the small patch of grass between the vicarage and the church.

Officer Stanley kept his tightly balled hands at his sides. "We are here to deliver condolences to the family," he said through clenched teeth. "Anything else is a matter for the courts."

Mrs. Crimp turned to go back inside. "Then your work here is done." With that, she closed the door behind her and retreated into the recesses of the house.

The policemen stood in stunned silence for a moment. Their radio squawked in the car, summoning them to the scene of a crime across town. Officer Stanley returned his cap, giving Bea a last sympathetic look. "I'm so sorry."

Everett walked over and grabbed Bea's hand, gripping it tightly as the officers drove away. His father's words rang in his ears. *I'm counting on you to look after your sister.*

"It's okay," Bea whispered, squeezing his hand. "You'll see. Daddy's not really dead."

Dying at a Funeral

Everett squirmed in the pew, unable to concentrate on the endless eulogy. The bishop droned on in his most preacherly voice about the "valley of the shadoooooow," as if drawing out the word made it more impressive.

How do you have a funeral without a body? Something felt wrong. But the investigation had concluded that Marcus Drake was almost certainly dead, and arrangements had been made.

Bea sat beside Everett on the wooden bench, swinging her short legs back and forth madly while drawing a maze on the funeral program.

Her acting normal was irritating. She hadn't cried once, insisting everyone was wrong and that their father was alive. Everett grabbed the program away from her. Bea scowled and tried to poke him discreetly with her pencil, but he reached down and broke the lead. It's hard to have a proper fight when you're in front of a bunch of unhappy grown-ups in a church.

Their future had been in question for a few days. Vicars

may be skilled at helping others manage the ups and downs of life, but sometimes their own affairs are in disarray, and, truth be told, Marcus Drake had never gotten around to drawing up a last will and testament.

No contingency plans had been made for the care of his children in the event of a tragedy. There were no longer any grandparents living, no aunts and uncles in the picture.

Some distant relatives in America might be able to take them, but Everett and Bea could not remember their names, and it would take time to track them down.

So the elders of St. Francis Church met again and voted unanimously that until such time as a replacement vicar could be hired or the Drake relatives found, the children would continue to live in the vicarage under the watchful care of Isadora Crimp.

Once again, the housekeeper found herself without recourse since she, too, had nowhere to go. And once again, she resented it bitterly, funneling all her angry energy toward the children.

Everett was no longer intimidated. With his father gone, the whole world felt flat. Now, as he sat through the torturously long funeral, he knew he should listen respectfully. But he kept envisioning his dad doing a spot-on impression of the dumpy bishop presiding with his grating, arrogant tone.

As Everett studied the clergyman's face now, he could see the man bore more than a passing resemblance to one of MC's enemies. The flapping jowls, the ice-cream scoop for a nose—it was all there. His father had drawn a thinly disguised (and most unflattering) caricature of the bishop into his comic! Everett almost laughed out loud.

The reception after the funeral was equally excruciating. The Drake children politely listened as a long line of parishioners offered condolences. Condescending men thumped their backs, and powdery grandmothers patted their hair. No one knew quite the right way to comfort grieving children, especially when Bea would inform them that they were mistaken about her father being dead.

When they ran out of words, well-wishers milled about in the garden, nibbling on miniature sandwiches and stale chocolate biscuits. Teary unmarried women dabbed at their eyes, dreams of snagging an eligible vicar now gone forever.

As the crowd dispersed, a young, dark-skinned woman approached the children. She wore a United States Air Force uniform and carried a briefcase.

"I'm so sorry for your loss," she began. "Could I speak with you privately? It's important."

Having never met an American before, Bea would have followed her anywhere. The three of them found a quiet corner on the lawn. In a hushed tone, the woman said, "My name is Abbie. I was a nurse at the site of the train accident."

She glanced around, then lowered her voice. "I know you've been told they never found your father's body, but that's not true. I tended to him on the platform after the crash."

Everett swallowed hard. "Did you see him die?"

The nurse shook her head. "That's what's strange. I don't know how he died. His injuries didn't appear life-threatening. The next thing I knew, a medic was wheeling him away. Now his body has disappeared."

Bea's eyes widened. "I knew it! He's still alive!"

Abbie pressed her finger to her lips. "I'm not saying that. He may have sustained internal injuries I couldn't detect."

She handed the dented briefcase to Everett. "I promised your father I would bring his belongings to you. He was adamant that he didn't even want your housekeeper to accept them. I thought the funeral would be my best chance to catch you alone."

Everett held the briefcase in front of him and a faint tingling sensation surged up his arms. He could picture all the times his father came bounding into the house with it. He thought of that painful last goodbye. How he wished he had returned his father's hug! How he wished he had gone out on the porch to wave. Staring at the battered leather case, he tried not to imagine how it had become so scraped up.

The nurse started to leave, then turned back, nodding at the case. "Sure is a strange pen he loaned me," she said. "I don't know if it was blessed because he was a preacher or what, but that pen seems to have powers. All the patients I marked with it recovered miraculously. Can you believe that? Every single one. Your father saved lives even while losing his own."

She bent down and pulled the children into a tight hug. "But you already knew he was a hero."

"Is," corrected Bea.

Abbie smiled sadly. Giving Everett a small card, she said, "You can reach me at the air force base. If you need anything, let me know."

As Everett watched her walk away, he caught sight of The Cramps eyeing them suspiciously through the kitchen window. He gripped the briefcase tighter and shoved the card deep in his pocket. If he and Bea had to live with that woman much longer, they would need all the friends they could find.

6 Undead

The unmarked lorry rattled northward. In the back of the truck, the Commander leaned over the unconscious vicar, who was still strapped to the gurney. The blotter pondered the family photograph in his hands, his wings twitching.

Two more blotters flanked him: a short, swarthy character named Dud and his lanky, dim-witted friend, Oafie. They were doing their best to stay standing as the vehicle shook and lumbered down the road.

"When will he wake up?" Oafie yelled above the engine noise.

"I'm keeping him sedated until we're back in Aberdeen," said the Commander, tapping the IV bag attached to Marcus. "By the time he wakes, there will be such high levels of Mind Murk in his system, he should be ready to cooperate."

Oafie scratched his misshapen head. "Won't the Murks make him forget what he knows about Stink?"

Dud shot an alarmed look at his partner. "It's not right to question the Commander!" Then he turned to his boss. "We would never dream of second-guessing you, sir."

The Commander ignored Dud and answered Oafie. "Mind Murk has different effects when delivered straight to the bloodstream. It proves quite useful in certain conversations."

"If anyone can get him to talk, it's you, sir," said Dud, continuing his flattery. "Where do you think he found that Stink?"

"Oh! I bet I know, Commander," Oafie chimed in. "What with him being on the train and all, it was probably that conductor you always—"

Without warning, the Commander extended a wing and shoved the top edge of it in Oafie's mouth. The slimy texture and bristles made Oafie gag.

"Never speak of that conductor. Do you understand?"

Oafie nodded, wide-eyed.

"Moron!" croaked a voice. It came from a raven perched atop a stack of crates, its beady eyes mocking the inept underlings. A black collar with needle-sharp spikes encircled the raven's neck. "Moron!" it repeated, as if to ensure the insult landed. The Commander made a *toc-toc* noise and the raven flew to his shoulder.

Oafie glared at the bird as if he wanted to bake it into a pie.

The Commander sat down and smoothed the raven's feathers. "There, there, Grip," he said. "I have something for you." He removed a paper clip from his pocket. "Go and play." The bird took the shiny object and flew back to his corner.

Now that the Commander was seated, his boots were more visible. Dud caught Oafie staring at their leader's left foot and cleared his throat. It was hard not to be curious about the famed appendage made of stone. But everyone knew that topic was even more taboo than the conductor. Oafie caught Dud's concern and shifted his gaze.

The Commander was busy scribbling out an order. "I'm sending you to search this vicar's home. Find me all there is to know about him"—he tapped the photograph—"and his offspring."

He stopped writing and looked from Dud to Oafie. "Most of all, destroy any stockpiles of this Stink you find on the premises. Then report to McLarch for rapid transport to Newcastle upon Tyne. I will take the prisoner back to headquarters and then meet you in Newcastle."

He held out his orders to Dud, who froze, staring anxiously at the page.

"What are you waiting for?"

Dud searched for a tactful way to raise his question. "It's just that, well, begging your pardon, sir, but to clarify, are you asking us to enter a . . . a . . . house of worship?"

The Commander rose to his feet again. "Not asking. Ordering. I do not want to see either of you again until you've demolished any remains of that unspeakable fluid. Is that clear?"

Dud's voice barely rose above a whisper. "Perfectly."

Curiouser and Curiouser

Gray suds slopped over the sides of the bucket as Everett lifted out the scrub brush and shoved it across the kitchen floorboards. He didn't scour them; he attacked them. With each swipe of his arm, he imagined scrubbing The Cramps out of his life. Scrubbing away all the horrid new reality.

It had been a rough few days since the funeral. Mrs. Crimp assigned an unreasonable number of chores to the children. For someone who called herself a housekeeper, she managed to avoid doing much housework herself.

Everett tossed the brush back in the soapy water just as the woman's shrill voice came from behind. "You, boy! Go pack up your father's belongings from his study."

Everett had had enough. "No," he replied coolly.

Like an owl diving on a mouse, Mrs. Crimp snagged his hair in her hand. "You're an impudent little fool!" Dragging him behind, she marched out of the house and across the lawn to the church.

"Let me go!" Everett yelled, slapping at her arm as he stumbled through the grass.

Bea ran after them, shouting, "Stop it! Stop it!"

Mrs. Crimp marched him through the doors and down the hall. When they reached the vicar's study, she gave one last yank on Everett's hair and flung him inside. "You will both stay here until every last scrap is boxed up."

"You can't make us!" Everett shouted.

"No." She seethed. "But if you refuse, I will throw all your father's belongings into the fire. You choose."

Spinning on her heels, Mrs. Crimp exited swiftly, slamming the door behind her. The children heard the scrape of a key as she turned it and removed it from the lock.

Bea ran over and peered through the keyhole. She watched for a long moment, then breathed a sigh of relief. "She's gone."

From somewhere inside her sweater, she produced two small wires and immediately set about picking the lock. "I should have us out of here in three. Two. One. Done!"

She gave the handle a victorious turn and the door swung open. "Skeleton key locks are too easy."

"Wait," said Everett. "We don't want to leave just yet."

Bea didn't appreciate having her accomplishment dismissed so lightly. "Did you even see how fast I was?" She couldn't imagine many scenarios surpassing an honest-to-goodness escape, but she shut the door and paused to hear him out.

Everett elaborated. "She won't be checking on us again for hours. Now's our chance to get that briefcase open without her spying."

Everett went to the secret spot behind the easy chair in the corner where he'd stashed the case after the funeral. It remained there, unopened. They'd wanted to look inside immediately, but Mrs. Crimp always hovered nearby, and they were not about to let her get a look at the contents.

This was their first private moment. Only one problem remained: Their father had left no instructions for opening the briefcase.

Everett sat on the study floor, pressing the latches, then sighed. "There must be a million possible combinations."

"Hooray!" Bea clapped her hands in delight. "My first chance to try a combination lock!"

Like an expert safecracker, she concentrated on the mechanism, running her small fingers over the numbers on the three wheels. She placed her ear on top of the case. Holding the sliding latch with one hand, she deftly moved the dials back and forth one by one as she listened to their movement.

Everett used to roll his eyes at Bea trying her Houdini act. But he had seen her open too many locks and untie too many knots to ignore her skill. For a little sister, she had some real talent. Talent he didn't possess, which made it slightly obnoxious, even when he had to admit it was helpful.

Click. The latch released. Bea herself was surprised. "That shouldn't have worked."

Whether by skill or by luck, the secrets of the briefcase

would finally be revealed. Everett's hands shook as he went to open the lid. What could be so important that their father had gone to such lengths to protect?

The hinges creaked as the top opened. The children peered anxiously inside. To their astonishment they found ... nothing.

Nothing exciting anyway. Just their father's Bible, a very old pen, and some rolled-up papers. And a large ink bottle that was about two-thirds full.

Everett unrolled their father's artwork. The pictures were wonderful, and normally, Everett couldn't wait for the next installment of MC. But this felt like a letdown.

He had expected some clue, some connection that would make it feel like his dad was not gone forever. Now as he stared into the briefcase with his sister, the fact began to sink in: Their father was never coming back.

Everett thought about Nurse Abbie delivering the case and how nice she was. It made Everett's eyes all watery. She was the first person to hug him since his father's disappearance.

He blinked rapidly to make the tears go away and walked over to the desk, scanning for anything that would provide some direction. But it looked the way it always did, covered with stacks of books. He picked up one. It was by D. L. Sayers, titled *Making Sense of the Universe*. As if anyone could.

"Do you hear this pen?" Bea held the antique writing

instrument next to her ear. "It's humming. I could hear it when I was working on the lock."

Everett took it and listened. He couldn't detect any noise. Bea and her wild imagination. He removed the cap. "Hand me one of those blank pages."

He pictured his father drawing incredible images with this pen, his hand moving skillfully across the page. All that smart dialogue and brilliant artwork that left Everett in wonder. For a brief moment, Everett could see himself following in his father's artistic footsteps—especially if he used the same pen.

He brought the nib to paper and the tiniest drop of ink appeared. That was it. His arm refused to move. It was as if the pen were cemented in place.

He frowned and pushed with all his might, and the small spot on the page grew into a slightly larger spot.

Maybe there was something sticky on the paper. He crumpled it, threw it in the trash, and took a fresh sheet. He shook out his hand and made another attempt with the same results—a single mark in the center of the page.

Everett's face grew hot, and he threw the pen back into the briefcase. "Stupid thing doesn't even work."

Bea picked up the sheet of paper and studied the small mark. "The humming wasn't from the pen. It was the ink. Now I can hear it from the page."

"Oh, hurrah for your ears!" Everett snapped sarcastically. He didn't know why he was feeling stirred up and irritable over not being able to use the pen. He reached out to crumple the second page, but Bea pulled it away.

"And it wasn't humming," Bea said. "It was *talking*!"

"Come on, Bea. Quit pretending."

She concentrated on the tiny mark. "No, really. It's saying . . . I *think* it's saying . . . *ASK DOT*. Ask Dot?"

She shrugged and held up the paper a few inches from her eyes and stared into it as if in a trance. Then she whispered dramatically, "Dot. Dear Dot, will you please help us?"

That was it. Everett couldn't take any more. He grabbed the page away.

"Give it back!" Bea wailed.

"Stop making fun of me! Just because I can't draw—"

"Why are you being so mean? I heard—"

She was interrupted by the ring of a bicycle bell coming from the driveway. It was a light, musical sound. Odd that they could hear it so clearly. But unlike when the police rang the doorbell, this time they both felt a surge of bubbly energy inside, as if whoever had arrived brought a most marvelous surprise.

Forgetting the argument, Bea raced out of the study and across the foyer to the front door of the church. She opened it just enough to see the vicarage door. Everett made his way to his sister and peered over her head from behind.

On the steps in front of the house stood the oddest, friendliest-looking little man waiting for the housekeeper to open the door. Not much taller than Everett, he wore a courier's uniform of sorts, with gray shorts and a gray jacket. Slung over his shoulder was a worn leather satchel, bursting at the seams.

His pencil-thin legs might as well have been soaked in bleach, they were so wrinkly and devoid of color. They disappeared into black socks and shoes below.

At the other end of him, a courier's hat perched atop disheveled tufts of wispy white hair. He glanced in the direction of the church. Peering out of the crinkliest face were eyes the color of a stormy sea, and just as wild-looking.

Right away, Bea liked the look of him very much and imagined what sort of grandpa he would make.

Everett gasped when he saw the man's face. His face was the same as the retired secret agent who warned MC seconds before the bomb went off back in issue seven. Just the day before, Everett had reread that story when he was evading the housekeeper.

A disapproving Mrs. Crimp was not nearly as impressed by the deliveryman's appearance. "State your business, sir."

"Are you the one known as The Cramps?"

Bea's hands flew to cover her mouth. How did he know what they called her?

Mrs. Crimp's face contorted in rage. "It is pronounced Crimp. Isadora Crimp."

The courier consulted his clipboard again. "Hmm. So it is. I'm going to need you to sign this."

Before she could object, he handed her the clipboard.

He then produced the most enormous feather quill pen from somewhere inside his jacket, as if he were Shakespeare.

Mrs. Crimp huffed her displeasure. "I am not using that monstrosity. I'll get my own pen." She stormed off toward the parlor. The courier turned and looked directly at Bea and Everett through the barely open church door, winking and smiling merrily as if a great joke were about to take place. Bea couldn't help but smile back, giving him a little wave.

Moments later, a flustered Mrs. Crimp returned. "Those hateful children must have hidden all my writing utensils. Give me that." She snatched the quill.

"Here, let me get the ink for you," said the courier, removing the stopper on a small bottle. Mrs. Crimp grunted in disgust and dipped the tip of the feather into the bottle.

No sooner had the quill touched the ink than the woman's arm froze like a stone. She stared down in bewildered aggravation as a thin blue-black film crept from the bottle up her motionless arm. "What's happ—" she began to ask, but didn't finish the question. A layer of dark-colored stone enveloped her in seconds.

Once Mrs. Crimp had been reduced to a silent statue, the courier tipped her back on her heels and dragged her inside the entryway. Her feet made a metallic scraping sound across the threshold.

"You can come out now," he called to the children. "It's all clear."

Since hiding seemed pointless, Everett and Bea made their way warily into the driveway. Everett hadn't thought it possible for The Cramps to look any uglier than normal. Until now. Her teeth gleamed like blue fangs. And those eyes locked in that permanent, hideous scowl gave him the shivers. Bea wouldn't even move toward the house.

Sensing her apprehension, the courier heaved and turned the statue until Mrs. Crimp's critical gaze faced the corner. Then he dusted off his hands and stepped back out on the porch. "Don't worry, she'll be fine. This is just Inkasement."

"Just in case of what?" Bea asked.

The courier laughed. "Never thought of it like that before. That's good. No—it's called INKASEMENT. As in Ink. Almost like paint, really, but hard as stone. It's a tough coating for her own protection. She won't remember a thing."

Everett looked the old man up and down. "Who are you?"

"Are you a magician?" Bea asked hopefully.

"Me? Oh my, no. My name is Osgood, and I'm in the delivery business. See? It says so right here." The man leaned in and pointed at his cap, tipping forward so the children could read it. Stitching that looked hand-sewn read: *Special Delivery.*

It was then that the children noticed the rickety bicycle in the driveway behind him. An impossibly large mountain of parcels balanced precariously on the back.

Bea was instantly suspicious. "You came on *that*?"

The courier crossed his arms. "Have you never heard of a bicycle messenger?"

"Which of those packages are you delivering to us?" Everett demanded, nodding toward the bike.

Osgood raised his eyebrows. "Hmm? What package do you mean?"

They all stared at one another blankly. Then a flash of understanding crossed Osgood's face. "Oh, right. I see what you're thinking—*special delivery*. That would make sense. But I'm not delivering anything *to* this place. I'm here to deliver something *from* this place. I'm here to deliver *you* from *her*." He pointed at the statue.

Everett folded his arms and shook his head. "I'm sorry. Just who exactly sent you?"

"Who sent me? Who sent me? Why, you did, of course!" The little man blinked repeatedly as if Everett had asked a nonsensical question.

Everett gave his sister a bewildered look. Her confused expression matched his own. This courier was clearly not in his right mind. Bea's voice came out a little shaky. "Excuse me, Mr. Osgood, but . . . we didn't send for anyone."

Osgood quickly became serious. "Is that so? Well, let me double-check to see if there's been a mistake." He rifled through his messenger bag, pulling out stacks and stacks and stacks of crinkly paper, some yellowed and curled as if it had been in there for centuries. At school, Everett had been studying volume, and he couldn't help but notice that the volume of paperwork produced far exceeded the volume of the bag itself.

"Aha! Here we go." Osgood gave the sheet of instructions a shake. "Most unusual. It was a voice-to-Ink communique. Came into Central Dispatch via the Ausculator: *Young male, age eleven, used father's Ink to make Dot. Sister, age eight, petitioned Dot for rescue. Please deliver immediately. Threat imminent.*"

"What threat?" Everett was starting to get a headache. He rubbed his temples with both hands. This man spoke gibberish. How had he listened in on their conversation and arrived so fast? "And if you're delivering us from Mrs. Crimp, why did you say she needed protecting?"

"Well, that depends," said Osgood. "Might you still have the note you wrote?"

"It was only a dot," muttered Everett, embarrassed to think about it again.

Bea ran to the study and retrieved the piece of paper. She handed it to the courier. He peered at the page with a furrowed brow. "Not much to go on, is it?"

Everett's face grew hot. "Something was wrong with the pen."

"The pen—yes. May I see that as well?" Bea ran back into the church and returned holding the pen. Osgood took it from her gingerly. He unscrewed the cap and waved the pen in a figure eight in the air, then stuck his nose in the same space and inhaled deeply. His eyes grew wide and he quickly replaced the cap, glancing all around. "Oh, dear," he said under his breath. "Oh, dear."

Everett stared at the courier. It was uncanny how much he looked and acted like that secret agent. He was about to ask the courier if he knew his father, but Osgood handed him the pen. "No time to waste. Now think carefully for a moment. Is there more of this Ink anywhere? Any other pages where it has been used?"

Everett nodded. "There's a big bottle in Dad's study and the drawings for his next comic."

"A big bottle? Oh, my. I'm beginning to see. Run and fetch them. Then we must leave here immediately. Hopefully we're not too late."

Something in the courier's tone was both entirely trustworthy and extremely serious. Everett had no idea what the danger was, but he ran to his father's study.

Bea stood still, her eyes flashing. "Mr. Osgood," she whispered, "is this a real live escape?"

He scanned the horizon, as if expecting trouble to appear. "Indeed it is, miss." He walked over to his bicycle and reached into the pile of packages.

Bea looked skeptically at the contraption, which appeared to be held together with nothing more than packing twine and tape. She searched for a tactful way to voice her concern. "It's just that . . . I don't see how we can all fit on your bike."

Pulling two sunflower seeds as large as pancakes from amidst the parcels, Osgood handed them to Bea. "My bike? Oh, yes, I see what you're getting at. Although she's got some rather unexpected abilities. But don't worry—I've arranged for other transportation."

Everett reappeared, winded from running his fastest, his father's briefcase in hand. "Got it."

"We're not taking the bike," Bea informed him, tapping the oversized seeds against each other.

Osgood cupped his hands together and brought them to his lips. Blowing air between his thumbs, he produced a low cooing noise.

Bea loved it. "You sound just like a dove!"

"Rock pigeon, actually," Osgood informed her. "That's how you'll be traveling."

"That doesn't make any sense," said Everett.

Osgood eyed the woods across from the vicarage. He made the cooing noise again. "Of course it makes sense. Homing pigeons are one of the oldest delivery systems in the world."

A tremendous crashing sound came from the shrubs on the far side of the church. The children could see the tops of the trees swaying above the roof. They both jumped back as an enormous gray feathered head peeked out from halfway up the side of the church, two giant eyes peering at them quizzically. Then the rest of the big bird's body tottered out—a frightening size. Fortunately, its face had a gentle kindness that offset the scariness.

"Ah, there you are, Ermengarde," said Osgood. "No one would ever think it possible to lose track of this girl's whereabouts, but she's got a knack for making herself invisible."

He took the large seeds from Bea and handed them to Ermengarde. As she bent to pluck them from his hands, Everett stepped forward to shield Bea from the gargantuan beak. Up close, he could see her feathers had tiny crosshatch lines like pen marks. "How is she so big?"

The courier looked up at Ermengarde. "This old girl flew straight out of a book. I take it you've heard of *Peter and Wendy*?"

Everett scowled. "There's no giant pigeon in that story."

"I told James—Mr. Barrie, that is—I told him she didn't fit," said Osgood, patting the bird affectionately. "But he liked her too much to just unwrite her, so he begged me to deliver her from the pages and find her a new home. A bit of a rare feat, but we did it."

Bea pushed out from behind her brother and pointed to the tag hanging down from Ermengarde's neck. The inscription read: I BELONG TO D. L. SAYERS. An address in Oxford was printed below.

"Oxford!" Bea said. "Daddy goes to Oxford all the time.

Maybe that's where he is! Ermengarde could take him a message!"

Everett was about to set Bea straight when the bird's head lifted skyward. She tilted it to one side and gave an alarmed cluck.

"They're coming!" Osgood rushed the children around to her side. Strapped onto the pigeon's back was a wicker gondola such as you might see dangling under a hot-air balloon, except larger. A rope ladder hung over the edge and down Ermengarde's side, reaching the ground.

"Hurry, children! Up you go!"

"What?" Bea exclaimed. "You want us to ride a bird?"

"It's perfectly safe. You must go now!"

Everett scrambled halfway up the ladder. "Who's after us?" he asked over his shoulder.

"Blotters!" Osgood lifted Bea onto the first rung.

Blotters. Everett had never encountered the villainous term before, but even the way Osgood spat the word from his mouth told him they were unsavory characters.

Before Everett could press for more details, the odd little messenger was swinging one leg over his bicycle.

"Wait," Everett said. "You're not coming with us?"

"I have more deliveries."

Bea frowned. "But we don't know where we're going."

"Homing pigeons always find their way home."

Everett hesitated. While this had all the makings of a

Max Courageous—worthy adventure, who in their right mind would entrust Bea to that flimsy box on top of a bird the size of an airplane? As he weighed the options there on the ladder, he spotted an unfamiliar black car racing down the lane toward the vicarage, thick plumes of oily smoke trailing behind it.

"They're going to see us!" he yelled, hoisting himself into the basket and pulling Bea in after.

"No, they won't," yelled Osgood from his bike. "Most folks only see what they expect to see, if they glance up at all. Besides, Ermengarde looks like clouds from below. It's how she was written. Even I have a hard time picking her out in the sky. Now go!"

No sooner were the words out of his mouth than Ermengarde launched herself into the air. Everett and Bea tumbled against the basket wall. Their ascent was breathtaking, the pigeon's powerful wings driving them higher and higher with every beat.

As soon as the great bird leveled out, Everett glanced over the edge. He couldn't believe how small the house, the trees, and even the church looked. Osgood and his bike had already vanished without a trace. How could such an ancient man pedal away so quickly?

The big bird banked to the right and the world Everett knew disappeared. Acres of unfamiliar towns and pastureland stretched away to the horizon. Had their driveway still been in view, he would have known that their departure was not a moment too soon. The black car screeched to a halt in front of the church. A thuggish driver stepped from the vehicle and sniffed the air, his pupils turning to liquid.

Flying without Seatbelts

An overgrown pigeon can travel at remarkable speed. Everett wrapped his arm around Bea, praying that the creature wouldn't go into a sudden dive and dump them out.

Yet once they grew accustomed to the rhythm of the wings, the two children found the experience rather thrilling. They soared along with the clouds, Ermengarde deftly navigating the airstream like a seasoned pilot.

Bea decided that pigeon was her new favorite mode of travel. She scooted out from under her brother's arm and peeked over the edge of the gondola. The wind rushed toward her, carrying scents from Ermengarde's gray feathers.

Not a bird smell—more like memories stored in the plumage from the pigeon's journeys to distant corners of the globe. What could Osgood have meant by saying he'd delivered her from a story? Visions of marketplaces and cobblestones and golden fields ran through Bea's mind as she imagined all the places Ermengarde must have flown.

If this rescue was necessary, Bea felt grateful to be aloft

on the back of this magnificent bird instead of teetering along on crazy Osgood's bike.

Thinking about Osgood's urgency made her worried for her father. Only something very serious could have prevented him from coming home.

She leaned back against her brother. "Ev—are you scared?"

"Not really. A little, maybe." Truthfully, he was afraid, but Bea didn't need to know that. It would only make her worry. He thought of how his dad would comfort her. He reached out and patted her hand. "This would sure make a good bedtime story, wouldn't it?"

He instantly regretted the reminder. Their dad wouldn't be telling them any more stories. The wind bothered Everett's eyes and he felt very tired.

"This will be better than a story," Bea decided. "It's a real adventure. We're flying to Oxford to find Daddy."

The mention of Oxford made Everett think of the tag around the bird's neck. There was a connection somewhere.

"What was the name of Ermengarde's owner?"

"D. L. Something." Bea frowned, trying to remember. "Sawyer?"

Now it came back to him. It was Sayers. D. L. Sayers. Everett had heard that name before. No, he had seen it! The book about the universe on his dad's desk!

"It's an author," he said under his breath. For some reason that fact felt hopeful and important.

His thoughts were cut short as he realized they were descending, headed for a yard behind a quite modest house.

They set down gracefully. Ermengarde lowered her body to the ground and tipped to the side, sending the children tumbling out of the basket. She broke their fall with her wing, sliding them to the ground.

Everett and Bea walked toward the house, hoping they were in the right place. "Do you think it's polite to knock on the back door?" Bea asked.

Before Everett could answer, a light came on in the window and the door opened for them. A no-nonsense—looking woman with hair pulled into a bun on the back of her head stood regarding them through round glasses. She wore a lumpy sweater and trousers, with her hands jammed in the pockets. The only showy feature of her wardrobe was the pair of large, brightly colored earrings hanging far below her ear lobes. Bea could not take her eyes off them.

The serious face broke into a warm smile. "Hello, children. Do come in. I've been expecting you."

Everett glanced back toward Ermengarde and was shocked to discover that she was quite well hidden. Her massive form inexplicably blended into the landscape.

Bea smelled cookies inside and skipped ahead.

"I hope the journey was bearable," the woman said, walking them into the kitchen. "Ermengarde rarely has riders these days. Did she behave herself?"

"Yes, ma'am," Everett replied. He hesitated, then

continued. "I don't mean to be rude, but we don't know why we're here or what's going on. Before we go any further, we need some answers."

The woman scrutinized Everett as if reading a map. "Direct and to the point. I daresay we are going to get along splendidly, young man."

"Are you D. L. Sawyer?" Bea piped in, hoping for a little recognition of her own. "Ermengarde's tag said she belonged to D. L. Sawyer."

Bending down to look Bea in the eye, the woman smiled. "Excellent powers of observation, Miss Drake. You're close. My name is Dorothy Sayers."

Everett couldn't wait any longer. "Did you know our father, Ms. Sayers?"

She regarded him carefully. "I don't think that's the question you most want to ask me, is it?" She gave him a quick wink. "But yes. And please—Ms. Sayers feels too formal. How would you children feel about calling me Aunt Dot?"

Everett and Bea stared at each other with their mouths open. Bea spoke first. "You're the Dot I asked for help?"

Aunt Dot smiled. "Have a cookie while I explain a few things."

Smells like Fire

9

The passenger door of the black car slammed shut. "Wait up, Oafie!"

Pulling on a pair of rubber gloves, Dud waddled over beside the driver, who now stood in the middle of the St. Francis churchyard, sniffing the air.

"Dud, get a whiff. Commander was right. This place reeks."

Dud widened his pockmarked nostrils to take in the scent. Immediately, he sneezed. A highly productive sneeze with a spray that landed directly on Oafie.

Oafie promptly brought a fist down on top of Dud's head, then mopped his face. "Watch it!"

"It weren't my fault! Stink allergies are the worst."

The two of them poked around the grounds for a few moments. Oafie stuck out his tongue. "I can still taste that wing. Awful."

Dud sniffed around a flower bed, then blew his nose. "Serves you right for mentioning You Know Who."

"You ever see it? The foot, I mean."

Dud glanced up and scanned the clouds.

Oafie squinted upward as well. "What are we doing?"

"Just checking for the spy in the sky."

"Huh?"

Dud gave an exasperated sigh. "The Commander's little raven friend. He flies around and reports what he hears."

Oafie ducked his head as if the bird were about to strike. "What about the *F-O-O-T*?" he whispered loudly, hoping ravens couldn't spell.

Dud lowered his voice. "I saw it one time. Commander had torn a hole in his boot and asked me to bring him a new pair. The foot was just sitting there out in the open. Gray as a London sky."

Oafie's jaw dropped. "Is it true he cut off his real foot himself? On purpose?"

Dud nodded. "Saved his life. He's every bit as tough as they say. You don't want him mad at you."

The two of them went back to work. A few minutes later, Oafie stopped. "What exactly are we looking for again?"

The Commander had not sent his cleverest subordinates on this assignment. Yet Dud's extremely sensitive nasal passages were useful, particularly when it came to detecting trace amounts of Stink (or, "going on the Sniffers," as the blotters called it). And though Oafie was no bright bulb either, he was the only driver willing to tolerate Dud for more than a few minutes.

The two continued their search by examining scraps of

garbage and digging in the flower beds. Then Dud spotted the door of the vicarage, still ajar. He slapped Oafie's arm. "Look! It's open!"

"You think someone's home?"

"Let's find out."

They tiptoed up the front steps. Oafie pushed the door all the way open and they both jumped as they confronted the unmoving form of Mrs. Crimp. Oafie put his face up next to the statue's.

"What happened to her?"

"She's covered in the stuff. I didn't know it worked on humans."

Oafie sighed. "And a face like that. Pity she ain't a blotter."

Dud grabbed the feather quill from her hand. He ran it under his nose, analyzing its meaning. His pupils not only went to liquid—his eyes began to swell.

"Oh, my. This is fre—this is fre—freshHOO!"

A second sneeze burst forth.

Oafie tried to duck out of the way but didn't make it in time.

Disgusted, he wiped his arm on Dud's back. "You check the house. I'm going to see about the church."

Dud's puffy eyes widened ever so slightly. "You can't go in there! You know what happens!"

"Don't worry 'bout me. Just do your job and let's get out of here."

Dud made a cursory examination of the remaining rooms of the vicarage but didn't smell anything obvious. He took out a dingy handkerchief and blew his nose again. The place made him nervous. He dug through just enough papers to learn Everett's and Bea's names and ages, then kept going.

By the time he checked the turret, he was moving faster than his short legs could handle.

Down the stairs he fell, bouncing like a ball.

A big thud echoed off the walls as he landed at the bottom.

He lay there for a minute to make sure nothing was broken. Slowly rising with a few groans, Dud limped outside to find his fellow blotter.

Oafie stood perfectly still in front of the church, eyes closed. He breathed out and extended his gloved hands toward the building. His shadow began to stretch away from him, gliding like black smoke under the church door, curling past the sanctuary and down the hall until it reached the vicar's study. The shadow spread out slowly across the floor, as if scanning the room for clues, lingering an extra moment by the garbage can.

One piece of paper, crumpled up in the bottom, caused the spreading darkness to stand still. The shadow slithered underneath the paper, creating an air current that lifted it up and floated over the edge of the trash can. It smoothed itself out in midair and floated down the hall and under the door, all the way out of the church.

When the shadow had withdrawn back to Oafie's feet, he

opened his swirling eyes, leaned over, and plucked the paper from the ground. He stared at the dot.

Then he smelled it, just to be sure.

The stench triggered a gag reflex. "Phew! That can't be more than an hour old. This must be all of it, right? There's no other Stink in the whole place."

Oafie held it out for Dud to smell. The miniscule mark on that page contained enough allergens to send Dud into a sneezing fit that lasted a good five minutes. He leaned over and pulled his shirt up over his nose. "Take that away. Let's get this over with and leave."

The blotters went to the trunk of the car. They removed two cans of gasoline and doused the front of both buildings. Tearing the paper with the dot in half, they lit the two halves and threw them toward the trails of gasoline. Soon both buildings were engulfed in an unearthly looking crimson inferno.

Dud was relieved to see the place consumed in flames. "There's something about a fire. So destructive."

"We done good," Oafie agreed. "They might even give us a promotion."

They stood there, relishing the ruin they had brought.

"Come on," said Dud. "We best go before this smoke starts me sneezing again."

By the time firefighters arrived on the scene, nothing remained of the church and vicarage except smoldering heaps of blackened stones. Along with a somehow uncharred, very lifelike statue of an unpleasant-looking woman.

10 A Talking Bottle

Dot and the children sat around the kitchen table with glasses of milk and a plate of cookies, as if Everett and Bea were on an ordinary visit to a favorite aunt. She listened attentively as they related events since the train crash.

Everett still wanted to know what Dot meant when they first arrived. "Why did you say it wasn't my real question when I asked if you knew my father?"

Dot sighed. "That wasn't very helpful of me, was it? It's what comes of writing too many mystery novels, I suppose. Always listening for subtleties."

She got up to fetch napkins from the cupboard and continued. "You asked if I'd *known* your father. But I believe what you're wondering most is if I *know* your father."

"Yes!" exclaimed Bea, jumping from her seat. "Didn't I tell you, Ev? Didn't I? He's still alive, isn't he?"

"I cannot say with certainty. Yet. But I have known your father for many years. And I have two good reasons to believe he is still with us."

"What reasons?" asked Everett.

Dot grabbed both children by the arm and squeezed. "You. The clues in your story all point to a search and rescue for Marcus."

Those words sent Everett's mind reeling. Could it be true? Had Bea been right about their dad all along? His mind searched for a thread. The policemen. The funeral. The nurse. The briefcase.

"Does this have something to do with his pen?" he asked.

Dot leaned forward. "It has everything to do with it. Did you bring it with you?"

Everett set the briefcase on the table and tried to open it but realized with frustration that it was locked again.

He felt all out of sorts and needed some air. "I thought the pen was in my pocket," he fibbed. Sliding the briefcase toward Bea, he said, "You show her this while I go check the backyard to see if I dropped the pen."

It was a thin excuse, but before anyone could question it, Everett slipped out the back door. The night air cooled his flushed face as he leaned against the side of the house. He could scarcely allow himself to hope their father was truly alive. How had Bea known the whole time when he didn't? It wasn't fair. Why was she the one who got to solve everything, hearing the ink and opening locks?

Max Courageous didn't have a little sister, but even if

he did, he wouldn't need her help. Everett turned and caught his reflection in the window. He looked and felt about as useful as Osgood's bicycle.

Taking several slow, deep breaths, he decided it didn't matter. Their father was out there somewhere. Alive! That revived his spirits. Everett would do anything that could bring him home. He slipped back through the door.

"We found the pen, Ev!" Bea said excitedly. "It was in the briefcase."

Dot examined the pen from all sides and adjusted her glasses. "One of the more beautiful pieces of workmanship I've seen." Suddenly, she froze with the pen in midair as she glanced down at the open briefcase and noticed the bottle of ink for the first time. "Where did Marcus find a bottle that size? I don't believe it."

She located a pair of white cotton gloves in a drawer, pulled them on, and gingerly lifted the ink bottle as if holding the world's most valuable diamond. As the light above the table struck the ink, it appeared to glow from within.

Everett could not see what was so significant about having extra ink. Who didn't keep a spare bottle in a desk drawer somewhere? Unless this was some expensive brand. But on a vicar's salary, his father never wasted money on extravagances.

Dot exited the kitchen and moments later returned pushing a very squeaky cart. Atop the cart sat what looked like half a cantaloupe, except made of brass and covered with typewriter keys. It was suspended by tubes and bars above a spool of paper. A single cord stretched from the keys to the mouthpiece from an old-fashioned telephone.

Bea wished she could push all the golden buttons. "Is that a fancy typewriter?"

"Of sorts," Dot replied. "It's an old Hansen Writing Ball. Osgood modified this one to listen to Ink and type what it hears. He's very proud of what he calls his Ausculators."

She placed the Ink bottle on the cart and positioned it next to the telephone mouthpiece. "This one's not always reliable," she admitted. "There can be a lot of static. But at least it will tell us if the Ink is sending any messages."

Bea elbowed Everett in the ribs and whispered, "I *told* you I heard it—"

"Shh! Let her concentrate," replied Everett, more harshly than he intended. He was not interested in one more word about what Bea could do that he couldn't.

Dot, however, was keenly interested. "You can hear the Ink?" She held up the mouthpiece. "Without a listening device such as this?"

Bea nodded, suddenly feeling rather shy.

Everett then said something he wasn't proud of later. "Bea is always pretending to talk to her toys. She makes things up all the time."

From the expression on his sister's face, he knew the jab had hit home.

Dot disregarded the comment entirely, her attention

fixed on Bea. "A human Ausculator. I read of such a thing once, but I didn't believe it."

"An ask-you-later?" Bea tried to repeat.

"Just a big word for someone who can hear and be heard by Ink. When you asked the Ink for help, the Ink heard you say the word dot and assumed you meant me. That explains it."

"Not really," said Everett, whose head was beginning to pound. "Ink is liquid—not a person. It doesn't have ears or a mouth. How can it hear and talk?"

Dot smiled at him. "A skeptic. Good! Always press into the questions. Truthfully, I know very little about how Ink does what it does. It might not actually 'hear.' But I can tell you it acts more like a living organism than a chemical compound. It is always sending and receiving energy waves—light, sound, smell—most of us can't perceive at all."

She turned to Bea. "Tell me: Do you hear the Ink now?"

Bea's face flushed. She tilted her head to the side and squinted her eyes, concentrating. "I . . . well . . . kind of. I mean . . . I hear it, but I don't understand what it's saying."

"A lot of good that does," Everett muttered under his breath.

Bea ignored him. "I don't think it's a real word. It sounds like *Ellzbid*."

Dot gasped and dropped the telephone mouthpiece with a clatter. "To think I almost opened such a priceless treasure."

She rose from her chair and swiftly returned the pen and Ink to the briefcase. "Your hearing is very good. It's not *Ellƶbid*—it's *Elspet*. Not a word, per se. The Ink is giving you a name. And another clue that makes finding your father even more urgent. We have to leave immediately."

"Wait." Everett could tell Bea was bothered by something. He had been giving her a hard time, but he could see the seriousness of her expression. "That's not all you heard, is it?"

Bea slowly shook her head. "It kept saying something over and over again, like *bounce* or *pounce*. The Ink was talking fast, the way I do when I'm nervous."

Everett looked to Dot for a reaction.

The color had drained from her face. "Pounce is a powder used for drying ink. In centuries past, people kept it in pots on their writing desks and sprinkled it over a page to make ink set more quickly. There is an ancient rhyme that says, *'Whene'er the pounce pot hath been spilled, the hands of time shall soon be stilled.'*"

The foreboding words of the rhyme sent a wave of coldness down Everett's spine. "What does that mean?"

"Metaphorically, pounce is equivalent to an overturned hourglass. The Ink just told us we're working against a clock."

"Who is out of time? Is it talking about our father?"

Dot measured her words carefully. "Possibly. The source of this Ink may also be in danger of being shut down, which would be a travesty. What is clear is that we must make haste. I need to take you to The Bird immediately."

Everett moved toward the back door.

"Oh, Ermengarde isn't the bird I meant," Dot said, pulling on an old fur coat. "It's a pub. The Bird and Baby. Technically, The Eagle and Child. It's a short distance from here, so I can drive you myself."

They all hurried out a side door to a garage. Bea looked around, confused. "Where's your car?"

"I don't have one." Dot turned to Everett. "Would you mind giving me a hand?" On one side of the garage was a large object covered by an old army tarpaulin. Each of them grabbed a corner and pulled it back to reveal a vintage motorcycle and sidecar.

Everett was awestruck. "Is that a Triumph Model P?"

"It is indeed! It belonged to my father." Dot rummaged around the shelves in the garage, collecting riding gear for the three of them. "This may be a little big on you," she said as she strapped a white helmet on Bea. Even fully tightened, it slumped forward on her small head as if it might tip her completely over.

"I believe I have a second one in that cupboard over there." She motioned for Everett to retrieve it. "You two should wear them—I'll use goggles and earmuffs on this trip."

Everett found the other helmet and pulled it on quickly. The thought of riding in a sidecar for the very first time provided a welcome distraction from the churning inside.

Bea kept rapping her knuckles on her helmet, saying, "I can't even feel this!" She and Everett fumbled their way into the sidecar. Everett was glad neither of them were any bigger in the cramped space.

Dot strapped her handbag and the briefcase to the rack above the rear tire. "All right, children, here we go!"

She kicked down the starter pedal. The engine backfired twice, then gave a throaty yell and vibrated so strongly, Everett thought the sidecar might fall off.

Dot opened the throttle wide, and the scenery flew past. Riding so low to the ground in the sidecar gave Everett the sensation of hurtling through space in the rocket that took MC to Mars.

He glanced up at Dot, hunkered down over the handlebars, grimacing behind the goggles. She would have looked like a mad scientist if not for the fur coat and those earrings flapping wildly below the earmuffs.

It hardly seemed real. Here they were, miles from home, careening down a highway with a strange woman they had just met, headed to someplace they'd never been, to do something that was supposedly urgent. Everett wondered what all this had to do with his father. And what was the secret behind the Ink?

Bea was far less concerned. All the excitement of the

day caught up with her and she somehow managed to fall asleep, bundled snugly in the sidecar with her big brother. She looked little and helpless. Everett felt a pang of guilt for how he had been treating her.

Dot turned down a street with a row of shops and parked the motorcycle illegally in front of a small cream-colored building. A sign above the door had a picture of an eagle in flight, carrying a baby. It seemed a bizarre picture—until Everett thought about their own trip on Ermengarde earlier in the day.

Dot turned off the engine, which brought Bea back to life, rubbing her eyes and full of chatter. Leaving helmets and goggles in the sidecar, Dot grabbed the briefcase and her handbag. The three of them hurried into the pub.

Two silhouettes watched their entrance, then strode briskly across the street to follow them through the door.

11 A Dark Place

Marcus woke up.

At least, he thought he did. He worried his injuries had left him paralyzed and blind, until he realized he was strapped to a bed in a pitch-dark room. By touch, he identified an IV needle protruding from his arm with the torn sleeve. Was he drugged? He felt strange.

His last memory was talking to that nurse. He knew he wasn't on the train platform anymore, although he was still wearing the same clothes. There were only two options: Either the nurse had taken him to a medical facility for further care, or that blotter had found and abducted him.

Clearly, this was no hospital.

From what he could tell, he was lying on the same gurney from the train station, and the straps holding him down were not as tight as he had first feared. Whoever had restrained him must have been more concerned about him falling off than running away.

He quickly shed his bonds and sat up a little too fast. He had to lie back down or he'd black out again. What was shooting into his veins right now? Was it safe to pull out the needle? Cotton seemed to cloud each thought. He lay in the dark, feeling helpless and uncertain. In his current condition, escape was out of the question.

A scratching sound in the corner made him catch his breath.

"Hello? Is someone here?" Silence. Had he simply imagined the noise?

He reached into his jacket pocket to check on his pen and nearly panicked before remembering what he had done with it. He breathed a sigh of relief. At least by giving it to that nurse, he had kept the Ink out of his enemy's hands. Whoever was after him had not gotten what they wanted.

Something remained in his pocket, though: his glasses case with the soaked handkerchief inside. Marcus found it comforting to have even a token of Ink with him.

He needed a plan. More than that, he needed his strength back. Marcus said a quick prayer, thought about his children, and drifted off into a fitful sleep.

12 Answers and Inklings

Evening customers packed tightly into The Eagle and Child. Dot led Everett and Bea to a closed door with a sign above it that said RABBIT ROOM. She knocked twice and ushered the children inside.

Bea instantly decided the Rabbit Room was a very friendly place, with its warm wood paneling and a blazing fire on the hearth. She saw no sign of rabbits, but still she liked being there. It smelled of tobacco and onions and books.

Seated at a table across the room were two men with mugs and plates in front of them. Their half-eaten meals were shoved aside and papers were strewn about the tabletop. One man had a roundish face without much hair on top, while the other had a full head of thick gray hair and smoked a pipe. Both rose to their feet.

"Sorry to interrupt, boys," said Dot, "but we need your help. These are Marcus Drake's children, Bea and Everett."

The gray-haired man stooped down to greet Bea. With

a kind, crinkly smile, he took her hand in his as if she were a princess. *"Elen sila lúmenna omentielvo."*

Bea was completely enchanted. "I don't know what you said, but I like the way those words sound."

"Me too," he said. "They mean 'A star shines on the hour of our meeting.' My name is Ronald. This is my friend Jack."

Jack peered at Everett closely. "You're the spitting image of your father," he said. "We are deeply saddened that he is gone."

"I'm not so sure he is," Dot said. "We have every indication he's alive and in trouble."

Everyone sat down on the padded stools, and Jack ordered two frothy hot chocolates for the children, who gratefully accepted them. Nothing is quite so calming as a warm mug of something while sitting by a crackling fire after an upsetting day.

Dot recounted events for her friends. Her tale was punctuated by numerous murmurings of "Oh, my!" and "Yes, I see" from the two men.

When she finished, they were silent. Jack sat scribbling notes on a pad while Ronald took a long draught on his pipe, sucking in his cheeks until Bea thought they might touch each other. Realizing he had an audience, Ronald blew an enormous smoke ring that rose high above the table while both children watched in admiration.

Finally, Jack set down his pencil and spoke. "Tell me, children, how are you at keeping secrets?"

"That's what I do best," said Bea, as if applying for a job. "I never tell Ev when I know what he's getting for Christmas."

Jack turned to Everett. "And what about you, young man?"

Everett thought for a moment. "It depends on the secret."

Jack nodded, satisfied. "A fair point. What we are about to share with you is probably the biggest, most important secret you will ever keep. Few other children know it, and not many grown-ups, either."

"Will it help us find our father?" Everett wanted to keep the conversation on task.

Ronald leaned in. "My dear boy," he said, "it's the only thing that will help."

Jack rose and stood by the fire, gazing into the flames. "We find ourselves in a serious situation that will require a great deal of bravery from you both."

"Those," Ronald couldn't help but comment, "are the very conditions of a great adventure. We must—"

"Gentlemen," Dot interrupted, "this is not one of your books. Can we *please* forgo the melodrama and get to the point?"

"Quite right, quite right," said Ronald. "Let's start at the top. Have you children ever heard of a group of people called the Inklings?"

"Inklings is a funny name," Bea said.

Dot smirked. "That was Ron's idea."

Ronald defended himself. "It's a very sensible name. A modern name for a very ancient group. We are a band of men—"

Dot gave a loud cough.

Ronald caught her meaning. "We've been over this, Dorothy. *Of course*, there are women. The Oxford chapter of the Inklings is a band of authors and artists who have been entrusted with the use and keeping of the Ink in these parts. Other chapters around the world do the same, but the task grows more difficult as the supply is disappearing."

The name of the group sounded vaguely familiar to Everett. "Was . . . *is* our father part of it?"

"He was helping form a London chapter," replied Jack. "I take it you're aware of the pen in his possession?"

Everett held up the briefcase. "It's in here."

"Well, it writes with no ordinary ink."

Jack collected all the papers from the table in one stack and held it out with both hands. "What if I told you children that all the great stories—I mean the best of the best—what if I told you they all came from the same Ink?"

"We have buckets of ink at school," Bea informed him.

"A different substance," said Jack, "that only has trace amounts of real Ink in it."

Ronald pointed his pipe at the children, punctuating each word he spoke. "Not all ink is Ink; And Ink is not ink at all." He crossed his arms and sat back, pleased with his riddle.

"Is it magic? Bea asked.

"Oh, Ink is far more powerful," Jack replied. "Deeper Magic from Before the Dawn of Time."

"Liquid imagination, that's what I call it." Ronald set down his pipe. "Liquid imagination! Properties beyond comprehension."

Jack could see the children's confusion. He returned the papers to the table. "Consider this: One Ink connecting Shakespeare, Newton, Rembrandt—"

"I thought Rembrandt painted," interjected Everett.

"Quite so," said Ronald. "But did you know he did his preliminary drawings in pen? He was particularly fond of a certain shade of brown Ink. Remind me to tell you more about that later."

"The point is," Jack continued, "this Ink is behind the greatest creative works in all fields. Poetry. Music. Even mathematics. It is the key that unlocks creativity itself. When you have it in your possession, the possibilities are limitless."

Ronald picked up a dinner roll from the table. "You've heard, perhaps, of the fountain of youth?"

Bea perked up. "Oh, yes! Explorers tried to find that water in the New World, but it was made up."

"A legend, yes. But based on a reality. *Except it wasn't water.*"

Ronald rotated the dinner roll and tapped his finger on different spots. "Down through the ages, small pockets of Ink have been discovered around the world. Inkwells—or fountains, if you like—with pools of pure creative energy."

He pinched off a bite of bread and popped it into his mouth, savoring the taste while the children processed his words. "Liquid imagination!" He raised his pint for a swig.

Jack elaborated. "Ink is not really an adequate term for what comes from these wells, because it does much more than write. It exudes energy in the form of what we call Ink Waves. It finds all kinds of ways to bring the best ideas to fruition. Making things. Mending things. It enlightens and inspires."

Everett could hardly believe what they were saying. "How can Bea hear Ink and talk to it?"

"It isn't hearing in the traditional sense." Jack picked up a fork from the table and flicked it with his finger. "Have you ever seen a tuning fork before?"

"The man who tuned our piano used one, but it didn't look like that," said Everett.

"He has you there, Jack," laughed Ronald. "Tuning forks only have two tines."

"True," Jack conceded. "My visual aid notwithstanding, a tuning fork resonates on a single frequency, producing a pure tone. But then"—and here he reached for Ronald's fork—"if you place it next to another fork like it, something magical happens: The second one will pick up the wave and begin to hum the same tune. Sympathetic vibrations."

He set both forks back on the table. "A few rare souls, your sister included, resonate on the same frequency as Ink. Some pick up the sound. Others can catch the scent. We don't know why. However it happens, something inside Bea 'hums' the same tune as the Ink."

The whole concept was a bit over Bea's head. But she did like humming. And the smell of that dinner roll. The fresh aroma made her mouth water, and she wished she had taken a second cookie from Dot's kitchen.

Ronald took another drink, then wiped the foam from his mouth. "Tell me, Everett. What's the first book you loved?"

Everett thought back to a favorite his father used to read to him. *The Magical Land of Noom.*"

"Oh, yes!" agreed Bea. "That's a good one."

Ronald's eyes shone with excitement. "Johnny Gruelle. Excellent! You know, he never sketched his illustrations with pencil first—he went straight to Ink. What I want to know from you is this: Why do you like his work?"

Everett didn't need to think twice. "It makes me want to go there."

Ronald pressed his face so close, his nose brushed Everett's. He tapped him on the chest. "Deep down, you feel there is something more—some bigger reality than ordinary life. A place of goodness and joy. You ache for it. It calls to you. And certain authors take you there, if only for a moment."

Bea laughed. "But those places are just pretend."

"Are they?" Ronald sat back and drew another long breath through his pipe.

The dramatic pause was too much for Dot, who rolled

her eyes and rose. "I need to park my motorbike around back before a policeman gives me a ticket." She slipped out as Jack picked up the dialogue.

"When you read a good book, what do you wish?"

Everett remembered how for days after finishing *The Magical Land of Noom*, he pretended he was Johnny and Bea was Janey. "I wish I could be in it."

"What if you *are* a part of it?"

"I'm from the Land of Noom?"

Jack shook his head, placing a hand on Everett's arm. "It would be more accurate to say both you and Noom come from the same place—the source of all creativity."

Everett felt he almost understood, but a question still bothered him. "Can only famous people use Ink?"

"Hardly!" Ronald said. "Ink draws out the very best talent and personality within each person, regardless of their station or merits. Jack has a way with fairy tales and theology. I find myself able to write about mythical kingdoms and even create other languages. Dot is brilliant at solving mysteries. What might it be for you?"

Everett's face grew warm. The pen certainly hadn't worked when he tried it. What was wrong with him? A frightening thought crossed his mind: What if he didn't have anything worthwhile for the Ink to find?

The nap in the sidecar had been too short for Bea, and she was feeling impatient with the lengthy explanations. She tugged on Jack's tweed jacket. "What about Daddy?"

Everett welcomed the shift in spotlight. "Yes. What about him?"

"Marcus and I met several years ago," Jack said, tossing a log on the fire. "At the time, he was the editor of a church publication called *The Anvil*, and I wrote articles for him.

"One day your father shared with me that he had begun writing comic books. I read his first issues, which I found most delightful."

Bea laughed. "But you're a grown-up. You can't like comic books."

"And why not?" Jack said. "The best children's stories speak to all ages. I'm keen on a well-told tale in any format. Your father had bigger dreams for Max Courageous. To my knowledge, Ink had never been used in comics, so an experiment seemed in order."

"Was that when you gave our father the bottle of Ink?" Everett asked.

"Oh my, no," exclaimed Jack. "Ink has been exceedingly scarce for many years. In several regions of the world, Inklings have run out of reserves. Here in Oxford, we have been diluting our supply and rationing it carefully to make it stretch. We hadn't seen fully concentrated Ink since before the war.

"No, we had no bottle to give your father. We gave him a pen. Ordinarily, one full pen can last many years, even at half strength."

Ronald's face lit up at the memory. "The moment your

father began to draw, Ink flowed in blazing colors. Vivid, realistic stories poured out. Extraordinary."

Looking back, Everett knew exactly when the quality of MC's adventures had changed. The pictures in the newer issues were more vibrant and the plots far more riveting. Still, something didn't quite make sense. "If the Ink does all these things, how is it a secret?"

Jack dug through the stack of papers and pulled out a graph showing the number of Inkwells throughout history. Jack pointed to a high point on the line. "Centuries ago, the Ink flowed freely. Everyone knew about it and shared it openly."

He moved his finger farther down the line where the graph dropped sharply. "Today, the enemies of Ink are shutting down wells. They are on a mission to eradicate Ink completely."

Bea was alarmed. "Can they do that?"

"They nearly have." Ronald patted her hand reassuringly. "But Ink is the source of all the stories where good triumphs over evil. It's hard to imagine its own story being any different."

Everett studied the chart. "Does this say there's just one now?"

Jack nodded. "As far as we know, only one remains active: Elspet's well. Prior to your father acquiring that bottle, we feared it might also be gone for good."

Everett stared at the briefcase. "So this bottle we have is from that well? Is it what got Dad in trouble?"

At that moment, Dot returned, shutting the door and leaning against it. She closed her eyes. "Eddie Montbanks."

"Here?" asked Ronald.

"At a table just outside the door."

Jack began to pace, one hand rubbing his forehead. "Montbanks is a perfect example of why you've never heard of Ink, Everett. It becomes dangerous in the wrong hands, and his are undeniably wrong. We were warned he might be coming. I didn't expect him so quickly."

"You're sure it's him?" Ronald asked Dot.

"His picture came across the Ausculator a few days ago from Inklings in America. Wisp of a man with a king-size bodyguard."

"Who's Eddie Montbanks?" whispered Bea.

"He used to be an Inkling in the States," Jack explained. "Then he went bad. He began forging money with Ink. The bills were undetectable counterfeits. He would have made millions, but he grew careless. He went to prison and was banished from the Inklings for life."

"Good," said Bea.

"He broke a sacred trust, and has gone from bad to worse," continued Jack. "He served his time and was released last year. He has been attempting to steal more Ink, using his 'bodyguard' to intimidate other Inklings. But every Inkwell in America has dried up. There's none there for him to steal. Many Inklings have even had to leave the country."

"McCarthyism!" Ronald exclaimed. "Not a good time for creative types across the pond. It all stems from—"

Dot cut him off. "Two weeks ago, someone broke into the Inklings' New York headquarters and stole the list of all the chapters worldwide. No doubt it was Montbanks. It appears he's expanded his search internationally."

"Should we call a policeman?" Bea asked. "Ev and I met some nice ones."

Everett had a more pointed question. "Did Mr. Montbanks kidnap our father?"

Dot shook her head. "It's far more likely he was captured by . . . that is to say . . . "

"Those blotter people?" Bea asked. "Osgood said blotters were coming to our house."

The grown-ups looked at one another as if trying to decide how much to say. Finally, Jack spoke. "Yes. From the evidence you've shared, it would seem blotters are behind his disappearance. They are even more despicable than Montbanks. Which is why we must be going."

He cracked the door open and peeked into the pub. "Unfortunately, we can't just waltz past Montbanks and out the front door."

Everett thought of what MC would do when cornered. "What about a diversion? Mr. Montbanks doesn't know me. I could create a distraction while the rest of you sneak past."

Ronald smiled. "That's very Tookish of you, young man. You're full of pluck. But there's no need. Did you see the sign above the door as you came into this room?"

"Oh, yes!" exclaimed Bea before Everett could respond. "It said this is the Rabbit Room."

Ronald walked over to the corner by the fireplace. "Here's how it earned the name."

He slid an entire section of the wood paneling to the side, revealing a large round tunnel.

"A rabbit hole!" Bea said in wonder. Immediately, she grew serious. "Is there a giant bunny in there?"

Dot laughed. "You've been around Ermengarde too long! No giant rabbits."

Ronald waved his arm toward the opening. "All right, children, let's quietly make our way into the tunnel and get this Ink bottle safely away before Mr. Montbanks and his muscle man invite themselves into the conversation."

13 · A Pet Peeve

T alk."

Marcus startled at the voice. "Who are you?" he replied softly.

"Talk."

If Marcus had been awake earlier, he would have recognized the raspy voice as the Commander's. Even in a single word, the tone and inflection were recognizable.

But it was not the Commander who spoke.

There was a rustling and flapping, then Marcus felt a weight land on his chest. Instinctively, he tried to bring his hands up to push it away, but to his dismay he discovered that the restraints had been retied much more securely.

It took him a moment to realize the nail-like objects pressing into his sternum were a bird's talons.

The Commander had left his pet raven, Grip, to watch over the prisoner until he returned from Newcastle. Like a parrot, Grip could mimic anything he heard and repeat it at will. The bird's intelligence let him use that skill to great effect.

"Talk," he repeated, hopping up and down on the vicar. "Talk. Taaaaaalk!"

The raven leaned down until the tip of his beak grazed Marcus' eyelashes. He hovered there, as if contemplating stabbing downward. Then he snapped his beak open and shut.

"What is it you think I have?" asked Marcus. "Important secrets?"

"Important secrets!" mimicked the bird.

Grip moved up until he was standing on Marcus's neck, crushing his windpipe. He bent down and swiftly pecked at the vicar's forehead. He repeated the motion again and again in multiple places, drawing blood.

Combined with the pressure on his throat, the effect was terrifying. Unable to draw a breath, Marcus struggled against the rising panic. He tried to break his hands free of the restraints, but he could not.

Just when he started seeing spots, the bird moved back down to his chest. Marcus gulped in air as the bird jabbed sharply at his torso.

There was a ripping sound as the raven pulled a button free of his shirt.

The door burst open and Grip flapped back to his cage with the button. The Commander's uneven footsteps brought him alongside the gurney. He leaned in so close, Marcus could feel his dry, ragged breath on his face.

"I see you two have been getting acquainted," said the Commander.

"I don't know what you want," yelled Marcus.

"I have . . . important secrets," Grip said, in a perfect impression of the vicar.

"That is not what I said!" Marcus strained against the ropes. "That bird is twisting my words!"

The Commander sighed. "Perhaps it's time to increase your medication." He reached over and adjusted the IV drip.

"Can you at least turn on a light?" Marcus asked quietly.

"Oh, I assure you, it's quite bright in here. We've wrapped your brain in a nebula. Think of it as a mental fog."

Marcus looked around. "This darkness—it's not real?"

"Oh, it's real," the Commander said. "But it's personal."

"What?"

"Don't worry. Sight eventually returns, at least some of the time."

Marcus grew exasperated. "What is it you want?"

"You will save yourself a great deal of discomfort if you tell me where it is."

"I . . . I don't know what you're talking about."

"Well, then, Reverend, you're in luck." The Commander summoned Grip, who flew to his side. "I have a great deal of experience in making myself understood."

If Walls Could Talk

14

With the exception of Bea, everyone had to duck their heads to step inside the tunnel. Bringing up the rear, Jack grabbed a flashlight from the mantel and pulled the paneling shut behind them.

Dot rummaged through her handbag and produced a light of her own. She led the group farther into the dark. It went on and on, much farther than could possibly be within the confines of the building that housed the pub.

As they walked single file, Everett extended a hand and ran his fingers along the wall. "It's like *Alice in Wonderland*," he observed.

Ronald chuckled. "You recognized it!"

Everett was unsure what he meant. "Recognized what?"

"Oh, do stop being so cryptic, Ron!" Dot shouted from the front of the line. "You always talk in shorthand and then smudge it."

Jack came to his friend's defense. "He's just having a bit of fun, Dorothy. Everett, do you know who wrote *Alice in Wonderland*?"

"Lewis Carroll?"

Ronald jumped back in. "His real name was Charles Dodgson. An Inkling of a previous generation. Did you know he coined the word *chortle*? One of my favorites. I—"

Jack quickly broke in before Dot became further annoyed. "While a student in Oxford, Charles discovered this tunnel. It leads to a labyrinth of tunnels used by Inklings from bygone civilizations. The tunnels formed connections between wells worldwide. Sadly, most are now stopped up."

Dot brought everyone to a halt. "I hope you children still enjoy a good slide."

She directed the beam of light ahead of them. A long metal chute sloped away into the blackness with no trace of the bottom.

"We're going on that?" Bea asked incredulously.

Dot winked at her. "The perfect exit for a budding escape artist, wouldn't you say?" With that, she abruptly sat down in the chute, pushed off, and slipped out of sight. "See you all beloooooooooooow!"

"Bea, Everett, in you go," Jack said, motioning with the beam of light toward the slide. "We old men require time to fold ourselves into that contraption, so we will follow last."

Bea paused a moment, staring down the chute, looking small and pale in the light of the flashlight. Everett took her hand, which she clutched gratefully. He tried to reassure her. "Remember riding with Dad on the toboggan last winter?"

That memory gave her the courage she needed. She

settled in, a determined expression on her face. Everett sat down behind her with his arms around her, holding the briefcase in front of her like a shield. "Ready, Bea?"

She swallowed hard and shut her eyes. "Ready!"

Everett shoved off before she could change her mind. Down and around they went. It did feel quite similar to a toboggan ride. The speed was incredible, with untold numbers of twists as it wound downward through the dark.

As the descent leveled off, a faint bluish glow appeared up ahead. The chute flattened out, and the children slowed to a stop in a most peculiar room.

It was a simple, box-shaped space with no windows and no visible way out, other than the chute. The blue light was emanating from the ceiling. But the walls were what set the room apart. Handwriting covered every inch of the entire room like graffiti. And the notes appeared to have been scribbled by thousands of different people in all sorts of languages and penmanship. Everett and Bea joined Dot, who stood scrutinizing one section of a wall.

Moments later, peals of laughter punctuated the stillness as Jack and Ronald tumbled into the room. They smiled broadly, like two schoolboys who had just shared the best joke.

"What fun!" Ronald clapped his hands.

Jack wiped his brow with a handkerchief. "Exhilarating! It's been years since I've done that." He looked around. "Children, you are standing in Writer's Block."

Everett looked at the walls covered with Ink. Scientific formulas and drawings of animals. Poems and signatures. Lines from plays and bits of speeches.

Not only was every space filled—the Ink was layers deep. Words sat on top of pictures on top of numbers. But the remarkable thing was that with concentration, you could read whichever layer you wanted, simply by focusing your vision. Even when one word was scrawled over another, the layer beneath it could still be deciphered.

Everett glanced over at his sister. Bea stood with her hands covering her ears, her eyes squeezed shut. "What's the matter?" he yelled.

She opened her eyes and yelled back. "IT'S TOO LOUD IN HERE!"

"Oh, my dear," said Dot. "A thousand apologies. I forgot about you hearing the Ink."

She reached in her handbag and pulled out her earmuffs from the motorcycle ride. "These should dampen the sound."

Bea placed them over her ears and gave a sigh of relief.

Everett turned his attention back to the walls. "What are we looking for?"

"A needle in a haystack. There are at least ten thousand one hundred seventy-three exits from this room, and we need the right one," Dot said.

Everett frowned. "I don't see any."

"That's the maddening thing about Writer's Block," Jack replied. "Every way out is hidden in the words and numbers."

"I find that to be the fun part," said Ronald. "Getting lost in the minutiae while you—"

"Time is of the essence, Ron," said Dot. "I am specifically searching for an exit that will take us to the Harrow and Wealdstone train station, where your father was last seen."

Harrow & Wealdstone. Everett was stunned. "That's miles and miles from here."

"You'd think so, wouldn't you?" Ronald said. "From Writer's Block, London is just as close as Oxford."

"That doesn't make any sense."

"Allow me to demonstrate." Ronald paused, studying Everett's shirt. "Take these top two buttons on your shirt. How far apart would you say they are?"

Everett estimated the distance. "Maybe three or four inches?"

"So it would appear," Ronald concurred. "But is that always the case? Can you bring them closer together?"

Everett thought for a moment. Then he reached down and folded up a section of his shirt so that the lower button moved up and touched the top one.

Ronald's eyes danced with amusement. "You see? Given the nature of fabric, you can pinch the space between them and bring the two points side by side—presto! Suddenly, two objects become much closer than they naturally appear."

Everett's mind was reeling. "You squeezed Great Britain and brought two places together?"

Ronald smiled. "Oh, no, my boy. Exits from Writer's

Block are some of the naturally occurring Pinches in the world, shrinking the distance from one place to another. They're similar to wormholes through space."

Jack joined in the conversation. "For decades, Inklings passing through Writer's Block tried to understand how the secret exits worked." He looked at Bea. "It was a gifted girl about your age by the name of Madeleine who first sorted it out. Years ago, she described them as 'wrinkles.' I do hope she'll write out her theory one day. We're not doing it justice."

Everett chafed at the idea of someone else younger than him who understood the Ink. Yet if it gave them a shortcut to finding his father, he could live with it.

Bea tugged on Dot's sleeve. With the earmuffs on, she spoke louder than normal. "WHY DO YOU WANT TO GO TO THE TRAIN STATION? DO YOU THINK DADDY IS STILL THERE?"

Dot bent close to Bea. "I doubt he's there. But I know a train conductor who may be able to help us find him."

Jack put on his spectacles and turned his face to the nearest wall. "All right, Dorothy. Give us some instructions."

"We write to discover," said Dot. She took a handful of Ink markers from a nearly invisible shelf on one wall and passed them around.

"Free association. Look for something related to our search. A picture of a train . . . mention of London. Be sure to check the lower layers as well. Then write whatever comes to mind. That will lead us out."

Bea took her marker straight to a corner and set to work. "I'M DRAWING DADDY."

For the next half hour, no one spoke as everyone scoured the walls. Everett felt like he was in a trance. The numbers and letters seemed to move and arrange themselves in ever-changing combinations. He found himself drawn in by a story of a knight on a quest. Then his attention was diverted to a short verse from a poem about a tiger, then a picture of a most lifelike ship. On and on it went, until the letters *HW* caught his eye as if they were floating toward him.

His heart began to gallop. This had to be it! *HW* must stand for *Harrow & Wealdstone*. Placing the tip of the marker on the wall, he tried to think of something fitting to write. But his mind was a complete blank. Nothing. As moments passed, panic set in. Then he remembered: He couldn't write with the Ink!

Should he tell someone? It was humiliating, not being able to do something as simple as write. Even people who couldn't read knew how to write a big *X* for their name.

A big *X*. That could stand for exit! Everett dragged the marker all the way across the *H* and *W*. It resisted him, but he managed to pull it back in a second line, scrawling a single letter. It was legible even if it wasn't pretty.

Instinctively, he reached to touch the *X*. Right away, his fingers tingled the way an arm or foot feels when you've had all your weight on it for too long and it has fallen asleep. The

X grew and moved away from the wall until it was hanging in midair.

"Over here!" he shouted. "I think I found it!"

The group gathered around and stared at the giant X. "Interesting," mused Dot. "Not what I was expecting. What made you think to draw an X?"

Everett didn't want to explain. "X over HW stands for *exit to Harrow and Wealdstone*."

He crossed his arms and looked at Dot expecting validation, but she appeared unconvinced. The expressions on Jack's and Ronald's faces showed similar skepticism.

"What's wrong?" asked Everett, feeling the color rising in his cheeks.

"Nothing at all, my boy," said Ronald, patting him on the back. "That was a fine bit of deduction there. It's just that in these sorts of situations, a giant X is generally considered a warning rather than an invitation."

"That would be my take as well," conceded Dot. "It's as if the H and W are crossed out as being off limits. Let's search a bit longer to see what else turns up."

Everyone drifted away to continue looking, but Everett remained brooding in front of the X. He was sure he had found the way out. Just because he couldn't write with the Ink didn't mean he was wrong. But if he was right, why was no exit appearing?

Everett lightly touched the X with his fingertips. There was that same tingling sensation. He set down the briefcase and grabbed the *X* with both hands. As he did, it transformed itself into a spoked handwheel, the kind found on the door of a bank vault. It was asking to be opened, no matter what the grown-ups thought.

He turned it to the left.

Instantly, all the writing on the wall behind it began to swirl in a counterclockwise motion, pulling in the letters and images until there was one large circle of solid Ink spinning in the air, like a sideways whirlpool.

But it wasn't solid. As Everett peered into the Ink, he looked right through the wall into another tunnel. This *was* the way out!

"Ev, wait!" shouted Bea, but she was too late. Everett grabbed the briefcase and stepped forward, through the circle and out of Writer's Block.

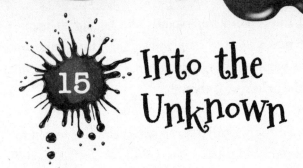

Into the Unknown

Dropping the marker and earmuffs, Bea ran after her brother into the swirling portal. Not about to lose the children, the three grown-ups followed. After everyone crossed into the new tunnel, the spinning hole closed behind them, leaving the group in total darkness.

Dot and Jack switched on their flashlights.

"Well, our choice has been made," observed Jack, rapping his knuckles on the now solid wall. "There's no going back."

"Are we in a Pinch?" asked Bea.

"Perhaps in more ways than one," muttered Dot.

Everett couldn't bring himself to look at her. Suddenly, he felt far less sure of his choice.

Ronald grunted as he bumped into something. "Oh! I say. This will be helpful."

There was a loud creak as he moved a lever, and a string of lights hummed to life overhead, revealing a passageway. The lights cast the same bluish hue as in Writer's Block.

As he stared at the row of radiant orbs, Everett recalled how the Ink appeared to glow when Dot held it under her kitchen chandelier. "The lights—are they blue because they use Ink Waves?"

"One of the most intriguing and useful properties of Ink," said Jack, "is its ability to shed light." He studied Everett's face. "An impressive bit of deduction, I must say. You're very observant."

Everett shrugged off the compliment. His father often told him he was good at that—observing things. He wanted to be strong and brave like MC. He would settle for being better than his little sister at something. Instead he had to content himself with being "very observant."

Dot wrapped an arm around Everett. "Well, young man, it remains to be seen if *HW* is indeed the train station. But you succeeded in finding a way out of Writer's Block, which is a most impressive feat in and of itself."

Everett felt relieved. Maybe now they were one step closer to rescuing his dad.

"What's that?" Bea pointed down the tunnel toward a short column rising from the ground.

Dot led the way to the object. It was an ancient-looking stone pillar that stood about three feet high. She excitedly motioned for Bea and Everett to come close. "Children, take a look. It's not every day you get to see a Roman mile marker in England. Especially underground."

Everett walked around the pillar. "How did it get down here?"

"Roman Inklings used these tunnels," said Jack. "They marked them the same way they marked roads above ground."

Near the base of the column, Everett could see letters etched into the stone. Parts of the words had crumbled away, but what remained said:

FON

ATRAMEN

Bea scrunched up her face, trying to decipher the words. "Someone couldn't spell very well."

"Latin," said Ronald. "The words once said Inkwell."

"Of course." Jack slapped his forehead. "I should have made the connection to the Romans when we first saw the initials *HW*."

Everett's heart sank. "You mean it doesn't stand for *Harrow and Wealdstone*?"

Jack shook his head. "Unfortunately, no. We have traveled to Hadrian's Well."

"You mean Hadrian's Wall," corrected Everett, suddenly feeling irritable.

"Hadrian's *Well* is why the Romans built Hadrian's *Wall* across northern England," said Jack. "It was one of the most fertile sources of Ink ever discovered. Almost mythical, which is why Roman Inklings felt the need to protect it from the barbarian hordes. And why blotters shut it down."

"But that means . . ." Everett was too sickened by the thought to finish his sentence. Hadrian's Wall was far to the north—hours from the station. His impulsive choice had cost them precious time, and they were further than ever from rescuing his father. And now there was no going back to Writer's Block to find the correct exit.

Dot took off her glasses and began cleaning them with a cloth from her handbag. "Marcus once told me he wanted to write a story about Max Courageous fighting a battle at Hadrian's Wall. Wouldn't it be splendid if we could tell him all about this place when we rescue him?"

She perched her spectacles back on her nose and gave a satisfied nod. "That's better."

It cheered Everett to picture his hero in the same spot. He patted the top of the milepost. "MC's never seen anything like this."

With a clearer sense of their bearings, they set off to find the well, which they were now certain must be nearby. More blue lights overhead illuminated the way, but Everett noticed that several had been smashed, as if someone purposely broke them to make it darker.

"Look!" Bea pointed to the silhouette of a large mound several yards ahead of them, right in the middle of the tunnel.

Walking closer, they could see the mound wasn't dirt— it was broken pieces of something. Everett picked up one of the shards. Heavy sadness came over him the moment he touched the material.

"Oh . . . oh, no!" Bea's hands flew to her ears and her eyes filled with tears. "I think the pile is crying."

Everett turned the piece over in his hand. It reminded him of dry spaghetti noodles, excepted that it was dark blue and full of curves and bends. "It's dried Ink." He held it up for the others to see. "It's as if someone scraped millions of words out of books and piled them here."

Jack took the piece and examined it. "Tomecide."

Bea tried to process the word. "Thomas who?"

"The destruction of books. When blotters shut down a well, they routinely raid the surrounding towns, sniffing out and destroying anything created by the Ink."

His flashlight swept across the ground, revealing a footprint.

"We're not safe here," whispered Dot.

It was grim news. Yet there was no returning to Writer's Block. They had to move forward.

Dot quickly took charge. "Jack and I will sneak our way to the other side of the pile. Ron—you stay here with the children until we signal you with the flashlight that the coast is clear."

Bea clung to Everett's arm. They stood stock-still beside Ronald, awaiting their cue.

From the far recesses of the tunnel came a faint but chilling wail.

"Did you hear that?" Everett asked Ronald.

"Hear what, exactly?"

"It sounded like an animal howling."

Ronald paused to listen. "Perhaps a breeze? Airflow in these tunnels can deceive the ears. I wouldn't worry yourself about it."

But the way Ronald said it was the way grown-ups say things to convince themselves not to worry. And Everett *was* worried. Because he knew what he had heard, and it was no breeze. No trick of the ear could fake the evil in that howl.

He was sure of that.

16   Eddie Goes Hunting

Eddie Montbanks finished his dinner. A glance at the clock validated his impatience. He motioned to his mammoth bodyguard, Mr. Lugg, who went to ask the waiter for the check.

It had been hours since Eddie had followed the Sayers woman into the pub and watched her enter the Rabbit Room with some children. Children didn't attend normal Inkling gatherings, at least not back home. Something must be up. Time to find out what.

Traveling overseas made him feel cross. His stomach didn't appreciate English cooking. But his research led him to believe the Oxford Inklings were his best bet for acquiring more Ink. And he needed more. So he made the trip.

Eddie had given up his money-printing scheme. That now seemed so passé. His new plan was much bigger.

While hunting for more Ink in America, he had strong-armed enough people to realize just how scarce the commodity truly was. There was none to be had. The very lack of this resource made it more precious. It was the law of supply and demand. And a great big flash bulb of an idea went off in his brain.

Instead of forging money, he would forge Ink. He would create a synthetic version for mass production and control the supply himself. He just needed a sample to replicate.

The demand would be enormous. Every starry-eyed would-be author would want it so they could write a best seller. Every starving artist would pay any price to create a masterpiece. It was a fortune waiting to be made. The Inklings who disowned him would soon come begging. He would have his revenge, and it would be delicious.

Far more delicious than the steak pie he'd just finished. He wiped the remaining crumbs from his lips as Mr. Lugg returned. "The waiter's bringing the bill."

"Time to make our move."

Eddie walked with Mr. Lugg to the door of the Rabbit Room. He knocked once, softly. No answer. He knocked louder, and still no response. Mr. Lugg opened the door.

The room was empty. The two men scanned it for a back door. They checked under the tables and chairs. Nothing. The fire crackled in the hearth and there were half-full steins on the table, along with most of a dinner roll. Stacks of papers were strewn about.

Eddie riffled through a few. They were all written in pencil. Where did everyone go? In a fit of frustration, he flipped the table over, sending papers flying.

"Excuse me, gentlemen—did you say you were ready to

pay?" The waiter stood at the door with the bill, trying to ignore what he just saw.

"Yes, here you are." Smoothing his tie, Eddie smiled unnaturally, took out his billfold, and handed the waiter enough cash to ensure he went away without asking more questions. "Keep the change."

As he surveyed the room one last time, Eddie noticed something on the floor in the far corner. He went over and picked up a small porcelain figurine that had been knocked off a ledge with several other figurines above the paneling. He contemplated it a moment, then looked more closely at the wainscoting on the wall.

A thin crack separated two sections of the paneling beneath the trim. He snapped his fingers, and Mr. Lugg came to his side. "What do you make of this?"

The bodyguard looked at the gap and grunted. Taking a penknife from his pocket, he wedged the blade into the opening, widening it until he could get his ample fingers in the space.

With a single shove, the entire section of paneling slid away to reveal the secret tunnel.

Eddie's eyes narrowed as he took in how everyone had escaped him. He grabbed a kerosene lantern from the mantel and used his lighter to bring it to life. Mr. Lugg moved to enter the tunnel, but Eddie stopped him. "I can handle the bookworms and the woman. Stay here and guard the entrance. Don't let anyone follow me."

Mr. Lugg handed him the knife. "Better take this, then. You never know what you might run into."

Eddie slipped the knife into his pocket. Then he turned and entered the blackness.

Everyone Loves a Log Ride

17

Dud would not leave the car.

Oafie rapped on the window. "We don't have time for this!"

Crossing his arms, Dud slumped further in the seat. "Why can't we just drive?"

"Have you been dipping in the pounce again? Driving would take hours!"

Oafie slapped a piece of paper against the window glass for Dud to read. "Orders is orders. You want the same punishment as last time?"

With a big sigh, Dud unlocked the door and got out. "It's not fair. Other blotters have wings. Why couldn't I have a pair? Then I could fly myself places."

He was no sooner out of the car than a sneezing fit caused him to double over.

Oafie paced back and forth in exasperation. "There's not even any Stink around here!"

Dud blew his nose. "I'm allergic to pain, and I got a bad feeling this is going to hurt."

The two blotters walked down a steep path that led to a valley tucked out of sight of the road.

"Do you think we're going by airplane?" Dud gnawed on his fingernails.

"Dunno." Oafie consulted the orders. "Just says *'When mission is complete, report to McLarch immediately for rapid transport to Newcastle.'*"

"I ain't never flown before."

They soon came to a low stone cottage, with flower boxes at the windows and smoke rising from the chimney. A homely garden gnome on the lawn smiled impishly at the visitors.

"See, Dud?" Oafie said. "What's so scary about a cozy little place like this?"

He knocked on the door. A few seconds passed, then a small porthole opened and an eyeball evaluated the visitors, followed by a giddy gasp. Then came the sounds of multiple bolts being loosened, and the door flung wide to welcome them.

It took Dud and Oafie a moment to realize they were looking at a woman.

Her expansive form filled the door frame, and her ape-like arms nearly reached the floor. All the layers of powder caked on her face made her head resemble a rising lump of dough. It was punctuated by what could only be called a snout, which bubbled and wheezed with every breath. She tossed her stringy blond hair in a nauseating attempt at flirtation. But her crazed, unblinking eyes told Dud and Oafie she would snap them like twigs if provoked.

The pasty face cracked into what passed for a grin, revealing a handful of teeth with debris in between. "Why, hello."

Oafie squirmed and cleared his throat. "Um . . . hello. We're . . . we're looking for McLarch."

The woman tittered and curtsied clumsily. "Look all you want. I'm McLarch. MISS McLarch."

To call her ugly wouldn't capture the reaction she generated. Horrifying was more like it. Perhaps the best way to describe Miss McLarch is to simply say that she was too terrifyingly hideous for even a blotter to find attractive.

The nauseatingly powdery scent emanating from her set off a sneeze attack for Dud. Miss McLarch stepped out onto the porch and shoved a well-used hanky in his face. Her thick fingers slid it roughly back and forth across his nose.

"I can't recall the last time two gentlemen callers came asking for me." She clucked and cackled, pinching Dud on the cheek. "To think I was worried I would never have another suitor."

The two blotters glanced uneasily at each other.

"Well, Miss McLarch, the thing is . . ." Oafie searched for the right words. "This isn't exactly a social call. We're here for transportation."

The woman's eyes darkened and narrowed menacingly. She crossed her arms, the smile gone. "Transportation?"

Oafie extended his paperwork in front of them. Miss McLarch snatched the orders from his hand and studied them. Her bottom lip began to tremble and she burst into tears, her shoulders heaving up and down.

"It's always the same!" she sobbed, throwing the orders back at Oafie. She took the handkerchief that had soaked up Dud's sneezes and buried her face in it. "Nobody ever wants to see me!"

The wailing grew louder. Worried they might never get the ride they needed, Oafie tried to reassure her. "That's not true, miss. Why, Dud and me was just saying on the way over here how much we'd heard about the pretty Miss McLarch."

She sniffed and dabbed her eyes. "Is that so?"

Dud caught on and played along. "Yes, indeed. Oafie told me how next time we get to London he wanted to come back and pay you a visit when we ain't on duty."

Miss McLarch's mood brightened considerably. She fluffed a few strands of hair and grinned at Oafie, who gulped in fright.

Coaxing her along, Dud said, "The sooner you help us leave, the sooner he can come back to you."

The woman laughed. "Silly boys. I can't help you go anywhere." She waddled off the porch toward the garden gnome. Dud and Oafie followed her.

"You can't?" Oafie asked.

"You have the wrong McLarch."

Oafie checked the orders, confused. "We do?"

"You need my brother." With that, she placed a heavy foot on the garden gnome's head and stomped it completely into the dirt. The ground shook, knocking both blotters off their feet. Behind them, the entire cottage lifted up and tilted to the side like the lid of a jar, revealing a gaping hole underneath.

"ANGUS!" Miss McLarch bellowed. "VISITORS!"

Up out of the ground came not a man, but a giant.

If you've ever seen the gnarled roots of an old, fallen tree, you have a fair description of Angus McLarch. He sported a matted, rusty beard and long hair that looked like it had never seen a comb. Northern giants are not known for their hygiene as much as their strength. His arms were as thick as Dud's waist. Above his black kilt he wore a sheepskin vest, which looked alarmingly capable of bleating.

Blotters collaborated often with giants, so Dud and Oafie had seen many of their kind up close. But this one filled them with a dread they'd never experienced before.

Angus bent low to inspect his visitors, his rancid breath hot against their faces.

Dud let out a nervous sneeze.

The giant turned and scowled, then burst out laughing.

He poked Oafie in the belly. "Well, curse me if you two ain't adorable!"

Oafie did not appreciate the insinuation that they were anything less than intimidating. "We're here on official business. The Commander sent us." Once again, he extended his paper for inspection.

Angus brushed it aside. "I know why you're here. Caber toss, same as always. What is it with you blotter types and the caber toss? Let's go out back."

As he moved. Dud turned to Oafie, wide-eyed. "Did he just say 'caber toss'?"

Angus led them behind the cottage to a large, open field surrounded by acres of conifer trees. "Wait here."

The giant lumbered off into the woods.

His sister sidled up to Oafie and wrapped her arm in his. "I'm glad we have a few minutes to ourselves."

Oafie thought he might be sick when Miss McLarch leaned her weighty head on his shoulder. The three of them watched as the top of one of the trees in the forest shook, then disappeared. Soon Angus came plodding back toward them, dragging a tree in his wake.

He stood it on end and began snapping off branches by hand, pine cones dropping to the ground.

"I'm the only one in my family who can throw logs," Angus boasted. "The rest are all about the boulders. Too much of a stereotype, I say. All giants throw rocks."

"I'm only half-giant," Miss McLarch cooed at Oafie. "But my heart is all blotter."

"So, you do this often, then?" Dud asked Angus, desperate for anything reassuring.

"It's been a while since my last toss," the giant confessed.

"I used to keep a supply of spare logs, but after the accident, I . . ."

Dud waited anxiously for the conclusion of the story, but it never came. What accident was he talking about? Why was he playing with trees? Wasn't the giant supposed to be taking them to Scotland?

Angus finished stripping the tree of its limbs and looked around. "Now, where are those ropes?"

Miss McLarch went and rolled a large bin on wheels to her brother's side. "You stopped using ropes, remember? The issue with reentry."

Angus searched his memory banks. "Ah, right you are. Chains it is, then."

He opened the bin, removed two sections of chain, then turned to his visitors, who were now both visibly shaken. "Have either of you lads gone for a log ride before? No? Well, it's pretty simple, really. Except when, you know, it ain't."

He kicked at the log on the ground. "We'll strap you lads to this caber, then I give it a good toss."

"Wait," Dud said, trying to comprehend. "What's happening?"

The giant demonstrated by moving his arms in an underhand throwing motion. "You go up in the air here and land in . . . you land in . . . where am I sending you?"

"Newcastle," squeaked Oafie.

"Right. And not to fill me own bagpipes, but I nearly always get close to the mark."

Without another word, the giant scooped up the blotters and set them lengthwise atop the log, Dud at one end and Oafie at the other.

Miss McLarch took the chains and soon had the two blotters tightly secured, looking ready to roast over a fire.

She leaned close to Oafie's face. "Hurry back to me, love." Then she planted a slobbery kiss on his lips, leaving a thin trail of drool. Oafie stifled a scream.

Angus lifted the log and carried it to the center of the field. "Let's have our own Highland Games, shall we?"

He tipped the log up on end with Dud upside down. All the blood rushed to Dud's brain as the giant fiddled with his grip. When Angus finally picked up the log, his hand slipped, dropping Dud squarely on his head.

Dud let out a whimper as stars floated in front of his eyes.

"My sincerest apologies," said Angus with embarrassment. "If it's any consolation, I'm told the toss gives riders a pounder of a headache anyway."

With that, he crouched down and cupped his hands underneath the end behind Dud's head, leaning the log against his shoulder. Then he stood up and ran with the log straight up and down.

As Oafie bounced above the giant's shoulder, he could

see Miss McLarch behind them, tearfully waving her hanky. "Goodbye, my sweet prince!"

With a mighty heave, the giant yelled *"Alba gu bràth!"* and hurled Dud and Oafie into the stratosphere.

Up they went, end over end, their mouths open in silent terror. Faster and faster, they rose through the clouds like a runaway propeller.

Then with a flash, they disappeared altogether.

Well, Well, Well

A circle of light flashed once, then twice on the stone wall next to the pile of Ink.

"That's the signal, children." Moving on tiptoes, Ronald led Everett and Bea around the base of the mound. Dot and Jack stood next to a small hatch in the tunnel wall. Jack's shoes were covered with dust.

"It's all right," he said. "The coast is clear."

Dot aimed her flashlight toward the hatch. "This way." She ducked through the opening.

When the group had stepped through, they found themselves in a large, round room. "It's just like the turret!" exclaimed Bea. And it was in a way, except for being twice as wide and having no ceiling. Stone walls rose high in the air, with the bottom layers of stone looking as though they had been coated in dark blue paint. A few empty burlap sacks littered the floor, along with a rusted-out wheelbarrow and several grimy work gloves. A thick layer of powdery dust coated everything.

Ronald tapped Everett's shoulder and directed his

attention upward. "The source of the breeze you heard earlier, eh?"

Far above them was a patch of light. It took Everett a moment to realize it was the moon.

"Are we standing in an underground castle?" asked Bea, tipping her head back and turning in a slow circle.

"Something even more impressive," said Ronald with a hushed reverence. He went over and traced his hand around a blue stone in the wall. "This was Hadrian's Well."

Bea put her hands on her hips and looked around. "Then where's the Ink?"

Dot picked up one of the burlap bags, coughing in the billows of dust it released. "Gone. It must have taken countless bags of pounce to dry it all out."

Ronald lowered his voice. "It's a wonder we haven't seen any patrols down here."

"Why would someone patrol a hole in the ground?" Everett wondered aloud. "All the Ink is gone."

"Ink never truly runs out, it is simply buried deeper," Jack explained. "Given a chance, it will resurface. Blotters monitor every well they shut down."

At the mention of that word again, Bea instinctively stepped closer to her brother. "What exactly is a blotter anyway?"

Jack hesitated. "My dear child, some evils you needn't concern yourself with yet. Suffice it to say that blotters are deplorable creatures who—"

Everett stopped him. "Wait. Creatures? Are you saying they aren't human?"

"Most of them can pass for human when they want."

"Are they elves?" Bea asked.

Ronald grunted in disgust. "Blotters are nothing like elves. At least not Light Elves. More like chimera. Some even have wings. I thought they were Jötnar from Norse mythology until—"

He caught sight of Dot's exasperated grimace and turned his back toward her. "Blotters are their own miserable breed, bent on ruin."

"Do they have superpowers?" asked Everett.

"They are no comic book villains, if that's what you mean. Jack—you're more familiar with their background than I am. What can you tell us?"

Jack stuck his hands in his coat pockets and cleared his throat. "During the Dark Ages, a nefarious king sought world domination. Expanding his power required a vast army."

Bea kicked at the dust. "I don't like bad people," she muttered.

"The king learned that one bishop of Rouen in France possessed a rare ability with Ink. This bishop not only wrote fantastic tales—he had translated some of his creations from the page to the real world."

"You mean like Ermengarde?" Everett asked.

"Precisely. The bishop exercised his unusual gift

sparingly and with great caution. But the king viewed him only as the secret weapon he needed. He arranged an audience with the bishop, pretending to bring a spiritual request. He commissioned the bishop to write a story with the most evil creatures imaginable. The king said he wanted 'a work to frighten the masses away from their wickedness.'

"Initially, the wary bishop hesitated. But the king would not relent until he wrote it."

"It was a terrible tale!" Ronald exclaimed. "Menacing ogres and fearsome giants and schools of sea serpents. Then there were the *Malignus Macula*—blotters. Why, one of them—"

"Enough, Ron," scolded Dot as she saw Bea scooting closer to her brother. "What were you saying, Jack?"

Jack continued. "When the story was complete, the king revealed his true intentions, insisting that all the horrid creatures be brought to life.

"The bishop refused. But the king tortured the poor man until he broke. Blotters and the other fiends poured from the realm of imagination into our world. Then the king threw the bishop in a dungeon for the rest of his days."

"I'm glad he was locked up," Bea said fiercely. "He sure made a mess with his words."

"True," Dot agreed. "But he also created glimmers of hope. Fearing the king would misuse the story, he secretly wrote in three safeguards. First, he made it so that blotters and the others cannot come in contact with Ink. If Ink touches their skin, they are Inkased in stone."

"Gargoyles!" said Ronald, striking a pose.

Everett shuddered. "Wait. The gargoyles on top of our church—they were blotters once?"

"That brings up protection number two," said Dot. "Being a man of the cloth, the bishop wrote in a rule that all houses of worship would be sanctuaries for anyone fleeing the creatures. Blotters even attempting to enter such a place instantly become Inkased as gargoyles."

"He should have made it so they disappear," said Bea. "They're too ugly."

"What's the third safeguard?" asked Everett.

"Fomentori," said Dot. "My favorite. The bishop wrote of a magnificent class of beings endowed with special powers to fight evil. They are strong and swift and exceedingly intelligent. The Fomentori wield Ink in ways ordinary humans cannot. They are guardians and messengers who are more than a match for any blotters. When the king released the evil creatures from the scroll, he unwittingly released the Fomentori as well."

A connection formed in Everett's mind. "Osgood . . . is he one of the Fomentori?"

"Indeed he is," said Dot, smiling. "Swift communication is a formidable ally in times of need."

Bea remained unconvinced. "How come I've never seen a blotter anywhere?"

"The gloomy skies above the British Isles are no accident," Jack replied. "Blotters have seeded the clouds with their Mind Murk that blinds people to certain realities."

Everett swallowed hard. "Did blotters cause the train crash?"

Dot placed an arm around Everett's shoulders. "We don't know. That's why we need to get to the train station."

At that moment, they all jumped as a loud banging startled them from overhead, echoing down the walls of the well. It was followed by a horrific metallic scraping.

Dot pointed her flashlight skyward. The dark outline of a large object hurtled toward them, gaining speed as it drew closer. Each bump against a wall of the well generated a shower of white sparks.

Bea stood transfixed as she watched whatever was careening toward them. Everett knew his sister was moments away from being crushed.

Leaping through the air, he tackled her to the ground and rolled to the perimeter of the well. It was none too soon. He felt metal brush past the back of his shirt just as the ground shook with a tremendous boom. The landing sent thick plumes of pounce into the air.

There was a long silence, followed by much coughing and hacking as the dust settled. Dot shone her light around the group, then turned it toward the large object that had descended upon them.

It was a giant iron pail—as wide as a car and nearly as

tall as Everett. The handle above it was attached to a thick cable stretching up to the surface.

Bea squirmed out from under Everett's arm and looked at the big bucket. "I guess we really are in a well."

"Where's Ron?" Dot grew alarmed. "Oh, please don't tell me! Ron? Ron?"

Everyone looked around, fearing the worst.

"Over here," came a voice. Ronald emerged from behind the far side of the pail, wiping the pounce from his sleeves. "Was that concern I detected in your voice, Dorothy?"

Ignoring him, Dot pointed upward. "What do you make of this? Could we use this pail as a lift to the top?"

Ronald frowned skeptically. "Possibly. The real question is: Did it drop by accident, or did someone up there lower it?"

Everett handed Bea the briefcase. He grabbed the top edge of the bucket and pulled himself up on his toes so he could see inside. A large lump lay unmoving on the bottom. The shadows made it difficult to see clearly.

Curious, he dropped inside for a closer look. He took two steps nearer, then froze.

Backing quickly to the edge, he scrambled out. His mouth had gone completely dry, and he could hardly form the words.

"There's a body in there."

19 Water Isn't Worth It

A *dead* body?" asked Dot.

An icy chill crept up Everett's spine. "It's not moving "

Jack moved toward the bucket. "I'll climb in and have a look."

"You'll do no such thing," retorted Dot, stepping quickly in front of him. "None of your chivalry nonsense. Death and mysteries are my territory, and I won't have you meddling with the scene of the crime."

With that, she pulled herself up and into the bucket before Jack could protest. Everett, Jack, and Ronald peered over the side. Bea hopped up and down trying to see, but she couldn't jump high enough. Not to be deterred, she set the briefcase down and dragged the wheelbarrow close and climbed in for a better vantage point.

It was a boy. Not much older than Everett, his leg twisted at a funny angle. His face looked ashen and his lips were blue. Blood pooled on the floor beneath his wavy black hair.

Dot bent down for a closer look, then bolted upright in surprise when the boy groaned. "He's alive!" She felt the boy's forehead. "I wish we had water to give him. And something we could use as a splint. His leg looks badly broken."

An idea came to Everett. "I'll go back to that pile of dried Ink. There were some bigger pieces I think would work for a splint."

He grabbed a burlap bag off the floor to collect shards, then darted out of the well.

"Wait for me!" shouted Bea, jumping down from the wheelbarrow. She handed Ronald the briefcase and took off after her brother.

When he reached the mountain of Ink, Everett scrambled over it, searching for any pieces large enough to brace a leg.

Bea caught up to him but stood still at the foot of the pile with her eyes closed and her hands folded.

"Why follow me here if you're not going to help?"

Bea kept her eyes shut. "I am helping. Daddy says to pray when we are in trouble, so I am praying for water."

Everett shook his head and kept looking. He knew his dad would pray, but he didn't like that he hadn't thought of it first. Plus, standing motionless with your eyes closed didn't seem practical when someone's life hung in the balance.

Whoever made this pile seemed determined to break the Ink into the smallest chunks possible. And the shards stuck out like needles, making it a challenge to find safe footing.

Everett dislodged several pieces he felt confident were

solid enough. He grabbed a variety of lengths and shoved them in the sack. On impulse, he also grabbed a smaller, sharper piece that he stuck in his pocket in case they needed something to cut up one of the burlap bags for tying the splint together.

Bea was still mumbling her prayers. Everett sighed in exasperation. "Come on, Bea. Time's up."

She opened her eyes and looked around, as if expecting to see a canteen lying at her feet. "Hmmph," she huffed, turning to go.

As they headed back, Everett felt another twinge of guilt over how impatient he'd acted with his little sister. "You've been really brave today, Bea."

"Do you think so?" She brightened at the thought, skipping along beside him. "I liked the slide part best. It wasn't scary at all."

They had reached the hatch to the well when Everett stopped. "Shh. Do you hear that?"

Bea strained her ears. There was a faint gurgling off in the distance straight ahead of them, farther down the tunnel. "It sounds like the creek by our house." She gasped. "I got what I asked for! Let's go!"

Everett found himself feeling irritable again. Bea hadn't made anything appear. Water doesn't suddenly materialize.

"Dot needs these splints. Let's go back."

Bea would have none of it. "We're supposed to get water." She grabbed his hand, tugging him behind her.

Everett clenched his teeth. "We don't even have a cup to collect any."

Bea dropped his hand and raced down the unexplored section of tunnel beyond the well. "We're so close—it's getting louder."

Everett deliberately dragged his feet as his sister skipped happily around a curve in the bluish light of the tunnel.

Somehow, the cheerier her actions, the darker his mood became. He knew it was childish, but he didn't care. He didn't want to reach the water. Why should Bea get to be right all the time?

He slowed to a full stop and waited.

She never liked being by herself. She would come running back soon.

Her shrill, terrified scream changed his mind. Everett dropped the bag and ran toward his sister. As he rounded the bend, the tunnel widened into a cavern where two sights stopped him cold. The first was the source of the sound they had heard—a small waterfall pouring out of a boulder and into a deep chasm. The second sight was Bea. She was standing on the boulder above the waterfall, pressed up against the cavern wall. Below her, a black wolf snapped and snarled at her, bits of foam flying from its mouth.

"Leave her alone!"

The enraged monster whirled around, and Everett nearly passed out. Its teeth were viciously long and yellow. But its bloodshot eyes were worse. The pupils swirled like pools of swamp water.

Everett reached in his pocket for the small Ink blade, but before he could grab it, the incensed animal charged.

Leaping through the air, the wolf knocked him to the floor.

He kicked and pounded his fists against the mangy fur. The animal bit and clamped down on his right shoulder. White-hot pain flashed through his body.

Everett twisted his left arm around until he could grab the shard knife from his pocket. Summoning all the strength he had left, he slammed it into the side of the evil beast.

Howling in fury, it released Everett's shoulder.

He pulled the scrap of Ink back and stabbed blindly at the creature that was still pinning him down. After the third blow, the knife pierced the hide and stuck. The animal froze, letting out a brief whimper that was cut short. A blue film spread out from the knife, enveloping the entire body and Inkasing it, just like The Cramps.

Breathing heavily, Everett rolled the dead weight off his chest with a thud.

"Ow!"

Something sharp had scraped his hand. He looked near the wolf's neck and saw that it was wearing a collar covered with spikes.

The beast had an owner.

Everett's right arm throbbed and blood seeped from his shoulder, but he ignored it and walked to the bottom of the boulder.

"You okay?" he asked Bea.

She nodded, her lip quivering. Flattening her back against the wall, she inched her way slowly toward him.

"Be careful—those rocks are slimy."

Everett felt sick to think how close he had come to losing his sister. All because he let her go ahead by herself. He couldn't bear the thought of anything happening to her.

"If that wolf had reached you . . ." He couldn't finish the sentence.

"I can't believe you Inkased it." Bea hopped down to the ground. "You're like Osgood."

Even Everett found it hard to believe he had just won a fight with a wolf. But in the heat of the moment, he had known what to do.

He walked back over to the carcass to collect his Ink knife. The tip of the blade broke off, but it still might be useful. Now that the animal was motionless, it looked smaller and less intimidating.

Wanting to wipe the blood off the blade, he picked up a rock. As he scraped the Ink shard across the stone, sparks flew everywhere. It made Everett think of the time MC had to start a fire in the wilderness using nothing but flint and steel.

It occurred to him that he had just done something the resourceful MC never had. That felt good. He had a sudden urge to start singing *"Who's afraid of the big bad wolf?"*

"Come on, Bea," he said. "The others will be getting worried."

Before she could respond, they heard it. The same sound he had heard earlier. A high, wailing howl, followed by another, and another.

He had forgotten wolves always travel in packs.

Blocked

Eddie set the lantern down in the middle of Writer's Block. He was not easily impressed or surprised, but this room left him stunned.

He knew without a doubt every scribble on the walls had all been done with Ink. This place held the secret to his future fortunes.

Yet there was no sign of Dorothy Sayers and company. Just a marker and a pair of earmuffs on the floor. He could see no other way out of the room except for the chute that had brought him there. Another hidden exit, perhaps, like in the Rabbit Room?

For the next hour, he searched high and low, tapping and listening, sliding his hand along anything that looked like an edge. He cursed as he nearly tripped over the earmuffs, then kicked them across the floor.

He spent a moment recalibrating. Maybe there was another way to tackle the problem. With Mr. Lugg's knife, he went to the nearest wall and scraped off some Ink shavings, catching them on a piece of paper from his notebook.

Tucking that away, he then picked up the marker from the floor and sniffed it. The lid had been left off, rendering it completely dry. Still, along with the shavings, it might give his scientist enough chemicals to analyze.

Satisfied with his new plan, he looked around and committed the space to memory. Then he stepped into the chute for the long climb. One way or another, Inklings around the world would learn that Eddie Montbanks meant business.

21 Hounded

Bea saw it first.

This wolf looked even hungrier. One of its fangs extended far past the other, like a golden tusk. All its ribs could be counted under its matted, oily coat. It licked its lips and snarled, anticipating a long-awaited meal.

Everett and Bea had made it back as far as the burlap sack full of Ink shards, right where Everett had dropped it. Now the beast blocked their path, standing between them and the well.

And it wore the same collar as the first.

Everett slowly turned his head to confirm what he feared.

Two more wolves stood only yards behind them.

They prowled back and forth, their roiling eyes never leaving their prey. One had a nasty scar across its snout, while the other was missing a front paw and foreleg.

Clutching his knife, Everett knew he couldn't fight off three of them at once.

But he had Inkased one already, which meant they weren't invincible.

He kept his voice calm. "Bea. Stand with your back to mine and watch the wolves behind us."

While she moved next to him, Everett dumped the Ink shards from the sack.

The wolves stepped closer.

"Bad dogs! Go away!" Bea clapped her hands and stomped her feet, trying to sound more cross than frightened. The animals bared their teeth, but stopped advancing.

"Good. Keep yelling at them!" Choosing a shard as long as his forearm, Everett wrapped the burlap sack in a ball around its top. He then grabbed a stone and scraped the Ink knife across the surface, generating sparks.

The wolf in front gave a signal, and all three tightened their perimeter.

"Ev! They're getting closer!"

Placing the stone right next to the burlap ball, Everett struck it with the knife again and again. His hands were shaking so much it was hard to control the direction of the sparks. Eventually, a few showered onto the burlap. The cloth began to smoke, then burst into full flame.

Everett raised his makeshift torch. The wolves all took a few steps back, snapping in frustration.

"Come on, Bea," he said in a low voice. "We're going to walk toward the well."

They made their way forward, Everett sweeping the torch in a circle to keep the animals at bay.

It was agonizingly slow. They had not covered much ground when the torch started to sputter.

Panic pinched Bea's voice. "It's going out!"

Sensing renewed fear, the animals tipped their heads back and howled. Everett looked desperately at his torch, willing it to stay lit. Not only was it dying—the shard was getting shorter. The heat was melting the Ink.

He held the torch over his free hand. A puddle of hot Ink quickly formed in his palm, and he remembered Dot's words in the well. *If Ink touches their skin, they are Inkased in stone.*

Just then, the wolf in front of them charged.

Everett threw the now-smoldering stump of a torch at the animal's head.

It missed completely.

As the beast lunged for him, Everett flung the Ink from his hand directly in the animal's face. The moment the molten Ink made contact, the beast stopped in its tracks as a sheet of blue spread from the snout to encircle the entire body. The wolf tipped and fell to the side, now nothing more than a block of stone.

Everett whirled around. He moved between Bea and the other two wolves. With their leader a statue, the beasts were unsure of their next move.

"Two down!" Everett yelled. "Which one of you is next?"

The one with the scarred face took the bait. It shot forward in a flash.

Everett grabbed another Ink shard and braced himself. Out of the corner of his eye he saw the three-legged wolf slinking around to the side.

"Bea! Watch—"

His warning was cut short as the scarred wolf pinned him to the ground. The shard sailed from Everett's hand, leaving him defenseless. He felt the hot breath as the beast opened its jaws and prepared to clamp down on his neck.

There was a loud *thwack* of metal on bone. The wolf crumpled to the floor, unmoving.

Jack stood over Everett, flashlight in hand, worry creasing his face.

The third wolf had run away, not liking its chances anymore.

Bea remained curled in a tight ball. Jack threw his jacket around her and gently picked her up. "Oh, children. What have we let happen to you?"

22 A Bucket of Trouble

Everyone huddled inside the bucket, Dot keeping one arm tightly around the traumatized Bea. Everett related all that had happened.

"Unmistakably dye hounds," said Jack.

"Dye hounds!" Ronald exclaimed in disbelief. "Among the more detestable of the bishop's creatures. But underground? Hardly their natural habitat."

Everett shared the bit about the dye hounds wearing collars.

"That explains why there are no blotters guarding the well," said Dot. "Their pets do the dirty work. Dye hounds have an even keener sense of smell for Ink than blotters. They go into a frenzy over the scent, whether fresh or dried." She squeezed Bea tightly. "You poor dear."

Ronald noticed Everett's chattering teeth. "You're shaking!" He handed him his corduroy coat. "Take this. You've been through a harrowing ordeal."

Everett wanted to say he didn't need the jacket, but it felt so comforting, he forgot to worry about acting all grown-up.

Dot looked at him with admiration. "I can't forgive myself for letting you go alone. But that was terribly courageous of you, young man. Your father would be so proud."

Everett hung his head. Would his dad be proud that he almost got Bea killed? Would he be proud of the last time they saw each other? Everett had behaved so badly, sulking over having to stay with The Cramps. And he had botched the one job his father gave him to do while he was away.

What happened with the dye hounds wasn't courage. It was either fight or die. "I always thought I wanted an adventure, but not like this."

Jack agreed. "Adventures are never what you expect while you're having them."

Dot inspected Everett's shoulder. "We need to clean this to prevent infection."

"It's not deep," Everett said. The pain, however, was intense. And the skin around the bite was beginning to swell. But he couldn't bear any sympathy at the moment.

"I dropped all the Ink shards I had found for a splint."

"We didn't bring back any water, either," Bea confessed, wrapping Jack's tweed blazer tight.

Dot placed a hand on the unconscious boy's arm. "I honestly don't know if he's going to make it, with or without those supplies. He lost a lot of blood."

Ronald sighed and held up the briefcase. "If only this were a first aid kit." The mention of first aid stirred a memory in Everett. "Nurse Abbie! Remember what she said, Bea? She marked patients with Dad's pen after the accident."

"Oh, yes!" Bea recalled. "She told us all of them got better. Can the Ink heal people?"

"Healing is one of the creative arts," Ronald replied. "As I said, Ink is not ink at all. It has surprising properties. It couldn't hurt to give it a try."

"Actually . . . it *could* hurt," said Jack with a frown. "There is a high probability that using the pen on the train is what exposed Marcus."

"What are you saying?" Bea didn't like any suggestion that her father was at fault.

"For all its benefits, the Ink can bring danger, particularly a full-strength bottle," Jack continued. "If blotters are near, they can immediately detect when it is being used. Opening the pen now may alert them to our location."

"Did Ink cause the train wreck?" Everett asked.

Dot shook her head emphatically. "We can't blame that misfortune on the Ink. All risks aside, how can we withhold a potentially lifesaving remedy from this poor young man?"

"Quite right," Ronald agreed. "Fear of what we don't know cannot stop us from acting on what we do know. The Ink has cured other wounds. I say we give it a chance."

Everett opened the briefcase and took out the pen. As he went to remove the cap, he remembered the last time he tried to write with it. He handed the pen to Dot.

Dot drew a small *X* on the boy's forehead, trying to copy the little they knew of Nurse Abbie's technique. Then she turned to Everett and did the same. A powerful jolt coursed down his neck to his wounded shoulder. He startled involuntarily at the shock. As the sensation subsided, it left his skin tingling the way it had back in Writer's Block. Within moments, the pain in his shoulder had faded to a dull ache.

Dot quickly replaced the lid on the pen. "No sense attracting more attention than necessary."

"Look!" Bea pointed at the boy's forehead.

The *X* was disappearing—absorbing into the skin like water on thirsty ground. Moments later, the color in his face went from deathly gray to a natural, golden brown. Soon after, he opened his eyes and looked with confusion at everyone staring at him. He blinked several times.

"Where am I?"

"You have fallen into a well from a very great height," answered Jack. He gestured to their surroundings. "We're in a large pail."

"Can you remember your name?" asked Dot.

He thought for a moment. "It's Trey. And I didn't fall— I was thrown, I think. It's blurry."

He sat up and rotated his shoulders. "I almost got away from them, but a big one stepped in front of me and lifted me off the ground. He threw me so hard."

Gingerly, he ran his fingers over the back of his head. "I can't believe I'm alive."

Trey's eyes darted from one face to the next with growing concern. "Wait—am I alive? How are all of you down here?"

Before anyone could answer, a violent shake sent them all to the floor of the bucket as it rose with a groan.

23 Waking Up Is Hard to Do

It was a pretty meadow, all in all, with yellow buttercups and white daisies and purple heather.

But when you are lying facedown, chained to a heavy log, natural beauty can go unnoticed.

"AaahCHOO!"

Dud returned to full consciousness with a sneeze and immediately winced. The goose egg on top of his head throbbed.

"Oafie!"

There was no sound from the other end of the log. Dud rocked himself back and forth until the log rolled and he was facing the sky.

"Oafie, wake up!"

Oafie finally stirred. "Whaaa? Where am I?"

"It worked! We survived the toss!"

The two blotters shared a moment of elation over their survival before realizing they were still chained to a tree with no one around to set them loose.

From his end, Oafie had a bit more of a view than Dud.

"Hold on. I think I see the outpost."

Sure enough, the meadow sloped down to a gravel road with a military bunker just beyond. Three blotters stood talking outside the bunker.

"Over here!" Oafie yelled, but the sentries were too far away.

"We need to get a little closer. On the count of three, let's roll to the left. One, two, THREE."

They heaved and strained and didn't move anywhere. Oafie raised his head and looked at Dud, who was still struggling to roll. "I said left."

"This is left!"

"Well, I meant my left."

They gave it a second try, pulling in the same direction. This time they managed to roll the log a full rotation, scraping their faces in the dirt along the way. Oafie yelled again, but the guards were still out of earshot.

"One more roll and I'm sure we'll be close enough."

They repeated their efforts, but with slightly too much vigor. The log rolled far enough to reach the slope, continuing its revolution without any assistance from its passengers. It picked up speed as it went, crashing through the tall grass, rolling over and over, across the road and into the side of the bunker. They ended facedown again, noses in the dirt.

The three surprised blotter sentries came running.

"I hate Newcastle," groaned Dud.

24 A Surprise Visitor

The bucket continued inching upward.

"It's them!" Trey was nearly hyperventilating. "They're going to kill us all!"

"Who do you mean by 'them'?" Jack asked.

"Soldiers. But I don't think they're even human," Trey told him. "Their eyes—their eyes are . . . "

"Blotters," Jack said, shooting a glance upward. "Our use of Ink must have attracted their attention."

"Wait," said Trey. "You know about Ink?"

"We're beginning to wish we didn't," Dot said under her breath.

For several more seconds, the bucket moved haltingly toward the surface. Then it vibrated and slowed to a stop as if being pulled the opposite direction.

"We must use this lull to our advantage and form an escape plan," Ronald said. "I propose—" His words were interrupted by a shriek from Bea, who was staring at the floor of the pail.

A thin blue line took the shape of a large circle as if being drawn by an unseen artist. Everyone moved to the perimeter to avoid contact with the line.

Ronald offered to help Trey up. "Can you stand, young man?"

For an answer, Trey leaped up on his own, his shattered leg now fully recovered.

The line became a trapdoor and opened inward. Jack held his flashlight at the ready, preparing to smack whoever, or whatever, was about to come through the floor.

To everyone's surprise, a train conductor's hat poked through, followed by a large man in uniform. He sat down on the edge of the hole, legs dangling below the bucket, a pen in his hand.

"Gilroy!" exclaimed Dot. "How did you find us?"

"Blotters aren't the only ones with a nose for these things," he said. "I'd know Elspet's Ink anywhere. Lovely scent. But we've no time. Everyone down through here— I'll follow you out."

Everett peered into the opening and saw a spiral staircase drawn entirely of Ink. It had obviously been scribbled in haste and didn't look particularly sturdy.

"It will hold," said Gilroy, seeing his hesitation. "If these stairs can bear my weight, you're sure to make it."

The group hurried down through the floor. The conductor came last, pulling the circle back into place over his head. With his pen, he retraced his previous line, welding the metal shut seamlessly.

As the group wound their way to the ground, Gilroy gave a twist of his pen lid and used the cap to begin erasing the stairs behind them, hoovering all the Ink back into the pen. Not a trace of it was left.

"Just a precaution," said the conductor. "We can't make it too easy for those blotters to follow us, can we?"

Everett peered below. They had risen far higher in the bucket than he had realized. The view made him dizzy, especially as the stairs swayed with their descent.

He focused his attention on Bea, walking just ahead of him, looking like a big ball of twine in Jack's tweed coat. Ahead of the whole group, Trey bounded down the stairs two at a time.

They made it to the bottom of the well, and Gilroy returned his pen to his pocket, the staircase nothing but a memory.

"We'd better keep moving." He pointed to the rope of Ink anchoring the bucket to the ground. "That tether I used to lasso the pail should buy us a few minutes, but not long. We'll need to head farther down the tunnel."

"We saw dye hounds out there," Everett said anxiously.

"Did you, now? I met one with three legs on the way in," said the big man. "He liked the special doggy treat I gave him. Let's just say he won't be waking up anytime soon." He gave Everett a reassuring wink.

Dot put her arms around Bea and Everett and made introductions. "These are Marcus Drake's children."

Gilroy's mustache turned up at the corners. "Why, so they are. So they are. Delighted to meet you both." He shook their hands vigorously.

Everett stared at his cap. "You're a conductor?"

"Aye, lad, that I am."

"Were you on the train with our dad?"

"I was. And I've been searching for him ever since." He leaned down close to Bea, his eyes twinkling. "Anyone feel like joining a rescue party?"

The words *rescue* and *party* were precisely Bea's language. She threw herself at him, hugging him tightly and bursting into tears. "Oh, thank you! Thank you!"

Gilroy picked her up. "There, there. You let it all out. We'll find him." He patted her back for a moment, then set her down next to Everett, who pulled her close.

The conductor then turned his attention to Trey for the first time. "And who might this young warrior be?"

Trey liked that label. He stood a bit taller and stuck out his chest. "I'm Trey, sir. I can't remember much else."

Gilroy studied his face. "You've got the look of someone fresh from the front lines."

Above them, the bucket creaked in protest as it strained against the rope of Ink.

Gilroy's face registered concern. "Time to move!" he said, ushering everyone toward the exit.

25 · Parting Ways

They all rushed out of the well.

"I still can't believe you're here, Gil," Dot said as they whisked down the tunnel.

"When my train pulled into Newcastle, I caught the scent of fresh Elspet's immediately. I expected it to lead me to Marcus, since he had the bottle. I was surprised to find you instead."

Ronald called up to him from behind, huffing and puffing. "Certainly glad. You're. Here. Might we. Stop a moment?"

Everyone slowed down and the conductor spoke. "I think we've covered enough distance to take a short breather."

They had reached the cavern where Everett battled the first dye hound. The unmoving form was right where he had left it, looking smaller to him now. And the Inkasement had faded to a grayish color.

Dot put her hand over her mouth when she saw the statue. "You poor children. It sickens me that you encountered such a beast alone."

Everett wanted to remind her they had actually faced four of them but thought better of it.

Bea tugged on Gilroy's sleeve. "How will we find Daddy?"

The conductor motioned to the briefcase Everett was holding. "I recognize that. Are the pen and Ink still inside?"

Everett opened it so he could see.

"Good. I have an idea."

Gilroy's plan was simple. "There are three likely places for the blotters to have taken Marcus. I've already scoured London. That leaves Aberdeen, where he acquired the bottle, and Oxford, where he was given the pen.

"You three know Oxford better than I do," he said to the Inklings. "I'll continue on to Aberdeen and conduct a sweep there."

"And what of the children?" asked Dot. "Their safety is paramount."

"Then I will take them with me." He looked at Bea and Everett. "That is, if it's all right with you two."

Only one question mattered to Everett. "Do you think our father is in Aberdeen?"

"Aye, I do. I believe the blotters want him to lead them to the source of Elspet's Ink. That well is the only one they haven't been able to shut down."

Everett and Bea looked at each other. Without a word, they both went and stood by the conductor. If their father was in Scotland, they were going there, no matter who went with them.

"You're the bravest children I've ever met," said Dot. "Rest assured, you'll be far better protected with Gilroy than the three of us."

Bea studied Gilroy's face and tried to recall her new vocabulary. "Are you a Foam . . . oh what was it . . . a Foaming something?"

"A Fomentori? Aye, that I am."

"Do you know our friend Osgood?" Bea asked. "He's nice."

Gilroy bent close and smiled. "I like him too. I guess that makes you and me friends right off the start."

He then turned to the entire group. "I suggest we split up the Ink as a precaution. Everett, why don't you keep the pen, and the Inklings can take the bottle."

Everett handed Jack the briefcase. Bea shared the combination with him, in case he needed to open it for any reason.

"Yes. Take out the Ink and remove the stopper at a few points along the way," the conductor said. "The smell might throw the blotters off our trail as we head to Aberdeen."

"What about me? Can I go to Aberdeen too?"

They all turned. In the midst of the decision-making, everyone had pretty much forgotten about Trey. "We need to get you to your parents," said Dot. "They must be sick with worry."

Trey's eyes grew wide with alarm. "I . . . I can't remember them."

Dot placed a hand under his chin and looked in his eyes. "You suffered quite a blow to the head."

"The blotters may have used their Mind Murk on him," Gilroy said softly. "It could be weeks before he regains his memory. I'll look after him until it comes back."

When he had given the Inklings directions to a tunnel that would take them directly back to Oxford, the conductor turned and surveyed his youthful wards. "Children, it's time to catch a train."

Everett and Bea returned their jackets to Ronald and Jack.

Dot handed her flashlight to Trey. "It might prove useful," she said.

Everett and Trey followed Gilroy, but Bea lingered a moment, biting her lip and watching Dot and the Inklings go. Ronald looked over his shoulder and caught her eye.

"Oh, Bea. I nearly forgot." He walked back to her, patting his various jacket pockets until he found the right one. Reaching in, he pulled out a small tin. Inside it were six candied jelly cubes covered in confectioners' sugar. "Jack calls this stuff Turkish delight, but I think of these as my Cheering Up Pills. We decided you should have them. Extra fortification for the journey."

Bea took the tin gratefully. "Would it be all right if I had one now?"

Ronald's eyes shone mischievously as he nodded. "I think that would be very wise indeed."

With that, he gave her a quick hug and left to rejoin Dot and Jack.

Bea popped one of the cubes into her mouth. She couldn't taste any magic, but it was deliciously sweet, and she felt her courage might be returning.

She caught up with Gilroy and the boys. "Shorry," she said through sticky teeth. "Bizhnesh."

Into the Rock

26

Gilroy led the way through the tunnels.

"Will we take another Pinch to Aberdeen?" Bea asked, hoping for another slide chute.

The conductor shook his head. "These passages are no longer secure. I have a different plan."

He stopped and put his ear to the wall. "It's right around here," he muttered.

Moving a step to his left, he listened to the wall again. Satisfied, he drew a small circle on the stony surface. Grabbing the circle like a doorknob, he gave it a sharp twist, and a rectangular section of rock opened as if it were on hinges. "Quickly everyone, inside!"

The conductor yanked the rock door shut behind them and sealed it tight with his pen.

As they examined their new surroundings, Bea gasped in wonder. They stood inside a corridor with bright, multi-colored arches spaced a few feet apart. They looked like miniature plaid rainbows and functioned the way posts and beams do in a mine shaft, propping open the passageway deep into the stone. The arches cast a colorful glow as if someone had strung Christmas lights overhead.

Everett went over and touched one of the Scottish-style rainbows. It was made entirely of Ink. He looked at Gilroy. "Did you draw all this?"

Gilroy's face reddened. "I was going through what you might call an 'experimental' phase in my work back then."

Neon-blue train tracks ran the length of the corridor. The wooden crosspieces supporting the tracks were a swirling mix of colors and patterns Bea had never seen.

She placed a foot on one and laughed in surprise as the hues swam around under her shoe, creating new designs.

"It's called tie-dye," Gilroy explained. "I found it amusing at the time. A little play on words. You know—since they're railroad ties. That was ages ago."

Trey was curious. "You've been to this well before?"

The conductor grew wistful. "Many times. Hadrian's Well had a particularly artistic deposit of Ink. I drew this route from the train station when it was still thriving. Why do you ask?"

"I think my mother might be an artist. Wait." Trey closed his eyes in concentration. Suddenly, they flew open. "She's a musician!"

Gilroy gave his back a hearty pat. "Wonderful! One memory may unlock others."

Bea interrupted, tapping the big man on the back. "The rainbows—they're talking."

"Can you make out what they are saying?"

She stood still, listening. "Bat? No, bad. Bad . . . at . . . well."

Gilroy removed the cap from his pen. "The blotters have reached the well. Time to speed up our escape."

He turned to face the children, gauging their height and weight. Then he spun and moved toward the train tracks, waving his pen in the air like a maestro. It occurred to Everett that the word *conductor* had more than one meaning.

A Fomentori in action is a sight to behold. His hand moved faster than Everett's eyes could follow. Ink flew in front of them, bending and forming itself into a rectangular shape.

By the time Gilroy replaced the lid on the pen, an old-fashioned handcart sat on the train tracks. It was the kind operated by two people pumping a lever back and forth to move under their own power. Except instead of a lever in the middle that tipped up and down, the conductor had drawn a giant seesaw. One end had three seats with handles, and the other end had a single, larger seat.

"I trust you kids aren't too old for a teeter-totter ride," Gilroy said with a grin. "By my estimate, the three of you might weigh just enough to lift me in the air."

Everett helped Bea up and they all settled into place. When Gilroy maneuvered his frame into position on the other end, the children were raised high above the cart. Bea squealed with delight.

Then the conductor straightened his legs to raise himself, and the seesaw began its work, tipping back and forth. Up. Down. Up. Down. The motion turned the wheels of the cart, and soon they were clacking down the line, with Gilroy facing forward to see where they were going.

It was exhilarating. For a short time, Everett forgot about blotters entirely and just enjoyed the sensation of his stomach falling and rising. He looked at Gilroy on the other end of the bench.

"How do you do it?" he asked as the big man tilted skyward.

"I just give a good push," Gilroy replied, "then up I go."

"No, not that. I mean all of it. You and Osgood. How do you do what you do with the Ink?"

Gilroy considered how to respond as he touched down and pushed off again. "I'm a conductor-class Fomentori, which means I conduct Ink Waves the way a wire conducts electricity. I don't write with Ink—I create things with it. Vehicles, bridges, shields. Anything that will be in the service of protecting Ink and Inklings."

"What about Osgood?" asked Bea. "What can he do?"

"He's courier-class," replied the conductor. "All things communication and delivery. He can send and receive Ink Waves, similar to Bea, except over long distances. Distress signals are his specialty. Plus code making and breaking. And he uses his skills to get those messages into the hands of Inklings."

"With his Ausculators?" asked Everett.

Gilroy laughed. "You saw one, did you? Os loves his inventions. He's always tinkering with a new one."

"And don't forget he can Inkase people," Bea noted, stretching her toes down to touch the floor of the cart. "Although I don't know what that has to do with messages."

"It comes from the old days," said the conductor, "when people would secure their parchments with wax before sending them. You could think of Inkasement as a seal to ensure a safe delivery."

"Are we riding this all the way to Aberdeen?" Trey yelled from the back. "I'm getting thirsty."

"We're nearly to our destination. Then we can take a short break." Gilroy peered down the tunnel beyond Trey. "Let's just hope we're in time."

27 Puppies Are Easy to Make

A loud sneeze echoed off the walls of the well.

Dud's allergies were killing him. So much dust down here. Even dried-up Stink made his eyes swell.

He held two dye hounds on leashes and did his best to keep up with them as they sniffed around the edges of the well. Their keen sense of smell was vital in these hunts, but that didn't make them cooperative. One darted left while the other went straight ahead.

"Take it easy, ladies! Give a bloke a chance to catch up!"

The animals ignored him, crisscrossing paths until he was in a hopeless tangle. Meanwhile, Oafie was attending to the Commander, following him around with an assortment of beverages.

"We've got a ginger beer or maybe a nice tart lemonade. Very refreshing at a trying time like this, I must say. Do you fancy a lemonade, sir?"

The Commander didn't respond. He had flown swiftly in from Aberdeen on the report of a strong Stink rising from the well, much too strong for one that had been sealed off.

He stood with his pupils liquefied, mentally processing what his nose detected.

It was a nauseating smell. He had rarely encountered such a highly concentrated stench, except—

"The train," he said aloud. He whirled and faced Oafie, his eyes narrowing.

"The mission in London. Did you or did you not complete it?"

The bottles Oafie carried began to clink against one another. He looked for support from his partner. "We did, sir. Ain't that right, Dud?"

"I found out about the children," Dud said. "The boy, Everett, is eleven and the girl, Beatrice, is eight."

The Commander looked from one to the other. "You already told me that. What exactly did you destroy at the church?"

Oafie kept going. "Oh, we found more Stink, all right. It was this piece of paper that had the smelliest dot on it you ever did smell. Wasn't it smelly, Dud?"

Dud abandoned ship. "I had to take your word for it. I had an allergic reaction."

"Silence, idiot." The Commander placed a hand on Oafie's throat and began to tighten his grip. "You're telling me you destroyed a piece of paper?"

Oafie's face turned a bright crimson and bottles of ginger beer and tart lemonade crashed to the ground. "It had a Stinky dot. That's all there was."

"Apparently not." The Commander could sense the eyes of the other blotters watching him. He needed to make a show of strength, to instill fear and prove he did not tolerate insubordination. He gave a single flick of his wrist and the dim-witted blotter transformed into a whining dye hound pup. Dropping him to the floor, the Commander fixed his attention on the second culprit.

Dud took a step backward, whimpering. "I told him. I told him the paper wasn't important. Who would ever care about a dot?"

"Then how is it you returned without continuing your search?"

"I was just about to. What I meant to say is that—"

Dud dropped to his knees and clasped his hands, sobbing. "Please don't turn me into a puppy again. I can't go back to the kennel. The other dye hounds almost ate me alive."

If there was one thing the Commander could not stand, it was sniveling weakness. "I'm sure your friend will come to your aid the way you came to his."

POOF!

A second hideously ugly puppy yipped and yapped beside the first one near the Commander's feet. He kicked them away. "Sergeant!"

A blotter joined him and saluted. "Sir?"

"Get collars on them and take them to the kennel for obedience training."

As the soldier complied, the Commander reached down and picked up one of the unbroken bottles of ginger beer, removed the cap with his teeth, and took a swig.

A chilling howl pierced the air, followed by a chaotic chorus of raspy barks. He would never grow tired of that music. He took one last swig of soda, then threw the bottle back to the ground and ducked out of the well and followed the others into the tunnel.

Presently, they came to the cavern with the dye hound statue. The living beasts circled it warily, growling with a mixture of fury and fear.

A young blotter in glasses squatted down beside the Inkased dye hound. His fellow soldiers called him Screech, since his eyes looked the size of a screech owl's through the thick lenses. The beaklike face mask over his mouth and nose only enhanced the effect.

Leaning in close, he reached a gloved hand into a crack in the statue.

"Sir! I found something."

He held up a tiny fragment of the weapon that had broken off inside. The Commander peered at the scrap and cursed. The fact that even an old, dried-up, discarded piece of that filth could still inflict so much damage made him livid. He made a mental note to have the pile burnt to ashes and buried so it could not be weaponized again.

"Come with me."

Screech discarded his mask and the messy gloves and

scrambled to catch up with the Commander, who, despite having one bad foot, moved remarkably fast.

For the first ten minutes, the smell of Stink grew stronger and more distinct. Then, oddly, it vanished.

The Commander backtracked a few feet, inhaling deeply. The Stink returned. There was a clear cutoff point. He ran a gloved hand over the wall surface. No obvious doorways or alcoves. But there was something.

"Bring your spectacles to me."

Screech quickly removed his glasses and handed them over.

The commander held them in front of his face like a magnifying glass. There on the wall was a very faint sketch of a small circle. It appeared to be freshly drawn.

"Do you see that?"

"I sure do, sir," Screech lied. He couldn't see his own hands without his glasses.

With one nostril right next to the wall, the Commander drew a deep breath and felt his nose hairs being singed by an acrid electrical smell.

This was yet another familiar stench, mocking him. The circle in front of him had come from the conductor's pen that kept him at bay on the train.

That infernal conductor ruined his life once. It would not happen again. A wave of pure hatred washed over the Commander.

He had to crush something.

The glasses in his hands never stood a chance.

Screech listened in shocked horror as his last pair of spectacles snapped and shattered.

"Sir..."

The Commander didn't hear him. He grabbed the circle on the wall, rotated it, and gave a tug. A large chunk of rock pulled away from the wall. Loose debris cascaded into the tunnel. He could see arches drawn of Stink in such garish colors, he had to shield his eyes.

The Commander could feel his throat closing off as the fumes wafted out of the opening. With one hand covering his nose and mouth, he climbed over the rocks and into the hidden tunnel, careful not to set his foot in any foul patches of Stink. When this was over, he would send down a team of burners to purge the entire area.

Rasping and wheezing, Screech hurried to follow the indistinct form of his commanding officer. In his haste, he caught the tip of his boot on a chunk of rock and tripped. Reaching to brace himself against the wall, he forgot he wasn't wearing protective gloves. The skin of his fingers touched a rainbow he couldn't see, and he froze, Inkased on the spot.

The Commander neither noticed nor slowed down.

He had prey to catch.

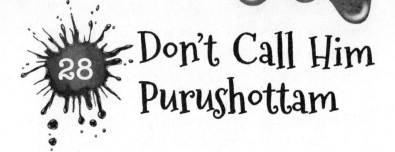

Don't Call Him Purushottam

The seesaw cart ride led to a wide, underground platform. Several feet overhead, a hand-drawn sky on the ceiling glowed a pale purple with bright orange clouds and a shimmering yellow sun. The mural on the far rock wall boasted an ocean in vivid blues and greens.

Gilroy noticed Everett gaping at it. "As I said before, it was an experimental phase," he said sheepishly. "I went a tad overboard."

Bea disagreed. "It's perfectly perfect."

The scene reminded Everett of going to the coast on holiday. That was where his father had taught him to swim. They had spent hours in the sea together, laughing and bobbing around on the waves. A lifetime ago. The memory left him lonely.

"Where are we?" Trey asked.

Gilroy pointed toward the ceiling. "We're directly beneath Newcastle station."

He pulled out his pocket watch. "If you'll excuse me, I need to make some calculations for the next leg of our journey." He walked to the far end of the platform, where he paced back and forth, tipping his head to the side and mumbling as he worked out the math.

Everett and Bea stood alone with Trey, suddenly at a loss for words.

Trey flicked his bangs out of his dark eyes and broke the silence. "We haven't even properly met. What did you say your names were?"

"I'm Beatrice," Bea said in her most mature voice. "But most people call me Bea. I almost died today too. This is Ev."

Everett elbowed her. "I can tell him my own name. It's actually Everett." He didn't want the older boy thinking his nickname was dumb.

Trey didn't seem to notice one way or another. He acted completely comfortable in his own skin, not trying to make a good impression or getting all sulky and withdrawn around new people. Everett wished he had half as much self-confidence.

"I've never heard the name Trey before," said Bea.

"It's a nickname, I think. Yes!" Trey's face grew animated. "It's coming back to me! *Trey* means *three*; I'm the third in my family with the same name. My real name is an Indian one. It's Purushottam."

Bea was sympathetic. "Trey is much easier."

Everett was more interested in his story than his name. "Why did a blotter throw you in the well?"

Trey shook his head. "I wish I could tell you. How did I survive that fall?"

"The Ink saved you," said Bea. With her finger, she retraced the *X* Dot had drawn on Trey's forehead and described how his injuries disappeared.

Trey internalized every word. "I think I knew about the Ink before meeting the blotters. Maybe that's why I went near the well. I'm not sure. I hope my brain returns to normal."

"All right, everyone!" Gilroy called, joining the group. "If my math is correct, it's time to board a moving train."

29 · Riding the Rails

The conductor leaned down and asked Bea, "Could I trouble you for some help? I need to remove two copper-colored hairs from my mustache, but silver and copper feel the same. Can you tell me which is which?"

Bea quickly identified two candidates. "Do you want me to pull them out?" she asked. She had extracted a tooth of Everett's for him once and wasn't squeamish about those things.

"Thank you, but no," Gilroy responded. "Fomentori hair removal requires a certain touch."

He grasped one of the hairs between his thumb and forefinger, gave a slight twist, and unscrewed it as if it were a lightbulb. When he twisted the second, it emitted a burst of light like the flashbulb of a camera.

Gilroy handed the first hair to Bea. She laughed in surprise. "It feels like glass."

He rubbed the second hair back and forth on the shoulder of his wool jacket. "Technically, they are triboelectric amber filaments. They connect Ink Waves to standard electrical current."

"What does that mean?" asked Everett.

"It's a bit complicated, but it means we will not be boarding this train in the usual way."

The conductor arranged everyone by height—Bea first, then Everett (who was nearly as tall as Trey), and himself last—and asked them all to hold hands. He grabbed Trey's right hand with his left and held the second copper-colored hair in his right.

"The train will slow down as it rolls through the station. The braking friction will generate a current that we will catch. Bea and I will touch the two amber hairs together and our molecules will be transported to the train above us."

Gilroy moved next to Bea, pulling everyone into a tight circle. "Now, I should warn you: I cannae control exactly *where* in the train we will arrive."

"Have you ever done this before? Caught a current?" Everett asked.

"More often than I care to remember."

Everett pressed further. "With people who aren't Fomentori?"

"Nearly every time," said Gilroy. "As long as we don't let go of one another's hands, we should be fine."

The whole concept sounded ludicrous to Everett. Transporting bodies through the air? How would their molecules not get jumbled together on the way? He was about to voice his doubts when it occurred to him that nearly everything about this journey would have sounded impossible before Osgood arrived.

The platform shook. Dust rained down from the sky ceiling as the locomotive rumbled through the station overhead. Everett fixed his attention on Gilroy, who was all concentration, holding out his strand of charged filament hair, listening.

"Now!" he shouted above the roar, bringing the hair into contact with the strand in Bea's hand. The instant the hairs touched, there was a white flash as their bodies shimmered and disappeared.

Afterward, Bea always described it as "going watery," the sensation of rushing along in a tumultuous stream. Everett felt as though every muscle in his body went into spasms, with bolts of lightning coursing through his veins. Then everything went black as he slipped into unconsciousness.

When he came to, he was unable to move. Trey and Bea were no longer holding his hands. Was he in a coffin? His mouth went dry and he got a panicky feeling in his stomach.

Then, to his relief, he heard Gilroy whisper, "Are we all here?"

"I don't like this place," Bea whispered, irritation in her voice. "I'm stuck."

Trey responded as well. "I think we're in the baggage car—a suitcase handle is pressing into my shoulder." A scraping sound followed, then a thud. "Hold on—I might be able to squeeze through."

Trey pushed the suitcase away and moved bags to let the others out. When he had dislodged everyone, they gathered in the center of the car.

Trey started to ask a question, but Gilroy raised a finger to his lips. "Blotters have been known to travel this route," he said in a low voice.

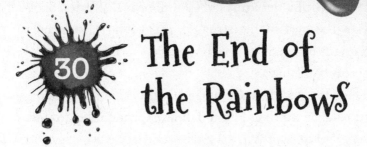

30 The End of the Rainbows

The Commander reached the hand-drawn platform. Dust was everywhere, and footprints.

Several sets of footprints. He identified the conductor's and the dead boy's immediately. Apparently, the fall hadn't killed him.

The other footprints were smaller. One set from a boy's loafers and the smallest prints made by a little girl's shoes.

So. The conductor had other young charges in his care. A boy and a girl connected with this mess. Could he be taking the vicar's children in search of their father?

The Commander retrieved the family photograph he had found on his prisoner. He studied the children's faces. Perhaps they would provide the leverage he had been needing.

His thoughts turned to the cursed conductor. Phantom pains still made his stone foot feel as if it ached.

He first crossed paths with that Fomentori a lifetime ago, as a much younger blotter. But the entire scene remained fresh in his mind.

The battle had been epic: An entire Fomentori regiment

challenged the blotter army over a well near Dumfries, Scotland. In the heat of the struggle, the young Commander intercepted the conductor, who was transporting a supply of Ink across battle lines.

They fought. The Commander knocked the conductor off balance, causing him to fall facedown on the ground. Blotters carried swords in those days, and he drew his from its scabbard for an easy kill.

But before he could finish off his opponent, the Fomentori stretched his arm forward and plunged his pen deep into the blotter's boot. Immediately, the Commander's foot began to turn to stone. Seconds before the Stink Inkased him entirely, he brought down his sword and sliced off his own foot.

It was like an animal caught in a trap, chewing off its own paw to survive. The gruesome act preserved his life, stopping the Inkasing process before it engulfed him.

Rather than be fitted with an artificial foot, he used his own Inkased foot as a prosthetic. He swore to wear it until the day he exacted his revenge. And the legend of his fearlessness was born.

But today, standing on the empty platform, the foot simply felt tiresome. The onslaught of light coming from the ceiling did not help the Commander's pounding head. He had to cover his eyes. His lungs burned.

No need to linger. There was no one here to apprehend. And the smell told him everything he needed to know about where they had gone.

He had to get out of this oppressive atmosphere, but first he would make sure no one ever used this tunnel again. The Commander pressed his gloved hand against the wall. The rocks shook violently until the roof collapsed onto the platform behind him.

He stretched his wings and flew back the way he came. Each beat of his wings required extraordinary strain, but it was a relief to be off his feet. He barely outpaced the collapsing arches as they sealed off the passageway.

So much Stink in the air! His breathing grew shallower and more labored as he neared the exit. He pushed past the statue of Screech, knocking it over, and stumbled through the rock door into the main tunnel. The startled blotter standing guard jumped to attention.

Wheezing and coughing, the Commander gripped the sentry's arm and pulled his face close.

"Must reach . . . train to Aberdeen . . . send Lt. Malo . . ." He fought the urge to fall.

"Are you all right, sir?"

"I gave . . . an order!" rasped the Commander, hoping a show of strength would mask his condition. After his subordinate scurried off, he again spread his wings. Despite the damage done to his lungs, he needed to return to Aberdeen immediately.

It was time the vicar started talking.

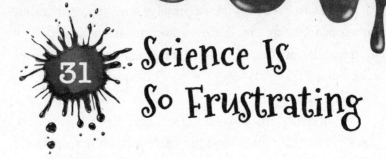

Science Is
So Frustrating

It was not a good day to be Dr. Pitz.

The pale green walls and fluorescent lights inside the laboratory made everyone look slightly sick all the time. But the middle-aged man in the poor-fitting lab coat felt as terrible as he looked.

Pitz worked for Eddie Montbanks, but not fast enough. He didn't want to work for him at all. Somehow, the American knew that Dr. Pitz had lied to get his job at Oxford and threatened to expose him.

Not that helping Montbanks would end better than a ruined career. At least four other scientists had disappeared under suspicious circumstances when they couldn't produce what Eddie wanted. Today, Dr. Pitz found himself in the uncomfortable situation of having to share disappointing results.

Eddie could not accept the explanation. "Perhaps Mr. Lugg could motivate you, Doctor."

The scientist's eyes darted to the imposing form of the bodyguard. He gulped nervously. "Please. I'm sorry. We're close. It's just that I . . . I can't change science. The surfactants can't be reconstituted from the available material."

He held out his trembling hand with a small packet of dark dust.

Eddie crossed his arms and refused to take it from him. "English, please."

Dr. Pitz adjusted the goggles that were sliding down his sweaty nose. He pointed at the packet. "This powder—I can't just add water to bring it back, as if it were dried milk. The chemical composition is unlike anything I've ever seen. Listen to this."

He walked over to a machine covered in dials and gauges. Dr. Pitz picked up a microphone and held it in front of the packet of Ink dust. Immediately a high-pitched squeal sent the needles on the machine jumping wildly. Eddie and Mr. Lugg covered their ears.

"You see?" yelled Dr. Pitz. "This substance sends out signals we can't even read. It's beyond the science."

Apart from piercing squeals, nothing irritated Eddie more than people who could not problem-solve. Especially when he needed them to. Yet finding a new scientist would delay the process further.

Eddie inhaled slowly and tried to speak calmly. "What about the book?"

In his research, Eddie had learned that an Oxford library housed the only copy of a journal written by an alchemist in the 1500s. Supposedly, the alchemist developed a secret formula for reproducing Ink and had hidden it in his notes.

Dr. Pitz removed his goggles, shaking his head. "I tried."

Eddie's face contorted in anger. "You tried?"

"It's in a private collection. The library won't give me access."

"Fine," grunted Eddie. "I'll get it myself. What else is stopping you?"

Dr. Pitz turned off the machine and pondered the question, running his fingers nervously through his thinning hair. "What else? You mean besides needing equipment that hasn't been invented?"

Eddie pounded his fist on the lab table, rattling beakers and test tubes. "Your future is hanging by a thread, Pitz. I'll ask one more time. What will it take to mass-produce the Ink?"

The man blinked rapidly. He looked toward the ceiling and mumbled to himself as he calculated. "Well . . . let's see . . . the solubilizers would be . . . if it's pigment based, I suppose . . ."

Mr. Lugg began to growl. Then he cracked his knuckles.

"At the very least, I would need a liquid sample rather than dried."

"How much?" Eddie hissed through clenched teeth.

"Not much, really, I wouldn't think . . ."

Mr. Lugg grabbed the poor doctor by the throat, lifting him off his feet.

Eddie repeated his question. "HOW MUCH?"

The scientist raised an index finger and choked out a response. "One! One bottle!"

Eddie watched his legs dangling in the air. "Let him go. He will be no use to us dead."

Mr. Lugg grunted and dropped him in a heap on the floor. The doctor clutched at his throat, gasping for air, a mixture of relief and hatred in his eyes.

Eddie gave a big sigh. He had wasted precious time chasing down that powder.

Time to exercise his "borrowing privileges" at Oxford.

32 Not All Trains Are Equal

The conductor led his young companions through several coaches full of sleeping passengers before arriving at the dining car. They entered the empty galley. The kitchen smelled of roast beef, reminding Everett he hadn't eaten any supper.

Gilroy walked over to an oven. Through the glass, Everett could see the roast. On closer inspection, he also could tell that the entire oven was drawn with Ink.

By now, he had witnessed enough examples of the Ink in use to expect the unexpected. But he was unprepared for what happened when the conductor turned the knob and opened the oven door.

"All right, in we go," said Gilroy, gesturing toward the inferno.

The three children stared back at him blankly as a wave of hot air blasted their faces.

Bea was indignant. "If you were planning to cook us for dinner, you should have said so up front instead of pretending to help."

Gilroy laughed out loud, which only aggravated Bea further. He tried to compose himself. "I see now how that looked. Like a page out of *Hansel and Gretel*—ha, ha!" He worked to regain his composure.

Bea failed to find the humor in it. "Why would you ask us to climb into a hot oven?"

Gilroy shook his head. "Oh, no, my dear. Not hot. It's truly not. See?" He shoved his hand into the opening—clear through the roast—then withdrew it. "The roast isn't real. Just a bit of an illusion."

No one was convinced. "What about the heat?" demanded Trey. "We can feel it."

"Easy enough to create with a small heater and blowers hidden in the outer edge of the oven."

"Don't the kitchen workers get suspicious?" asked Everett. "A roast that always cooks and never burns."

"The chef is a friend," said the conductor. "He's in on the ruse."

He could tell that the children needed more proof.

"Very well. Me first," Gilroy said, placing a knee on the oven door. "Watch."

The door creaked and groaned its protest under the load as the conductor hoisted his large frame all the way into the oven. Now it was the children who had to stifle their laughter as his ample backside squeezed its way through too small of a space. It reminded Bea of Winnie-the-Pooh getting stuck in the entrance to Rabbit's house.

She had an urge to give it a big swat but restrained herself.

Once through, Gilroy disappeared, completely hidden by the roast. "You see?" he yelled from inside the oven. "Perfectly safe. Who's next?"

Trey stepped forward, but Everett cut him off. "I think I should go first."

Trey didn't back down. "Why? Doesn't it make more sense for me to go since I'm the oldest?"

Everett knew it didn't really matter, but if there was one thing that bothered him, it was when people presumed they were right. "It's my father who's missing."

Trey frowned. "I came along because I thought you could use some help."

"Why? Because I'm too young?" Everett shoved him out of the way.

"Boys!"

The two of them turned around, looking for Bea. While they argued, she followed Gilroy into the oven herself.

They looked at each other a moment, realizing the silliness of the quarrel.

Still, Everett didn't wait for the debate to resume. He knelt on the open door of the oven and crawled in. A warm breeze hit his face initially, but the conductor had been right—the heat was just for effect.

Once inside, the oven was a surprisingly comfortable

temperature. Even more surprising was that the inside was far bigger than the outside. Gilroy was standing fully upright.

Trey followed right on Everett's heels, pulling the oven door closed behind him. Feeling rather sheepish about his outburst, Everett gave Trey a hand getting in as a sort of apology, which Trey gladly accepted.

Somehow, they were all side by side inside the nearly pitch-dark oven, and yet there was enough room so they weren't touching each other.

A whooshing sound broke the silence. "This will only take a moment," said the conductor. "The air has to pressurize."

"Like on a submarine?" Everett asked.

"Exactly."

With another whoosh, a back door slid open and Gilroy led them all through. He switched on a light. "Welcome to the Drawing Room," he announced.

They were no longer inside an oven, or even another train car, but a cozy sitting area with four comfortable-looking chairs around a table. A fire crackled in a small fireplace. Everett couldn't even feel the motion of the train anymore.

The table was set with a full supper for four. It looked mouthwatering—potatoes and carrots, buttery scones with Dundee marmalade, caramel shortbread, smoked salmon, strawberries, and large glasses of cold milk. And at the center of the table sat a plate of sliced and roasted Aberdeen Angus beef that smelled far more enticing than the imaginary roast in the oven.

"Is it real?" Bea picked up a scone.

Gilroy chuckled. "It most certainly is. Technically, the Drawing Room isn't for dining, but"—he pointed toward his middle—"I do need my sustenance."

The journey had given all of them a healthy appetite, and the conversation quieted as everyone dug in. No one was overly concerned with proper table manners, and the food was the most delicious Everett could remember eating.

As Gilroy passed a dessert plate around a second time, Bea pushed away from the table and patted her stomach. "I can't fit one more bite in here."

She turned her attention from the table to the room. The walls were lined with incredibly lifelike portraits, drawn in Ink. Right away, Bea spotted Dot, Jack, and Ronald in one of them, sitting in the very same Drawing Room.

"Who are all these people?" she asked, looking at the rest of the pictures.

"Some special passengers," the conductor replied. "Inklings one and all, just like the three of you."

"I'm an Inkling," Bea said to herself breathlessly.

Everett felt another pang of embarrassment. What if the conductor discovered he couldn't use the Ink? He didn't think Gilroy would kick him out, but . . . He quickly changed the subject. "How is this room part of the train?"

"Strictly speaking, it's not attached to the train at all.

Think of it as a small pocket of another dimension." Gilroy pointed to a portrait of an elderly man with long, wavy gray hair and a mustache. "This lad explained it to me, but the details are a bit soft in my head."

Everett stared at the photo. "Isn't that . . . Albert Einstein?"

Gilroy wiped some dust off the frame, a memory playing in his mind. "Not many people know about his secret trip to London back before the war. His mind made use of the Ink in ways I will never comprehend."

He pointed to the portrait next to it. "And that's my good friend Sir M. He's a fellow Fomentori, builder class. He took Einstein's theories and brought them to life as the Drawing Room. Another gifting with Ink that boggles my mind."

Trey pointed with a fork toward a bookshelf next to the table, where a collection of pens was on display. "Those are beautiful."

Many of their barrels had been turned from exotic wood, with gold and silver details forming the trim.

Gilroy beamed. "Glad you like them. They're a wee bit of a hobby for me."

Trey's jaw dropped. "You made them?"

The conductor smiled. "I wanted a little something to give to my favorite passengers—just the smallest amount of Ink intended for their own personal enjoyment."

He picked up one pen that had dark wood on the top half

and light wood on the bottom, then handed it to Trey. "Here's one I believe would suit you and your story."

Trey tried to remove the slotted cap by pulling on it, but Gilroy stopped him. "This one's different. No cap. See? It turns to open. And when you slide the barrel down . . ."

The conductor pulled a section of the pen away to reveal finger holes such as you would find on a penny whistle or recorder. Trey brought it to his lips and cautiously blew into the slot at the top. A single melodious note filled the room.

Gilroy handed him a small pad of paper, and Trey tried his hand at writing his name, once in all lowercase letters and once in uppercase. The pen glided over the paper with ease. A lump formed in Trey's throat. "This is the nicest gift anyone's ever given me," he whispered.

"You have things to write." Gilroy's words hung weightily in the air.

Trey looked up at him in surprise. "I do?"

"What happened to you back in that well—being brought back to life. That was no accident. You must record the details. Every sensation, every memory. Commit it to writing while it is still fresh. The more you write, the more your other memories will come back to you. They're all still in there."

The conductor then turned his attention to Bea, who could not take her eyes off the row of magnificent writing instruments. "Hmmm," Gilroy mused, letting his hand hover over each option before settling on which one he wanted. "Ah, yes. I think I know just the thing."

He picked up a mahogany-colored pen and placed it in Bea's palm, wrapping her fingers around it. Then he adjusted the two metal ends of the pen until he was satisfied. "There," he said. "Now this pen is locked. It will only open for you. No one else can remove the cap without your permission."

Bea took the lid off and replaced it again, over and over, listening to the click, scarcely believing what a perfect gift it was. Overcome with excitement, she startled Gilroy with a bear-worthy hug.

"It's got a few other secrets for you to discover later," he confided.

"Do the other pens have secrets?" Bea asked.

"One or two. Watch this." Gilroy picked up a miniature silver pen from the shelf and let go of it. Instead of falling to the ground, it flew to the metal base of the table lamp and stuck to it.

"Ink always emits energy waves, but the magnetic properties have been enhanced in this one," the conductor explained. "That might not seem like much, but it's gotten me through many a scrape." He picked up the pen and turned to Everett.

Everett hoped that magnet pen might be his. At least there was no writing involved with that one. He could feel the intensity of Gilroy's stare. His eyes seemed to bore right through him. Everett dropped his gaze. He was certain the conductor knew he couldn't use the Ink.

After a lengthy pause, Gilroy said in a soft voice, "Tell me what's troubling you, lad."

"His favorite color is blue, so he probably would like the blue pen," Bea blurted out, sensing her brother's discomfort and wanting to rescue him.

Everett shifted his weight uneasily from one foot to the other. "I don't really want one, thanks," he said, holding up his dad's pen. "I like this one."

Gilroy studied him some more. "Does it write well for you?" he asked quietly.

Everett wanted to scream. Why couldn't Gilroy leave him alone? He tried to brush it off. "I'm more of a reader than a writer."

Gilroy stayed silent a moment, then seemed to reconsider his options. He returned the magnet pen to the shelf and went to a bureau drawer. From it he withdrew two thin, gray metal sticks that were longer than ordinary pens and pointed on one end. He handed them to Everett. "Not everyone's connection to the Ink is through writing."

Everett turned the sticks over in his hands, examining them. They were nondescript and smooth. Boring compared to the beautiful pens given to Bea and Trey. Everett's disappointment showed in his voice. "What am I supposed to do with these?"

Gilroy's face became serious. "I cannae tell you how to use them. That's for you to discover."

33 Vicar under Pressure

Measuring the passage of time in thick darkness is difficult. Marcus felt like he had been there for years, but it could have been five minutes. He managed to work his hands free again, but he kept them in the straps so his captors wouldn't notice.

"Not a word, bird," he warned his unseen companion. The raven did not respond.

There was something unnatural about the pitch-black air. The harder he stared into it, the more fatigued he became.

He tried to recall one of the many psalms he had read on countless occasions to comfort his parishioners, but he couldn't remember a single verse. Not a one! Fear surged in his chest. The darkness drained his hope.

The door creaked, and the Commander reentered the room. He approached the bird cage first. "A shiny new pebble for my good boy, Grip," he said in an almost affectionate voice.

"Caw!" The bird squawked and flapped in appreciation. "Shiny!"

Marcus heard the familiar scrape as the Commander pulled up a chair. For a long moment he was silent. Then the blotter gave a painful-sounding cough. When he spoke, the words seemed to grind against one other.

"You don't look well, Reverend."

"You don't sound well," Marcus retorted.

The Commander cleared his throat and placed a clammy hand on Marcus's head, palming his scalp like a basketball. Marcus writhed in pain. Poisoned thorns seemed to be raking their way across his thoughts, clouding his brain with confusion.

"I know." The Commander's voice was low. "So difficult. This will all stop when you tell me about the well."

Marcus felt as if his head would explode. "I already told you! I don't know about any well!"

The pain was unbearable. The Commander continued talking in a calm tone. "The more you resist, the more uncomfortable you become. Start talking and the hurt goes away. It's very simple. Now then. What about the bottle of that Stink?"

"I don't have it!"

Marcus winced and sucked in his breath as the scraping sensation intensified.

"Ah, but you did. Who gave it to you?"

"I have no idea. You have to believe me!"

"I will believe you when you start making sense."

Five words from a psalm finally came back to Marcus: *I*

will not be afraid. Relief flooded his mind. The Commander seemed to sense the change in his mental state and withdrew his hand.

"I'm sure the answers will come to you in time. Your children are worried about you. What are their names again? Everett and Beatrice?"

The mention of the children produced the effect he wanted, with fear clouding the vicar's face once more.

The Commander stifled another coughing fit. Without another word, he rose and strode out of the room, Grip flapping noisily after him.

Marcus felt badly shaken and covered in sweat. The pain began to subside, but the sensation of thorns in his brain remained. He missed his children more than he could say, and it sickened him to hear the blotter speak their names.

He pulled his glasses case from his pocket and took out the handkerchief. Remarkably, the airtight seal had kept it from drying out completely. That comforted him somehow, like having an old friend turn up when you least expect it.

Impulsively, he wrapped the cloth over his index finger. Then he reached his arm underneath the gurney to write on the back side of the canvas beneath him. It was no use trying to form a picture without eyesight or a proper pen. Instead, he used the handkerchief to scrawl crude letters forming the word *HELP* where his captor was less likely to notice it.

It was as pointless as a castaway throwing a bottled message into the sea. Still, the small act of defiance felt good.

If that blotter hated the smell of Ink so much, maybe this would make him miserable.

# The Calamus Scroll

34

"How many Inkwells are there?"

Bea turned her pen over and over while she waited for an answer. The four of them sat around the table in the Drawing Room, giving their food time to digest.

"We only know of one that is currently active," answered Gilroy.

"That's all the Ink in whole world?" Trey alternated between jotting down notes on his pad of paper and figuring out the fingerings to play a simple tune on his pen flute.

"Ink itself is unlimited and eventually reappears," Gilroy explained. "Sometimes it returns to former wells, and sometimes it springs up in new places. But the blotters work tirelessly to shut down all the wells and keep them shut.

"There have been three periods in history known as the Blank Ages, where all the wells dried up. Some fear we're about to enter a new Blank Age. That's why it's so important to find and protect this last well."

"It's in Aberdeen," said Everett almost subconsciously. He still felt the sting of not being given a pen.

Gilroy looked incredulous. "How did you know that?"

Everett considered for a moment, unsure how to answer. The thought had just popped into his head and his hands buzzed like in Writer's Block. Hardly a reliable clue. He grasped for another reason. "Why else would our dad take a trip there?"

Gilroy nodded, continuing. "A century ago, a young lass by the name of Elspet McPherson served as a housemaid in Aberdeen. When her day's work was done, she would often walk home along the River Don. Always a free spirit, she liked to imagine the young postman, Isaac Forsyth, at her side, and she would dance along with him in a dream.

"One night, as the full moon cast its glow on the water, Elspet noticed a strange, dark, murky spot spreading on the surface of the river."

"An underwater Inkwell?" Trey asked.

"That it was," said the conductor. "Of course, the girl had no idea what she saw. But Elspet found it a wonder that the dark color didn't drift away downstream and that the moon could not dispel the darkness. It called to her. She grabbed a branch from a tree near the bank and waded out, dipping just the tip in the pool of Ink. With love on her mind, she took the stick back to shore and painted a heart on the tree with the initials *E* plus *I* in the middle."

"Oh," whispered Bea, her eyes wide at the notion of romance. Gilroy knew how to weave a tale.

"Well, Ink always favors true love. As soon as Elspet

wrote those initials, the tree burst into pink blossoms. Being a bright lass, she realized this was no ordinary Ink she had discovered.

"She ran and found a big glass jar and collected some from the river to take home. For months she experimented, learning how to write with it, going back again and again for more."

"And it still hasn't been shut down?" asked Everett. "Even after all these years?"

"Its exact location is unknown," said the conductor. "Being underwater, the scent washes downstream, making it impossible for the blotters to detect. No Inklings since Elspet have seen it."

Bea wanted to get back to the love story. "What about Isaac?"

Gilroy indulged her. "Eventually, the two of them married. It was a happy union, but with modest means, so they took in boarders to make ends meet. One was a college student, an aspiring author by the name of George MacDonald."

Trey jumped in excitedly. "Wait! Wait! I know that name!" The wheels in his brain were spinning madly to recall more details. "My mum . . . she read some of his books to me. He wrote fairy tales, didn't he?"

"That he did," Gilroy said, grabbing a volume off a shelf and handing it to Trey. "Like this one. Elspet had a hunch the young lad could write something wonderful with the Ink, so she shared her secret with him. Soon George began writing the most fantastic novels and poetry. Ask Jack and Ronald; Georgie boy was their hero."

Everett and Bea peered over Trey's shoulder at the old book. *There was once a little princess whose father was a king over a great country full of mountains and valleys . . .*

Gilroy kept going. "Young George took Elspet's Ink and shared it with his friend Charles Dodgson, who—"

"Lewis Carroll." Everett started to see the connections.

"Right you are!"

"Did Elspet and Isaac ever have children?" Bea wanted to know, still hungry for more personal details.

"As a matter of fact"—Gilroy leaned in close—"they had a boy named Peter. He was a sickly lad, staying indoors much of the time. He read a great deal. And when he got a hold of the Ink, the words from his pen wouldn't stop. He grew up to become one of Scotland's finest preachers."

Mention of another preacher piqued Everett's curiosity. "He used Ink for sermons?"

"Aye. No real surprise there. Like art, sermons express a greater story. At least those worth their salt. What was it Melville wrote? *'The world's a ship on its passage out . . . and the pulpit is its prow.'* But speaking of preachers, let's get back to your father."

"Yes, please!" Bea said. "That's who I want to talk about!"

Gilroy smiled at her. "Marcus quickly discovered that his new comic book project required far more Ink than ordinary writing, more than a single pen could provide. Or perhaps at least a more concentrated Ink.

"Jack and Ronald suggested he venture to Aberdeen. They had heard rumors Elspet's well had been rediscovered. It was a long shot, but they believed there were Inklings in town who might at least have a penful to spare for him. They never expected him to return home with a full bottle of Elspet's Ink."

"He didn't, exactly," Everett said sadly.

A loud clacking interrupted him. It came from a strange device in the corner.

When Everett turned to look, he was shocked that he hadn't noticed it before. It was a large wooden cylinder containing a spool of paper in the center. Rising from the base of the cylinder were three jointed mechanical arms. Each arm had a feather quill attached to it.

All three arms pivoted simultaneously, bending at the joint and dipping the quills into small Ink burrows set in the base. Then the quills rotated and began scribbling on the scroll, as if guided by invisible hands. Occasionally one would stop and dip itself in the Ink again, then continue writing.

"The Calamus Scroll," was all the explanation Gilroy gave as he walked over. The rest of them followed.

Everett was fascinated. "How does it work? Is it another Ausculator, like the one at Dot's house?"

"Osgood's pride and joy." Gilroy smiled. "The design

for the Calamus Scroll goes back to da Vinci, but it was Os who brought it to life. This one intercepts written, not spoken, messages. It has been fine-tuned to pick up the energy waves from emergency signals."

After a few moments, the quills stopped moving. Gilroy pulled a length of the paper and tore it from the rest of the scroll. There, in large fat letters looking as if they had been finger-painted was one word: *HELP*.

"Who's asking for help?" asked Trey.

The conductor turned to Bea. "Can you hear it? Is the Ink speaking to you?"

Bea concentrated for a long moment, then looked at Gilroy with a mixture of alarm and hope. "It's Daddy."

35 Inside a Camera

The creak was not loud, but it echoed conspicuously across the open rotunda as the narrow bookshelf swung slightly away from the wall.

Behind it, within the wall itself, Dot, Jack, and Ronald crowded close to peer through the sliver of light.

"We're inside the Camera!" Ronald exclaimed with recognition. "On the first level! I can see the—"

"Shh!" Dot chided. "Do you want to get us caught?"

When the three of them had parted ways with the others, they had taken the tunnel Gilroy had said would lead straight back to Oxford. The shortcut (another Pinch) deposited them inside the Radcliffe Camera, a famous Oxford library the Inklings knew well.

Built centuries earlier, the round building boasted two stories and a domed roof. It was just the sort of place you'd expect to be full of secret rooms and hidden passages.

Yet whoever went to the trouble creating the Pinch had somehow stopped short of including an inconspicuous way to step out of a wall into such a hushed environment.

Fortunately, the library was deserted at the moment, giving the opportunity to duck inside undetected. They left the shelf partly open to avoid repeating the creak. Jack led them toward the front door, but he froze suddenly and motioned for silence.

A voice much too loud for a library filled the air. A voice with a distinct American accent.

"It can't be," whispered Dot.

But it was. Jack tiptoed forward for a closer look and peered cautiously out from behind a column. Above him, next to a second-story railing, stood Eddie Montbanks and the unmistakable form of Mr. Lugg. They had their backs to Jack as Eddie argued with a matronly woman who appeared to be the librarian.

Her response was firm. "That manuscript collection is not accessible to the general public."

"So you said. But I can assure you, I am not the general public."

As Jack stepped back into the shadows, his heel caught the leg of a chair, causing it to scrape noisily across the floor. Mr. Lugg snapped his head toward the sound. He looked back at his boss, who gave a nod. Mr. Lugg moved toward the stairs.

Jack hastily rejoined the others. "The bodyguard's headed our way."

"We'll never reach the exit," said Dot. "We would have to walk right in front of him. What do we do, retreat into the wall?"

They heard Mr. Lugg reach the bottom of the stairs, moving steadily closer as he surveyed the area. The footsteps stopped. The three Inklings crowded behind a stack of books, holding their breath. Then the steps began to move again, slowly getting farther away. Ronald dropped to his knees and crawled to the edge of the shelf. He peeked cautiously around the corner, then rose to his feet. Inviting Dot and Jack to follow him, he took them around the outer edge of the rotunda, away from Mr. Lugg, to a back stairwell. The stairs led down into a cavernous basement, where rows of bookshelves stretched away, far past the walls of the building above.

"I've only been down here once," Ronald said. "But if memory serves, it's an underground link to a second library across the yard."

The three moved quickly and quietly between buildings. With no signs of being followed, they made their way back up to ground level and out to the street.

Jack breathed in deeply. "Fresh air at last!"

"Where to first?" asked Dot.

Ronald held up the briefcase. "We'd better do as Gilroy requested and leave a trail of Ink to throw off any blotters."

Jack grimaced. "I have to admit, I can't say I fancy the idea of having those creatures following us too closely."

A lone taxi sat out front, which gave Dot an idea. She looked at Jack. "Give me your shoelace. Hurry."

He knelt down and removed one. Dot retrieved the Ink

from the briefcase. She opened it and dipped the end of the shoelace in the bottle, covering it with Ink. Then she quickly replaced the stopper.

"Okay, Ron," she said. "Go speak with the cab driver for a moment. Distract him."

"I have nothing to say."

"That's never stopped you from talking before," she quipped. "I just need a moment."

Ronald rapped on the window of the cab. The driver rolled it down.

"Good day to you, sir," said Ronald. "Um . . . it's fascinating, you know." He pointed across the yard toward the Camera. "That building once had a copper sign on it that said: QUOD FELIX FAUSTUMQUE SIT. It was a wish for happiness and prosperity. Did you know that?"

The driver was unimpressed. "Listen, I have my own wish for prosperity that requires paying customers. Get in or get lost."

Ronald's face registered hurt. "I say. No need to be rude. I thought your next fare might appreciate knowing that this library—"

The driver rolled up his window and pulled away from the curb, leaving Ronald sputtering in a plume of black exhaust. Dot patted him on the shoulder.

"Perfect. I had just enough time to tie the shoelace to his bumper. The blotters can waste their time chasing a cab all around town."

Ronald smiled. "I'm glad to see you're starting to appreciate my winsome verbal skills. I—"

"Come on, you two," said Jack. "Let's hail the next cab. We have work to do."

Back inside the Radcliffe Camera, the reluctant librarian seemed to have disappeared, but Eddie now carried an ancient-looking book under one arm. He rejoined Mr. Lugg, who had discovered the ajar bookshelf masking the secret tunnel.

"Looks familiar," said the bodyguard.

Eddie was not listening. He stared in disbelief through the library window. The three Inklings were bundling into a taxi. He grabbed Mr. Lugg's shoulder and pointed at Dot.

"There! What's she putting in that briefcase? Is that an Ink bottle?"

Mr. Lugg's eyes narrowed. He moved toward the library entrance, but Eddie stopped him.

"Forget it. They'll be gone before you're out the door."

Eddie patted the manuscript tucked under his arm. "Let's get this to Pitz first. We know where to find the Inklings."

36 Magnetic Attraction

Everett paced the Drawing Room in frustration. "If our dad sent that message, we've got to go to him now!"

"It's all right, lad."

"No! It's not! He needs our help!"

"And he'll get it." Gilroy held up the paper from the scroll and pointed to the large letters on it. "The fact that he could send this message is very good news. Now we know for certain he's alive, which means the blotters have a use for him."

"Where is he, then?" Bea asked.

The conductor pondered the question a moment before responding. "We know the bottle came from Elspet's well. Someone he met in Aberdeen must have given it to him. The blotters will want your father to reveal his source."

He held up the paper from the scroll. "I have a friend in Aberdeen who may be able to tell us where this message originated."

"But you're a Fomentori," Trey said. "You conduct Ink Waves. Don't you know where they come from?"

Gilroy shook his head. "Messages transmit on a different wavelength." He then proceeded to give a very passionate and lengthy technical explanation of how all the Fomentori have different powers. None of the children had the heart to tell him they couldn't follow a word of it.

"How much longer until we're there?" Everett was growing impatient.

Gilroy placed a hand on his shoulder and said, "You'll be encouraged to know that when a communique comes to the Calamus Scroll, it goes through Central Dispatch."

"What does that mean?"

Gilroy smiled. "We're not the only help headed his way."

Everett looked at the machine. "Why would anyone want to fight the Ink?"

The conductor grew serious. "Many writers and poets have asked the same question. I suppose Mephistopheles gave the best answer: *'Misery loves company.'* The blotters despise all that is good and creative. Ink threatens their miserable existence."

"They don't act very worried," Trey said bitterly.

Gilroy disagreed. "They're not the all-powerful creatures they would have you believe. They have their weaknesses."

Everett pressed for more details. "Such as?"

"Well for starters, they can be Inkased."

"Dot told us about that," said Bea, looking disgusted. "Gargoyles. Do they stay that way forever?"

"Technically, it can be reversed," said Gilroy. "But who would want to? Blotters are far more useful as downspouts."

Trey put down his pen. "And the ones that aren't caught? What about them?"

"Well, since they cannae use Ink, they cannae create," said the conductor. "They can only cause havoc."

That didn't satisfy Trey. "Who cares if they can't create? If they destroy everything in the end, they win."

Gilroy grew quiet. "You're remembering something, aren't you?"

Trey strained to recall. "Patches of it. Like remembering parts of a nightmare. I was little. My mum was crying and I asked my dad why. He said bad people stole her music. I learned later the blotters had raided our town. All her compositions, gone forever."

Trey buried his face in his hands. Everett thought of the pile of Ink shards. So much creativity lost.

"Do you think you might be able to sing one of your mother's tunes for us, lad?" Gilroy asked softly.

"I don't feel like it."

"Please?" asked Bea softly. "Do you remember a happy one?"

Trey rubbed his eyes. "There's one, I suppose. My mum used to sing 'The Ballad of Eadfrith' to me. I always liked the story, even though the song sounded old-fashioned."

Gilroy approved of the choice. "Eadfrith was a splendid Inkling. Could you sing a bit?"

"If I can remember it."

Tentatively, he began, his voice a bit shaky at first, but growing stronger with each line:

When Eadfrith sailed to Lindisfarne
His holy book to write;
Despaired his heart, he ne'er could start
For lo, his quill was dry, oh-ho,
For lo, his quill was dry.

The monk, he rose and traveled far
To reach the River Dee;
Where Ink lay hid, 'neath shadowy lid
Below the current deep, oh-ho,
Below the current deep.

Then back went he to Lindisfarne,
His burrow filled to brim;
Began the saint to scribe and paint
And joy came flooding in, oh-ho,
And joy came flooding in.

Trey finished the lilting tune, the last notes lingering in the air. With eyes closed, Gilroy wore a peaceful smile. "See? Those blotters didn't destroy as much as they thought."

Bea was unable to suppress a yawn, which didn't go unnoticed.

"There's still a wee bit of time before we arrive. I suggest you all get some shut-eye while you can." Gilroy pointed to a small alcove off the Drawing Room with three cots side by side.

The exhausted children flopped into their makeshift beds.

"What about you?" Bea asked Gilroy. "Where will you sleep?"

"I'm going to do a sweep of the train for any threats," said the conductor. "Then I'll keep working on our plan."

Bea held up her pen and clicked it, giving another yawn. "Me too," she said as she drifted into sleep.

"What a crazy day," Trey said. "Almost dying is exhausting." He opened his notepad to write in the light of Dot's flashlight.

Everett couldn't turn off his mind. The fact that Gilroy gave him those knitting needles (or whatever they were) instead of a pen still stung. Everett held them like drumsticks in the dark, then swords, then wands. He waved them around, willing them to be magical, unable to see what good they could ever do.

Maybe Gilroy just wanted him not to feel left out. Give the boy a couple sticks and he can play pretend.

Everett dropped his arms and let the sticks clatter to the ground. They were useless. *He* was useless. How could he help find his dad? He went over all the clues in his mind, trying to think what MC would ask in this kind of predicament.

But the only question he cared about was whether or not his father was safe.

Why did his dad have to start using the Ink in the first place? None of this would have happened if he hadn't picked up that stupid pen. Everett felt angry with his dad, and guilty for feeling angry.

The sound of Trey's pen moving effortlessly across the page made it difficult to concentrate. Everett buried his head under his pillow to block the noise. It didn't help. The rhythm of the effortless scrawling kept going, taunting him.

Eventually, Trey closed his notepad and fell asleep, but Everett remained awake. He slid out of bed and tiptoed into the Drawing Room. Gilroy had gone to patrol the rest of the train.

Everett walked over and surveyed the shelf with the pens. It wasn't fair that he had to get sticks. There were plenty of pens to spare. Why didn't Gilroy give him one? He picked up the small magnetic pen. It was heavy for its size, but the weight felt good in his hand.

He wondered if the magnet would even work for him. He touched the end of the barrel to the base of the table lamp. It stuck fast. When he tried prying it loose, it refused to let go. In a panic, he gave a big pull. Nothing. He clicked the top, then tugged hard. The pen broke free, but dragged the lamp off the table and sent it crashing to the floor.

He held his breath and waited. No sound came from Trey or Bea.

Everett righted the lamp and went to return the pen. He wished he could keep it. If Gilroy knew how much he liked it, he probably would want him to have it. After all, didn't he say he made them to give away?

He slipped the pen in his trouser pocket.

Strictly speaking, was it stealing if Gilroy would give it to him anyway? He could always ask later if he could keep it. Until then, this was more like borrowing. And for a good reason, since they needed every available resource to rescue his dad.

Everett padded quietly back to his cot. He tossed and turned, working to justify the choice in his mind. Fatigue finally won out, and he drifted off to sleep. In his dreams, he was standing on one side of a river of Ink, with his father on the other, and there was no way to reach him.

Smell Anything?

37

Any passenger looking out the window of the train to Aberdeen might have thought they saw a large eagle swooping toward the locomotive. In reality, it was a blotter named Lt. Malo disguised by Mind Murk, straining his blotter wings to their limits in pursuit of the speeding train.

He alighted on the roof of the first-class compartment and made his way inside. His appearance morphed into that of an ordinary businessman.

From his pocket, he took out a canister. If any passengers grew suspicious and made a nuisance of themselves, one spray of Mind Murk would remove any memory of him from their minds. Mercifully, they were all asleep in their seats.

Lt. Malo began making his search from the front of the train, one compartment at a time. The Commander had provided few details, so he moved slowly and methodically, stopping frequently to inhale deeply and analyze what he smelled. By the time he reached the dining car, he was ready to declare the effort a bust.

The kitchen was empty at this hour of the night, but he

stepped inside for a quick inspection. Pots and pans hung from their hooks. The stainless steel counter had been wiped clean. Nothing to suggest a disturbance. He turned to go, then stopped.

It was the dead of night and no one was awake, yet a big roast was cooking unattended. He peered through the glass in the oven door. He could smell only the meat. Then he noticed the hand-drawn quality to the lines of the stove. He lowered his head for a sniff. His pupils began to swirl.

Opening the oven door, he stuck his hand inside. Realizing the roast was a smokescreen, he bent down and then climbed inside the oven to reach the source of the smell. No sooner had he crawled through than the oven door slammed shut behind him. A series of clicks accompanied a whooshing sound. Nozzles in the walls sprayed him with Ink from all sides. His face froze in an expression of shock as a red light flashed above him.

The Pipes Are Calling

The children awakened to the shrill sound of an alarm bell and flashing red lights.

Gilroy rushed in and pressed a button on the wall, silencing the alarm. "The oven's been compromised," he said. "Time to go."

Panic filled Bea's voice as the conductor rushed them through the Drawing Room. "What's going to happen to us?"

"Nothing, if we move quickly," said Gilroy. He walked by the bookshelf where the pens were displayed. Everett held his breath, hoping he didn't notice that the magnet pen was missing.

The conductor led them past the shelf to the hearth beside it. "I'm afraid you'll have to trust me once more," he told them. "Into the fire you go. I will come through last and secure the exit behind us."

The fireplace turned out to be the same sort of illusion as the oven. There was no hesitating this time. Trey led the way, with Everett and Bea right behind. Soon they found themselves stepping out of a giant steamer trunk and into a private train compartment with all the blinds pulled tightly shut on the windows.

The train came to a stop at Aberdeen Joint station. Gilroy gathered everyone around him. "The threat in the Drawing Room was neutralized. But from here on out, we are going to need to be very careful. Blotters have been alerted to our presence. Since they didn't catch us en route, they will be looking for us as we disembark. We will need disguises."

He looked each of them up and down, then clapped his hands and rubbed them together. "Trey, Bea—please hold your pens in front of you. Everett, you do the same with one stick in each hand. And all of you: Close your eyes until I say."

The children did as instructed, arms out, eyes tightly shut. Gilroy removed his own pen from his pocket and twirled it above his head as if throwing an imaginary lasso.

As the pen spun faster and faster, a cloud of microscopic colored dots formed in the air. The cloud moved above the children, raining Ink down on them in a fine mist.

When they were completely soaked, Gilroy lowered his pen and pointed it at them like a fire hose. He then proceeded to spray Everett, Trey, and Bea with a dark powder that made them all cough.

Just when they thought it was all they could handle, Gilroy flipped his pen once more. He removed a hair from his mustache, swiped it against his sleeve, and attached it sideways to the end of his pen. With a click, the hair began to rotate like a fan blade and a hot, strong wind blasted from the pen, sweeping across the children, leaving them dry.

The conductor then directed the cloud back over his own head, shutting his eyes and repeating the process. If you've ever tried to draw something without looking, you can appreciate the challenge he faced.

With one more click, everything became quiet.

"That should do," said Gilroy. "Take a look for yourselves."

Everett couldn't believe what he saw. They were now dressed in black-and-blue plaid kilts and tall furry hats. Trey and Bea held bagpipes, while he had a small drum strapped around his neck and his two sticks were now most definitely drumsticks.

The level of detail was staggering. Anyone would need a magnifying glass to see that the uniforms and instruments were hand-drawn. From a short distance, they were perfectly convincing.

Even more remarkable than the disguises was the fact that although their faces remained their own, somehow they all looked as grown-up as Gilroy. Everett could even feel a little stubble on his chin. He kept running his fingers across it in disbelief.

"You make a fine pipe band," Gilroy said approvingly,

holding a long drum major's mace in his hand. "I must warn you, illusions of this sort have a short life. I've stretched the Ink to where it is no longer waterproof, so keep the weeping and perspiring to a minimum." He smiled. "But it should get us off the platform. Once we're safely away from the train station, we can return to our normal clothing."

"Won't the blotters smell all the Ink?" asked Trey, holding his bagpipes to his nose.

Gilroy shook his head. "I added a coating to mask the scent. At least temporarily."

As he stepped down to the platform, Everett's heart sank; the station was crawling with blotters. Uninitiated travelers might take them for ordinary soldiers, but there was no mistaking the truth if you glimpsed their eyes. Several blotters were boarding the train.

"Ev—over there," Bea whispered, tapping his arm. "Are those . . . dye hounds?"

They were. Sniffing and snarling, the beasts prowled between passengers.

"Stay calm," Gilroy said out of the corner of his mouth. "If we don't act suspicious, they will pay no attention to us."

Trey grabbed the conductor's arm. "I don't think I'm supposed to be here."

Gilroy studied him. Even through the disguise, Gilroy could see the fear. "Are you having another memory?"

Trey nodded. "I've been here before. In Aberdeen. I was

leaving for somewhere. And I was scared of being caught then too."

"Well, I'm with you this time," said the conductor reassuringly. "You're going to be fine."

"Hey, Molly—look! Bagpipers!"

The loud voice belonged to a young American man walking straight toward them. Molly was sitting on a bench nearby, preoccupied with her luggage.

"This is amazing!" the young man said with a smile. "Are you fellas the real deal?" Gilroy gave a slight nod, looking every bit the professional.

"The name's Chet," the man said, shaking Gilroy's hand vigorously. "Could I ask you a huge favor? Would you mind playing a bit of 'Scotland the Brave'?"

Gilroy began to object. "Well now, I don't think—"

"It's just that it's our honeymoon, see? We're from New York, and I promised Molly the time of her life and it's all gone wrong. We missed our train and now I'm in a heap of trouble. But she loves bagpipes."

Without waiting for an answer, he yelled to his new bride. "Molly! Molly! These bagpipers are going to play a tune for us! Isn't that swell?"

Several blotters looked up to see who was yelling and took notice of the pipe band.

A single trickle of sweat made its way down the back of Everett's neck. He had no idea how to hold drumsticks properly, let alone how to keep a beat. And what about Bea?

Those fake pipes probably weren't even functional. The blotters would see through their disguise the instant they attempted to play anything.

Molly joined her husband, looking at them expectantly. An excruciating pause followed.

Gilroy cleared his throat. "We . . . normally prefer *not* to play without the rest of our band."

It was a thin excuse.

Chet's eyes pleaded for an exception.

Two blotters made their way over, sensing the awkwardness.

"How about a solo?" Trey said, looking straight at Chet and raising the blowpipe to his mouth.

Everett felt the fear rising in his chest. Maybe Gilroy should have explained to Trey that the illusion only included appearance—it would not give them talent.

But it was too late. He was already filling the bag with air. Everett braced for the sound, and then—the most hypnotic melody began to waft from the pipes.

Trey stood calmly keeping the beat with his toes, his cheeks puffed out as he played, fingers deftly finding the right places to land as if from memory.

The blotters lost interest about halfway through the march and drifted away. The newlyweds, on the other hand, were thoroughly enchanted and ended up kissing by the final note, which made Everett squirm and gawk at the same time.

When it was over and the couple had walked away, the

four of them huddled together on a corner of the platform. Gilroy had tears in his eyes. "I thought you'd lost your head, lad. Where did you learn to play so magnificently?"

Trey smiled. "I said my mum was a musician. The bagpipes reminded me my dad was too. He played them back in India."

Bea was surprised. "Bagpipes in India?"

"They're called mashak there. He was teaching me to play because he wanted me to see how my two worlds connected. He . . . He . . ."

His voice died out as he thought about his parents and his former life.

"Well, he would have been proud of that performance, to be sure," conductor said, beaming. "But we best be off before anyone requests an encore."

As they made their way across the platform, a sudden cloudburst brought a flood of rain. Walking behind Gilroy, Everett noticed that his drum major's mace left a bluish trail across the wet boards.

Alarmed, he tapped the conductor on the back. "We have a problem."

Gilroy kept walking. "I know," he said in a low voice, without turning. "They're going to smell us."

Everett glanced back at Bea. Her tall hat was melting, with large rivulets of black coursing their way down her face. Trey was no better. The bagpipes that had saved them were now nothing more than a dripping wet rag.

No sooner had they rounded the far corner of the station than a bark from the other end of the platform told them the dye hounds had picked up the scent. Another beast joined in, and the sound of howls and pounding feet came their way.

39 Walking Sticks

Without a word, Gilroy took his dissolving drum major mace and tossed it high into the air. As it twirled, it transformed, shrinking ever smaller, until by the time he caught it, it was his old pen again.

The conductor herded everyone under an overhang.

"Let's hope dye hounds have a bit of real dog in them." Gilroy drew feverishly in the air, creating what resembled a fluffy black cat with white paws. It was an excellent likeness, except that it was on wheels.

Taking his pen, Gilroy stuck it in the back of the cat and turned it several times like a key to a windup toy.

"All right, Mittens," he said. "Time to go to work."

Gilroy set the cat on the ground. Mittens rolled away from the building, leaving a hefty black streak as the cat's thick fur slowly melted into a stream.

"Meow." A very mechanical-sounding cat voice came from the quickly disappearing animal. But the farther away it went, the more believable the illusion became.

Gilroy then swept his pen through the air in front of the children to remove their disguises.

Everett felt as though hundreds of bandages were being ripped off his skin at the same time. All three children winced in pain as they returned to their normal selves.

Their discomfort changed to sheer terror as they heard five dye hounds and a clump of blotters barreling toward their corner of the station. They all pressed their backs up as flat against the wall as they could, barely breathing.

"Steady," Gilroy whispered. "Nobody move a muscle."

The animals charged down the side of the building, shrinking the distance in leaps and bounds. The lead hound came within inches of the corner, then halted, cocking its head to the side, unsure. It stuck its snout down into the puddle of Ink on the platform.

Mittens chose that moment to meow, and the dye hound howled its displeasure. The entire party raced after him in the opposite direction, pursuing the cat.

When the blotters were a good distance away, Gilroy gave a sigh of relief. "All right, children. Next stop is the post office. We must make haste."

The downpour ended as abruptly as it had begun, and the morning sun peeked through the clouds. It felt like relief shining down from the sky as the space grew between them and the blotters.

Bea skipped up alongside Trey. "How do you like your pen?"

His face brightened. "It's incredible."

"Mine too," Bea enthused. "I figured out one of its secrets."

Bubbly with excitement, she spent the next few minutes showing him all the features she had discovered. Listening to his sister describe her pen to Trey, Everett found himself feeling left out and a little bit cross. "Dumb pens," he muttered.

He was still holding his two sticks in his hands. He struck them against each other absently. As the sticks smacked together, a static shock jolted him and made him drop them to the sidewalk. It felt the same as when Dot had touched her pen to his forehead, except more intense.

He picked the sticks back up and hesitantly tried the same move once more, bracing himself. Again, there was a shock, one that produced a visible line of blue sparks in front of the sticks. But this time, he managed to hang on. Instead of the crackling kind of zap that flashes and is over in a moment, this shock continued as a slight tingling sensation up and down his forearms, pulsing back and forth. Could the sticks be picking up the Ink Waves Gilroy talked about?

It couldn't be a coincidence that it was the same sensation as when he found the exit from Writer's Block. The feeling continued as long as Everett kept the two ends touching each other.

What's more, he found that as he moved the sticks from side to side, the point where they touched would pull in different directions. The sticks seemed to have a mind of their own, almost like they were directing him somewhere.

"Gilroy! Look!" Everett said as the sticks led him toward the conductor. "They're returning me to you. Even in reverse. Watch!"

He turned and faced the other direction. The sticks rerouted him to face Gilroy again.

Gilroy watched the sticks leading Everett and gave a low whistle. "Keep at it, lad. We may need your skills with those sooner rather than later."

Unless the blotters were scared of static electricity, Everett couldn't see how this trick had any practical applications. Still, it gave him something to do while Bea and Trey talked about all they had in common.

As he lowered his arms, his hand brushed past his pocket with the magnet pen. He could feel the metal sticks being tugged toward it, nearly snapping his hand to his pant leg. He hurriedly raised the sticks back up and concentrated on following them, fighting to ignore the voice inside reminding him of what he had done.

Had he looked up, Everett might have seen the lone raven circling above, listening in on every word of the conversation happening below.

How Witch Hunts Start

40

Grip struggled to walk on tile. His talons clicked uselessly across the smooth hallway floor as he slipped and skidded his way into the office. Once through the door, he flew to his perch on the coat rack.

The Commander walked in and closed the door behind him. He reached in his pocket and pulled out a soda bottle cap. The glint of metal caught the raven's eye and he gave a loud squawk. The Commander put the cap back in his pocket. "Only after you tell me again what you heard."

Grip opened and closed his beak as if warming up for a performance, then said, "Gilroy! Look at the sticks!"

He repeated Everett's conversation with the conductor on the street. The bird even imitated the electrical buzz the sticks produced when they touched. It was as clear as a tape recording.

The Commander flicked the bottle cap in the air, and Grip added it to his pile of collectibles.

The sticks had to be Witching Sticks. Like the ones Fomentori had brandished long ago. As far as the

Commander knew, only certain enemies could use them, and they functioned primarily as guidance devices.

But most blotters knew another rumor about the sticks. It was said they could reverse Inkasement. The Commander looked down at his stone foot and imagined having full use of it again.

From what he knew, the sticks harnessed the powers of the Stink, yet required no direct contact with it. Therefore, they posed no threat to a blotter. If he had them in his possession, he could restore his foot. If he had the sticks, he could bring back all his Inkased comrades, for that matter. If he had the sticks, he could find and shut down the last well.

In short, if those sticks became his, there would no longer be any question who was the most powerful blotter in the world. He would be unstoppable.

The Commander strode down the hall to the room where Marcus was being held. The physical exertion aggravated his weakened lungs, which resulted in a violent coughing fit. He composed himself, then opened the door.

"Your son."

"I'm not talking to you about him."

The Commander held the vicar's arm in a crushing squeeze. Emotion made his breathing more labored. "Don't try me, Reverend. Your son has . . . abilities."

The vicar said nothing.

The fingers tightened, cutting off circulation to the arm like a tourniquet. "Tell me about the Witching Sticks."

Marcus was caught off guard. "Pardon?"

"Don't play games. Your son is a Stink Witch."

"That's absurd!"

"We've seen him."

"A witch?" Now it was Marcus who turned angry. "You don't know what you're talking about. We are Christian people. We do not practice witchcraft of any sort."

The Commander was about to argue, when he reconsidered. He didn't need to chase the boy. The boy was coming to him.

"Why don't we wait and ask him when he gets here?"

A dagger of fear stabbed Marcus in the heart. "What?"

"I think you're right not to talk about your children," said the Commander. "Let's change the subject."

"I beg you," Marcus whispered, his voice cracking. "Leave them out of this."

It was almost too easy. Children were such a reliable weakness.

The Commander pulled his chair closer to the gurney, studying his prisoner. He marveled at the lines of concern creasing the vicar's face, the fear clouding those sightless eyes.

This interrogation was going to be fun.

Horsing Around

41

Hiking from the train station to the post office took longer than anyone expected, so by the time they reached it, they were warm and dry again. Everett could tell the building was old. It still had a hitching post out in front where customers in days gone by would tether their horses while they conducted their business inside. Now a solitary old bike leaned against it, padlocked around the base below the rings that hung from the metal horse head on top.

Trey began to make his way to the front door, but Gilroy caught his shoulder. "We're not going in there, lad."

Trey was perplexed. "But you said we needed to get to the post office."

"I did, didn't I?" The conductor grinned. "A natural conclusion you reached there. I said 'post office' when what I meant was the Office of the Post."

Gilroy walked over to the old bike and set it to one side so he could examine the horse head atop the hitching post. Removing the lid from his pen, he said, "Bea, would you be so kind as to hold out your hand?"

She complied, stretching it out flat. Gilroy began drawing in the air just over her palm, and a small, three-dimensional cube formed. Then with amazing speed, he repeatedly touched the tip of the pen to the sides of the cube, making thousands of tiny dots in a matter of seconds. When it was complete, the artwork rested in her hand, much to Bea's delight. "It looks like a blue sugar cube."

"Let's hope it tastes like one," said the conductor, and he moved her hand directly below the horse head.

For a moment, nothing happened. Then the nostrils on the iron head flared, and the horse's lips stretched downward in search of what it could smell. Bea instinctively retracted her hand as it picked up the cube with its teeth and swallowed it.

The horse head came fully to life, raising its mouth in the air and neighing loudly, the two rings underneath clanking and rattling noisily.

"Hello, Kelpie." Gilroy grinned.

"You always bring the best treats," said Kelpie in a deep, booming voice. "Are you sure you aren't part horse?" He whinnied heartily at his own joke, then noticed the rest of the party. "What a fine string of colts you have here."

Gilroy made introductions, then produced the paper from the Calamus Scroll for the horse to examine. "My friends and I are on a life-and-death quest," he said. "I'm wondering if you might recall seeing this message pass through the post here in Aberdeen."

Flipping his head from side to side, Kelpie sent the two hitching rings flying up onto his nose to form a makeshift pair of eyeglasses. He peered carefully at the parchment through them, sounding out each letter.

"Hmm . . . *H-E-L-P*, it says. Help. Help. Not a word we horses use often. Did a dog send this?"

Bea scowled. "My daddy isn't a dog."

The horse head squeaked as he turned and looked at her.

"Ah . . . human writing. Of course. Well, that's a different matter entirely. Makes good horse sense. Let me check my memory banks."

His metal ears began to twitch back and forth rapidly. The sound of gears creaking and groaning could be heard coming from inside the horse head.

"Kelpie is a relay post," Gilroy told the children. "The message would most likely have been routed through him on the way to the Calamus Scroll."

"Ah, yes," said Kelpie. "Here we are. A distress signal came in directly via Ink Wave. We don't see much mail like that these days. Let me give you the address."

Kelpie opened his mouth. With a whir and a clank, he coughed up a narrow slip of paper. Gilroy promptly retrieved it.

"And there you have it," said Kelpie. "Straight from the horse's mouth." He neighed in amusement, then smacked his lips a few times. "Always a most disagreeable taste, ticker tape. I don't suppose you might have another of those sugar cubes?"

"I do," Bea replied, holding up her hand again. She had tried to mimic Gilroy's work on one of her Cheering Up Pills, drawing dots as grains of sugar all over the sides. But the Ink hadn't bonded well with the sticky surface, smearing into a blob of blue mess.

Kelpie eyed it rather dubiously, then gingerly bent forward to pick it up. He let it dissolve on his tongue, trying to make up his mind about the flavor. "Not bad. Not bad at all," he kept saying.

"There is one other matter," Gilroy said. "We also need to send a most urgent message."

"Then you'd better send it special delivery," said a voice behind them.

"Osgood!" shouted Bea, rushing to give him a hug.

"Did you bring Ermengarde?" asked Everett.

"Not this time. Just my trusty steed." Osgood gestured toward the old bike.

Kelpie snorted his disapproval. "That is no steed."

"Are you going to help us rescue our father?" Bea asked Osgood.

He nodded. "I was at Central Dispatch when I saw that the Calamus Scroll on the train had been activated. I came straight to Aberdeen to find where it originated. I stopped at the only address I had for the last Inklings I knew here, but they're gone."

Gilroy was shocked. "Gone? Where?"

"Neighbors said a family emergency came up and they left in a hurry."

Gilroy removed his hat and scratched his head. "I was hoping for some local help. But if they've left, I'm all the more grateful you came. We need to reach Dot and the Oxford Inklings right away."

42   Traveling in 2D

With Osgood on his way to fetch the Inklings, Gilroy returned his attention to Kelpie. He tapped the slip of paper.

"Approximately how far away is this address?"

Kelpie tilted his head, adding up the numbers. "Let's see, at a good gallop, I'd say no more than an hour."

"Hmm." Gilroy brooded. "That would take several hours for short human legs to cover."

The children's faces fell. They were already exhausted and anxious. Kelpie picked up on their disappointment. But being a horse, he did not want to say anything that might be taken as an insult.

"Have you been inside?" He nodded in the direction of the post office. "They have a wonderful mural from 1893. I believe a matching one can be seen in the local post office near the address on that piece of ticker tape."

Everett wondered how a post anchored in concrete could possibly know what was inside any building. And besides, with his father in imminent danger, who had time to stop and admire artwork?

Gilroy, on the other hand, perked up right away. "That sounds worth a look. Once again, I am in your debt."

Kelpie dismissed the thanks with a whinny. "Please. I owe you a great deal more than that."

As the group said their goodbyes to the horse, Bea slipped him one more hastily drawn sugar lump, which Kelpie graciously accepted.

Everyone bundled up the steps and into the post office. The run-down building had an equally unimpressive interior. There was a service counter to the left and banks of mailboxes to the right.

The gray-haired woman behind the counter looked as ancient as the building itself, her skin the color and texture of old parchment. She glanced up briefly as the children entered and regarded them silently, then returned to sorting parcels when it became clear they were not looking to buy postage or mail a letter.

Everett instinctively turned to the right and began walking past the bays of mailboxes. As he did, he could feel the magnetic pen tugging him toward the metal. Hoping no one noticed, he crossed to the other side of the corridor to reduce the pull.

The floor-to-ceiling mural Kelpie mentioned hung on the far wall. It was a colorful scene depicting a mail coach behind a team of four horses.

With one hand on the reins and one holding on to his hat, the mail carrier seated at the front of the coach wore a determined look on his face. It was the kind of picture that gave you confidence that your parcel or letter was in good hands.

"I see why Kelpie's fond of it." Gilroy went over and ran his fingers across the mural, inspecting it from inches away. He pointed at the driver. "And that is a very good likeness of the postman himself, Mr. Isaac Forsyth."

"Oh," said Bea admiringly. "He was handsome."

"Who painted it?" Trey wanted to know.

"There's no paint here," Gilroy said. "This is Ink."

Everett examined the mural more closely. The colors were vibrant enough to have been from one of their father's comic books.

"Definitely Elspet's," Gilroy added. "Everett, do you still have your dad's pen?"

Everett held it out.

Gilroy glanced quickly around to see if they were being observed, but apart from the inattentive postal worker, the place was deserted.

"This is a bit dangerous, but I don't see any other way. Ink is attracted to Ink."

"You mean like a magnet?" asked Bea.

Everett flinched. Did she know what he had done? Gilroy looked at him.

"Exactly like a magnet. We're going to use that property to catch a ride."

He had the children hold out the index fingers on their right hands, then turned to Everett. "One dot on each fingertip, lad."

Everett bit his lip as he removed the cap. What if he couldn't even write a dot this time? Or if the magnet pen in his pocket interfered with what Gilroy was trying to do? The Ink didn't like him. He was certain of that.

Gilroy sensed his hesitation. "Would you like me to show you how it's done?"

Gratefully, Everett handed the pen to the conductor. Starting with Trey, Gilroy pressed the tip of the pen against his finger. It left a perfectly shiny black drop.

The postal clerk froze in the middle of her sorting. She inhaled deeply, detecting an unmistakable scent.

Gilroy repeated the process on all of their fingers, including his own.

"When I count to three, we will all touch the mural at the same time. Ready?"

The clerk stepped out from behind the counter and headed toward the mural.

Her pupils shifted wildly.

Everyone lined up close to the wall, fingers raised. Gilroy gave the signal and the four of them simultaneously made contact with the wall. The moment their fingertips touched the surface, it felt as though a giant fist reached out and yanked them into the painting.

While everything about this journey had been strange,

Everett had no words to describe this experience. He could not move. He was sitting, but it felt as if his insides were turned sideways. He began to worry when he couldn't catch his breath, but then he realized breathing itself was strangely unnecessary. He had become two-dimensional.

Bea, or at least a drawing of her, was sitting directly in front of him. Her eyes were bright with excitement. It was impressive how well the Ink had captured his sister.

They were now part of the mural, seated across from each other inside the mail coach. The sound of horse hooves thundered at breakneck speed, even though Everett couldn't sense any movement. Gilroy must have been seated next to the driver, because his voice was shouting instructions to Mr. Forsyth about where to drop them off. And though he couldn't turn his head, with his peripheral vision, Everett could see Trey, hanging on the outside of the coach with one hand in the air.

The next thing he knew, he was catapulted forward and his limbs were flailing.

And just like that, they all landed in a heap.

For a moment Everett thought they might be back where they started, sprawled on a post office floor. But this post office was smaller and cleaner than the first.

Gilroy stood up, chuckling as he dusted himself off. "That old stallion was right. We jumped from one mural to another. We should be very close to finding your father now."

The conductor walked the children out of the post office. "I'm going back in to get directions. But I think it would be safer if you waited out here this time. That last postal clerk may have friends in this office."

A few blocks away, the telephone rang. On the third ring, the blotter on desk duty picked it up. He jumped and stood at attention immediately as the woman on the other end yelled urgently in his ear.

Then he ran to tell the Commander.

43 An Unnamed Source

Marcus pressed a palm to his forehead, pushing against the hammering inside. Thankfully, the bird had left with his owner after the most recent grilling, so at least the room was quiet.

The Commander seemed intent on wringing every drop of information about Ink from his brain. Yet Marcus couldn't answer the relentless barrage of questions about wells and Witching Sticks. He had not lied—he truly could not say how he found the bottle of Ink. It was more like the Ink found him.

When Jack and Ron sent Marcus to Aberdeen, they had not held out much hope, since the Inklings there had gone underground. As a starting point, they suggested he try Ma Cameron's, a pub nearly as old as The Eagle and Child.

"Inklings of previous generations gathered there," said Ronald. "At the very least, you can enjoy one of Ma's Sticky Toffee Puddings. Delectable!"

For nearly a week, Marcus followed their recommendation, scouring the city by day and returning to the pub every evening. Ronald had been right about the pudding, but no Inklings materialized in the establishment. By the fifth day, Marcus was certain his questions had attracted the wrong kind of interest and sinister eyes were watching him.

On the last afternoon before returning to London, he headed to the pub a final time. As he reached the entrance, the merchant from the spice shop across the street waved him over. "Good afternoon, sahib. We have a special on saffron."

Marcus smiled. "Not today."

The shopkeeper was undeterred. "Maybe some lavender for the young lady in your life? Someone named . . . Elspet, perhaps?"

Marcus locked eyes with the man, reading him. "All right. Let's see what you have."

The man ushered him inside, glanced out at the street, then locked the door. "Sorry for the charade, sahib," he said. "We are safe in here."

An overpowering array of competing fragrances filled the air. Open jars of basil and cardamon and garlic and mint all sat side by side on the shelves. Marcus coughed involuntarily. The shopkeeper grinned. "Not easy on the nose, but it covers the smell of Ink."

A ginger-haired woman emerged from behind the counter. Her eyes looked as though she had just had a good cry. "Hello, Reverend."

"This is my wife," said the man. "You can speak freely in front of her."

Marcus extended a hand. "Nice to meet you. My name is—"

The shopkeeper cut him off. "No names. Too dangerous."

He reached over and turned on the radio behind the counter. A Duke Ellington number blared through the speaker. "I apologize for taking so long to make contact. All the Inklings in Aberdeen have been forced into hiding. Blotters are everywhere now. They are energized by the possibility of finding and destroying the last Inkwell in the world."

"Elspet's is still operational, then?"

The shopkeeper nodded. "We believe so. We haven't located it yet."

"How do you know it's not already gone?"

"We don't." The man nodded to his wife, and she slipped into a back room. "Everyone assumed it dried up naturally, since no one had seen any new Ink from it in many years."

The woman returned from the back with a brown paper bag. Her husband continued. "Then a man came into the shop with this." His wife pulled a bottle of dark liquid from the bag.

"He was fishing in the river one day when a most beautiful smell arose from the water. He described it as a combination of citrus and cinnamon, only more delicious. He identified the scent as coming from a murky section of the river. He brought some in, thinking we might want to sell it in our shop."

The merchant shook his head. "It was completely odorless to us, but I asked him to leave the bottle with us for analysis. We were both sure it must be Elspet's Ink. We arranged to meet again in a few days, but he never made it. I tried in vain to find him and learn more. I fear blotters may have reached him first."

The woman held up the bottle and turned it from side to side. The Ink shimmered in the light. "The last bottle of full-strength Ink from Elspet's well. We'd like you to have it."

She put it back in the bag and slid it across the counter toward Marcus.

He looked at her in surprise. "What? If that's all there is, I couldn't possibly take it from you."

"You don't understand," said the shopkeeper. His voice took on a new intensity. "We've been through this with blotters before with another well. We've seen what happens. We need to get this Ink safely away from here before it's confiscated."

"Why not take it yourselves?" Marcus asked.

"We're on their watch list, and rather easy to spot," the woman replied, dabbing at her eyes with a handkerchief. "An Indian man traveling with an English woman? We've already sent our son away for his safety."

Marcus took the bag. "I don't know what to say."

"The less words, the better," the shopkeeper said. "We've said too much already."

He led Marcus to a back door that opened into an alley. "Whatever you do, do not open that bottle in public. Blotters can smell undiluted Ink from great distances. Use extreme caution." The two men shook hands, wished each other luck, and parted ways.

The next morning, Marcus passed by the spice shop on his way to the train station. It was boarded up with a sign that said OUT OF BUSINESS. The windows looked dark and empty. If he didn't have the bottle to prove it, he would have wondered if the exchange had even happened.

Now, lying on the gurney, Marcus wished it *hadn't* happened. He wished that blotter hadn't followed him onto the train. He wished he could just hand over the bottle and be done with the whole ordeal. But he didn't even have it in his possession. He had sent it—

Marcus bolted upright on the gurney, sick with the realization. That's why the blotter had asked so many questions about his children! "He's going after Everett and Bea . . ."

What was it the Commander had said—something about waiting until Everett arrived? It had been bad enough being the focus of these creatures' rage. Now they were simply using him to get to his children. He was nothing but bait.

He took a deep breath. "Fine," he said aloud. "Let's show them how bait has a way of squirming off the hook."

44 Confrontation

M r. Lugg stood on the roof of a brick building across the road from The Eagle and Child, staring through binoculars at the three people scurrying down the street toward the pub. He had been surveilling all afternoon, and his quarry had finally come into sight: the woman with the over-decorated ears, along with those two bookish blokes who always seemed to be shuffling after her.

The bodyguard went to the nearest telephone box and called his employer. Then he slipped into the pub himself to keep a closer watch. Once again, the Inklings had secluded themselves in the Rabbit Room.

Eddie arrived within minutes. "You're sure they didn't leave through the tunnel again?"

The bodyguard shook his head. "I've been listening at the door."

"And the briefcase?"

"No sign of it."

Eddie was preparing to interrupt the meeting when a

courier arrived at the pub, all breathless and in a rush. The man looked so odd and out of place that Eddie instantly pegged him as part of this whole business.

Sure enough, the deliveryman made his way toward the Rabbit Room. Before he reached it, Eddie intercepted him.

"I'm afraid you can't go in there. That's a private party."

Osgood frowned. "They won't mind. I have an urgent message for them."

Eddie held out his hand. "I'll see that they get it. They gave me specific instructions that they do not wish to be disturbed under any circumstances."

Osgood pursed his lips, sizing up the pushy little American and the human mountain standing behind him. He fished around in his messenger bag. "Very well, then. It was a verbal message, but I'll write it down."

He scribbled on a piece of paper, folded it in half, and handed it to Eddie, not letting go until Eddie looked him in the eye.

"Please give this to Dorothy Sayers. Tell her Osgood brought it."

Eddie smiled. "Oh don't worry, my friend. I will bring it to her attention immediately."

He watched the courier exit the front door. Then he unfolded the slip of paper:

ALL IS MELLOW IN AFRICAN UNDERGROUND.
SAME ESTIMATE COUNTING JOB PACKAGE.

He scowled, puzzled as to whether or not the note was a joke. If it was encoded, Eddie had no context for deciphering it. But it did give him leverage.

When he and Mr. Lugg burst into the Rabbit Room, Jack, Dot, and Ronald shot from their chairs.

"You're not welcome here, Montbanks," hissed Jack.

"You've heard of me? I'm flattered." Eddie shook his head. "Nice meeting you too. Although you seem angrier in person than in your books."

"I don't know how you live with yourself. You should be locked up."

Mr. Lugg took a step toward Jack. Eddie held up a hand to stop him.

"Do you know the real crime, Jack? May I call you Jack? You and your friends, hoarding all the Ink, robbing the world of great stories waiting to be written."

"We hoard nothing," Ronald objected. "Ink finds its own way into the hands of those who will use it for good."

"And who is to say my use isn't a good one?"

"You only want it for your personal gain," seethed Jack.

"Oh, stop acting superior!" yelled Eddie. "Who made you judge? You get paid for your books."

Dot moved directly in front of Eddie and pointed her finger in his face. "We know what happened in America. We're not going to help you print your counterfeit currency."

Eddie laughed. "You English have no imagination when

it comes to money. Why would I want to make fake money when I can make fake Ink?"

"You are sadly mistaken," replied Jack. "The power of the Ink cannot be manufactured. No amount of tinkering on your part will re-create its nature."

Eddie was unfazed. "You let me worry about that."

Ronald's eyes flared with indignation and resolve. "There is too little Ink left to waste it on the likes of you!"

Eddie walked over and put his face right in front of Ronald's. "Which is why I'm going to make more. All I require from you is a small sample."

Dot spoke up. "Even if we wished to give you the Ink, we couldn't. It's the same here as in the States: We don't have any left."

"Oh, really? Then what was that in your hand at the library?"

Dot fell silent.

Jack moved to stand between his friends. "Do your worst. We will not help you."

"Oh, I think you will." Eddie held up the message in his hand and turned to the others. "I have an urgent message for you all. I've already read it. If you'd care to see it, it will only cost one bottle of Ink."

"You don't know what you're asking," Dot said. "And how are we to believe this so-called message is authentic?"

Sensing they were cracking, Eddie divulged his secret.

"It was handed to me by a special-delivery messenger. I believe you know him, Ms. Sayers. His name is Osgood. He seemed very concerned."

This produced just the amount of alarm he had hoped. The Inklings appeared to be at a loss.

Eddie pulled his lighter from a jacket pocket and gave it a flick, waving the flame perilously close to the message in his other hand. "Please—take a moment to discuss what you wish to do."

The three formed a gloomy huddle. While they had no desire to help Montbanks, they could not risk losing an emergency contact from Osgood. The children might be in danger.

After a few minutes, they turned to Eddie. "We need to see that note," Dot said.

"So you agree?"

"We read the note now. If we determine it is authentic, then you get your sample. You'll have to take us at our word."

Eddie shook his head. "Not enough. I want to hear all of you promise. Look me in the eyes and tell me you promise as Inklings to do this."

The three of them gave their solemn word.

Eddie handed the message to Dot.

She laid it on the table. Jack and Ronald leaned in close to examine it with her.

ALL IS MELLOW IN AFRICAN UNDERGROUND.
SAME ESTIMATE COUNTING JOB PACKAGE.

Eddie tried to read their expressions, but they gave no indication they understood the contents.

"It's definitely Osgood's printing. I need my reading spectacles," said Dot. She rummaged through her purse and exchanged her everyday glasses for another pair. Then she reread the message. "Hmm," she said.

They all stood in silence, staring at the strange phrase. After a long while, Dorothy exchanged her glasses again and said, "Gentlemen, I hate to disturb our concentration, but would you excuse me a moment while I use the ladies' room?"

Eddie was instantly skeptical. "If you don't mind, Mr. Lugg will accompany you."

Dot glared at him. "I most certainly do mind. You may coerce us to cooperate, but private business is still private."

Eddie conceded. "He will stand outside the bathroom door to ensure you do not use the occasion to go elsewhere."

"Fine." Dot stormed out of the room with the bodyguard in tow.

As soon as the bathroom door closed behind her, Dot made her way to the window. She opened it as delicately as she could, hoping Mr. Lugg could not hear the wood frame scraping as it rose.

For a woman of her age, she pulled herself up and through

the window with uncharacteristic agility. She dropped down to the ground and briskly made her way around the back of the building. There, waiting for her, stood Osgood.

"You cracked it," he said with a grin.

"It was all I could do to keep a straight face," Dot replied, brushing dirt off her hands.

Osgood shook his head. "I knew that con man wasn't working for you. I had to write something on the fly. I wasn't sure if it would be clear."

"I was just glad I brought my glasses," said Dorothy. "Otherwise, I might not have found the hidden message."

Osgood had used a simple trick with the Ink, making certain letters stand out more than others when viewed through specially coated lenses he had invented. So his words read:

ALL IS MELLOW IN AFRICAN UNDERGROUND. SAME ESTIMATE COUNTING JOB PACKAGE.

I smell a fraud. Meet me out back.

"I don't have much time," Dot said. "What was the real message?"

Osgood got straight to the point. "Gilroy and the children have learned that Marcus is in Aberdeen."

"Are they sure?"

"The Calamus Scroll confirmed it. They're planning a rescue now."

Dot processed this new development. "We must get there to help them. Go to my house and collect Ermengarde. Then meet us back here."

Osgood raced away. As Dot climbed back through the window, she heard a rap on the door. "One more minute and I'm coming in, Ms. Sayers!"

For good measure, Dot flushed the toilet and splashed her hands in the sink as loudly as she could. Then, still holding a paper towel, she emerged, drying her hands.

"Some things cannot be rushed," she said curtly, then brushed past Mr. Lugg and returned to the Rabbit Room.

Jack and Ronald were still studying the note when Dot and Mr. Lugg reentered the room. With a straight face, Dot said, "Well, boys, when do we leave for Africa to get Mr. Montbanks his bottle?"

Ronald caught on to her ruse and played along. "Since the note says we are to count the job package in the estimate, I believe that would mean it is ready now."

"*Mellow* is the key word," Jack said dramatically, tapping his finger on the piece of paper for emphasis.

"Code for marshmallow, no doubt," Ronald agreed, barely containing his smile.

Jack pointed out something else in the handwriting. "Look at how all the *E*'s slant slightly right, suggesting we go east."

"Ah, yes. But the word *same* would indicate our usual drop-off point," Ronald enthused.

Dot began to worry that if the two of them kept this up much longer, Eddie would catch on. She drew attention back to the question at hand. "So, when do we go?"

247

"I will contact the Underground tonight and confirm the pickup," said Ronald gravely. "I'm guessing they will be ready for us within the week."

"You have until tomorrow," Eddie warned. "I will meet you back here in twenty-four hours to collect on your promise."

Mr. Lugg followed his boss to the door, where Eddie turned and gave a slight bow. "Cheerio, Inklings. Do not even think of crossing me. "

As soon as he was gone, the Inklings breathed a sigh of relief. Dot critiqued the performance. "That may have been slightly over the top, gentlemen."

"Do you think so?" asked Jack. "I felt we did rather well."

Ronald's fingertips danced against one another as he chuckled with delight. He tapped Jack on the arm. "Didn't you think the bit about marshmallows was brilliant?"

"Listen, both of you." Dot pulled the men in close. "Marcus isn't in Africa. He's in Aberdeen. Gil and the children need our help with a rescue operation."

After mapping out all the real arrangements, the three of them left The Eagle and Child.

In their haste, none of them took note that the door to the Rabbit Room had been left slightly open during their entire conversation. Had they peered into the dark corner, they would have seen the distinct shape of an oversized eavesdropper, a bodyguard barely concealed in shadows.

Running with Ink

Gilroy approached the lanky (and very ordinary) young clerk behind the counter.

"I'm trying to find directions to where a friend is staying." He took the slip of paper Kelpie had given him and slid it across the counter.

The clerk looked at it and shook his head. "Well, he's not staying at that address. Nobody lives there."

"Why do you say that?"

The clerk shrugged. "Easy. That's the old watchtower. Used to be a jail and now it's a museum. All about stockades and dungeons. Actors dressed as guards give guided tours. Don't waste your time."

Gilroy thanked him and returned to the children, who were sitting on the steps outside. He was surprised to find Bea laughing, with two puppies in her arms. An elderly woman in a shawl stood next to the children with a poodle on a leash. The boys knelt on the ground, petting the grown dog.

"Gilroy!" yelled Bea excitedly, trying to contain the

squirming pups. "Come meet—what did you say their names were? Dud and Oafie? They're adorable!"

She squealed in glee as one of puppies licked her cheek. The other one gave a snuffly-sounding sneeze.

Gilroy stood perfectly still. "Children," he said calmly. "Look at me."

They all turned to the conductor. He had his pen in hand and a bright light shone from it.

"Say goodbye to the animals and come with me."

It was as if his words and the light broke a spell, because suddenly the children could see through the Mind Murk to who was truly in front of them.

The elderly woman turned her head and glared at the conductor.

As he raised his pen, she removed her shawl and snapped it at him, momentarily obscuring his view.

Hideous wings sprouted from her back. She grabbed Bea, who screamed. Then she launched herself in the air and the two of them were gone, along with the puppies.

"No!" wailed Everett in horror. Watching the sky, he tore after them as fast as he could. Behind him, the grown poodle gave chase, dragging the leash behind it. The Mind Murk disguising the dog's body could no longer fool Everett's brain. He stole a glance over his shoulder and saw the frightening image of a full-grown dye hound bearing down on him.

A pair of blotters descended from the sky, flapping their

wings in front of Trey and Gilroy and blocking them from following Everett. Gilroy yanked two mustache hairs from his face and flung them at the creatures. The hairs stuck like needles, and the blotters were immobilized by a massive electric shock.

"Come on!" shouted the conductor, charging in the general direction Everett had gone. Trey did his best to keep up, but after a few blocks, both of them slowed to a stop.

The trail had already gone cold.

Everett's lungs were on fire as he raced through city streets. The dye hound was gaining on him, and he knew he wouldn't be able to outrun the animal forever. Gilroy still had his father's pen, which meant this time Everett had no Ink to defend himself.

Hoping to lose his pursuer, he ducked down multiple side streets, doubled back on his own tracks, and switched directions again and again. But every time he began to feel confident, the hideous snout of the dye hound would come into view and the hunt would continue.

In one moment when Everett had managed to pull ahead, he spotted a policeman on the corner in front of him. Finally! It was a relief to see an adult who could help. He ran up to the officer, and leaned over, trying to catch his breath. "There's . . . there's . . . a dog . . ."

"Steady, lad," said the constable, placing a hand on Everett's shoulder. "You look winded. Have you been trying to chase down your pup?"

"No, I—"

The constable looked past Everett and pointed to where the dye hound had just emerged from behind a building. "There! Would that be him? Why, that's a fine-looking poodle!"

He raised his fingers to his mouth and whistled. The dye hound broke into a run toward them.

"No!" shouted Everett. "He's not mine!"

But the officer didn't seem to hear him. He was down on one knee, holding out his arms. "Come on, boy! That's right! Come on!"

Realizing the policeman would be no help, Everett did not wait another second. He took off running and wove his way through several more side streets. He needed to get off the street, behind a door the dye hound couldn't open. Pausing out of sight next to a stack of pallets in an alleyway, he scanned frantically for a refuge.

Less than two blocks away, he could see the spire of St. Fergus Cathedral.

Everett knew all kinds of places to hide from Bea in their church back home. He had never been inside a Catholic church, but it couldn't be that different. There had to be plenty of dark corners inside where he would be invisible. And churches almost always stayed unlocked during the day.

He took off running down the alley and was halfway to the street when he heard a howl behind him. Without looking back, Everett raced into the street, causing cars to slam on their brakes and honk their horns. The dye hound bounded after him, closing in on its prey.

Less than a block to the church. Now Everett could hear claws on the pavement behind him. He lunged for the steps of the cathedral, scrambling up them two at a time. As he reached the top step, he felt his leg caught behind him.

The dye hound had the hem of his pants in its mouth and was holding on with all its might, growling viciously. Everett looked back and wished he hadn't. The monster's eyes swirled with hatred. Everett kicked and heaved forward with all his might to break free. But the dye hound gave a sudden tug that pulled him violently backward. He slipped and fell, smacking his head directly on the threshold of the church entrance.

Everything went black.

When he came to, Everett found himself lying on a pew in the sanctuary. A sturdy-looking nun sat next to him with her hand on his forehead.

"Well, now. That's better. You gave me quite a fright there, lad."

Everett sat up slowly and turned his throbbing head. "Where is it?"

"Where is what?"

"The dy—the dog," Everett said.

"No dogs allowed in here."

Everett shook his head. "It's not mine," he explained. "It was chasing me."

"I didn't see it." The nun paused, then laughed loudly. Everett looked at her and for the first time realized she was blind. He didn't know what to say.

"Sorry," she said, "that was an old joke. But no one was near you. Just you, face to the ground in the doorway. I nearly tripped over you. Father Murray helped me bring you inside. He ran to fetch a doctor. Why don't you lie back down?"

There was nothing he wanted to do more. But Bea couldn't wait. "I have to go."

He started to stand, but the nun grabbed his hand and made him sit.

"You'll be doing no such thing. You need rest. Is there someone I can call to collect you?"

From her iron-clad grip, Everett could tell that even without her sight, this woman was a force to be reckoned with. He changed tactics.

"My mum was just across the street. She said she'd be right back. She's probably worried I'm not there." It felt terrible, lying inside a church, but Everett didn't have time to explain the truth.

The nun put an arm around Everett's shoulder to help him up. "I will walk you out front and wait with you until she arrives."

Everett hadn't anticipated that response and kicked himself for not coming up with a story that would make it easier to escape. But he had to admit he felt lightheaded, and the extra support was a relief as he walked.

When the street came into view, a wave of panic hit him. What if the dye hound was waiting for him outside? What if it was lurking near the steps, ready to pounce the moment he stepped through the door?

He needn't have worried. Besides a few cars going by, the street was deserted. The nun kept a tight hold on his arm. He had to get rid of her.

Everett coughed a deliberate-sounding cough. "Could I trouble you for a cup of water? My mouth is dry." He had already told one lie. A second one couldn't make things much worse.

The nun stood beside him. "Do not mistake blindness for ignorance," she said quietly. "I'll humor you. Sit here on the steps. While you're waiting, you can admire our recent architectural improvements." She turned and guided herself back through the door.

Everett was not about to wait. The second she was out of sight, he bolted down the steps. He had seen enough churches and had no interest in sitting around admiring another one. Hurrying quickly down the sidewalk, he glanced back to make sure the nun hadn't reappeared. When he did, he froze in his tracks, fear giving way to disbelief.

Above the door of the church, next to a statue of St. Fergus, sat a brand-new bluish gargoyle in the shape of a dye hound.

Locked in a Dungeon

It's not easy to fly while carrying someone who is kicking and screaming, and Bea proved to be a handful for her kidnapper. The frightened puppies in her arms did not help matters, either. After only a few minutes in the air, the blotter grew weary of the struggle and returned to the ground, choosing to walk and give her wings a rest.

If Bea had one area of expertise, it was her knowledge of all kinds of getaways and elusive maneuvers. According to her Rules of Escape, the top priority when being abducted is to make as much noise as possible. As the blotter carried her down the street, Bea screamed and hollered at the top of her lungs, hoping someone would come to her rescue. But no one paid any attention.

When she turned to study her captor more closely, she abruptly stopped screaming.

"I know you," she gasped in recognition.

It was the female clerk from the first post office. Bea couldn't believe she hadn't seen it before. She had been too distracted by the old lady's dogs to pay attention. And now that this woman was wearing a floral dress and a woolen shawl, she looked very grandmotherly and innocent. Anyone hearing Bea's yells would assume she was a bratty child making life very difficult for Granny.

The dogs themselves changed too. They were no bigger, but they were decidedly uglier. Bea dropped them to the ground, where they kept nipping at each other as they trotted along behind.

"There, there, dear," said the blotter in a syrupy voice, tightening her hold on Bea. "We don't want to cause a row, now, do we?"

She covered Bea's nose and mouth with a handkerchief soaked in a Mind Murk solution, and it made Bea groggy straightaway. She tried desperately to follow the second Rule of Escape when being kidnapped, which is to take note of your surroundings, but her brain was in a stupor.

Eventually they came to an old stone building with a tower. The blotter stepped through a back door, carried Bea down a flight of stone steps, and set her down. The puppies skittered off, eager to be free.

The blotter patted the pockets of Bea's sweater. Discovering her pen, she ran it under her nose. Her pupils liquefied as she inhaled.

She noticed the pen was missing its cap and glared accusingly at Bea.

Bea shrugged, her eyes droopy. "I lose things a lot."

The woman reached into Bea's sweater pocket and

removed the tin of Ronald's Cheering Up Pills. She opened the lid, sniffing at the candies.

"I need those," said Bea, grabbing one and popping it into her mouth. "It's my medicine." With a determined glare, she took the tin and tucked it back in her pocket.

The woman led her to a cell and shoved Bea inside.

The metal door clanged shut.

The key scraped in the lock.

Bea was alone in the dark.

47 Worse than Lost

In his efforts to lose the animal chasing him, Everett hadn't given any thought to making sure he knew the way back to the post office.

He stopped in his tracks, unsure which direction to take. He couldn't even ask for help. Anybody might be a blotter in this strange city. Everett broke into a desperate run, up one street and down the next. Nothing looked familiar and everything looked familiar. All his instincts only took him in a circle. At last, he keeled over on the curb, utterly spent.

Maybe the Ink was punishing him. Maybe it knew he lied. Maybe it knew he took that magnet pen. He regretted ever wanting it. If he found Gilroy, he would give it back. He should probably return the sticks too.

The sticks! Everett took them from his back pocket. Could they guide him to Gilroy from this far away? He touched the ends together, and immediately the sticks lifted him to his feet.

They led him down streets and avenues he had never seen. It didn't seem like the right way back at all.

And it wasn't. He slowed to a walk as he found himself in an empty park nowhere near the post office. No sign of Gilroy or Bea or Trey—or anyone else, for that matter.

Disgusted, he shoved the sticks back in his pocket. Worthless. He walked up onto a grassy rise to catch a better view.

A river meandered through the park, just at the bottom of the hill. The sunlight danced along the surface, making it look like liquid gold. Except . . . there was one shadowy spot in the middle of the river. Trey's song rang in his ears: *Where Ink lay hid, 'neath shadowy lid . . .*

Could he be seeing what Elspet saw all those years ago?

"Everett!"

The voice sounded far away. Across the park, he could see Gilroy, with Trey standing beside him waving frantically. He hurried over to reunite with his friends. Gilroy wrapped him in a hug.

"We were beginning to wonder if we'd ever find you," he said, his voice breaking. Then he noticed the bruise on his forehead. "What happened to you, lad?"

Everett told them the whole story, including the part about the gargoyle. "How did it get Inkased? I didn't have any Ink."

"You said your head landed inside the cathedral when

you fell?" the conductor asked. Everett nodded. "If the dye hound was holding on to you at that moment, then technically it crossed the line with you."

Everett had forgotten that churches were safe havens from blotters. Gilroy handed him his father's pen. "From now on, this stays in your possession so you'll have some protection."

It was hard to concentrate on Gilroy's words. All Everett could think about was his sister and the horrible sight of her being whisked away by that blotter.

"We have to find Bea."

Gilroy searched for a silver lining. "No doubt they've taken her to the same prison where they're holding your father. The blotters don't know we have their location, which gives us the advantage."

All the emotions of the day caught up with Everett. In frustration, he lashed out at the conductor. "Stop trying to make it sound okay when it isn't! If you hadn't left us outside the post office, none of this would have happened!"

Trey stepped in to defend Gilroy. "He couldn't have stopped it. He—"

In a blur, Everett ran at Trey, tackling him to the ground. "You don't know anything!" he shouted through tears, pummeling the older boy with his fists.

The two of them tussled until Gilroy shouted, "Enough!" He took the boys by their collars and pulled them apart.

They stood for a moment, their chests still heaving from the fight, then Everett sank to the ground and buried his face in his hands.

Gilroy spoke up first. "I am truly sorry."

Everett couldn't bring himself to even make eye contact. He sniffed and wiped his nose with his sleeve.

Look after your sister. His father's words rang in his ears. He had to get her back.

Trey reached his hand down. "Ev. I want to help."

Everett accepted Trey's peace offering and pulled himself to his feet. "Well, staying here isn't doing anything."

"Very good," said the conductor with a nod. "Let's go rescue your family."

Three for the Road

48

"Why are we stopping?" Ronald looked up at Dot from the sidecar of her motorcycle.

She lifted up her goggles and pointed to the sky. "Osgood signaled me. I don't know why."

The Inklings were en route to Aberdeen. They had left The Eagle and Child as soon as Osgood returned with Ermengarde. Jack rode along with Osgood in the basket while Ronald chose the sidecar with Dot, with the briefcase strapped on the back.

Dot pulled off the road next to an open field and brought her motorcycle to a stop. Ermengarde landed in the field. Osgood walked toward them, with Jack following unsteadily behind. He looked even paler than normal.

"We're being followed," Osgood said. "The same car has been behind you for the past twenty minutes."

"Montbanks," said Ronald.

"He must have seen through our misdirection," reasoned Dot. "What should we do?"

Osgood looked back at Ermengarde, who could barely

be seen from where they stood. "We have to lose him between here and Aberdeen."

"Agreed. If we're caught, you fly on ahead. In fact . . ." Dot removed the bottle from the briefcase and handed it to Osgood. "I think this better go with you. That way you can still get the Ink to Gilroy even if Montbanks delays us. I will use some evasive tactics to try and shake him."

"Drives like a madwoman," said Ronald under his breath. "Are you all right, Jack?"

Jack had seated himself on the front of the sidecar, his skin clammy. "Might you have room for me on the back of your bike, Dorothy? No offense, Osgood, but I think my stomach is prone to air sickness."

"Man was never meant to fly," said Ronald sympathetically. "Since the days of Icarus, we—"

Dorothy revved the motor. "Hop on."

As Jack swung his leg over the back of the motorcycle, a black sedan appeared in the distance.

"Go!" shouted Osgood, running to Ermengarde. Dot opened the throttle, accelerating as fast as she could. The added weight of two full-grown men did not help.

Montbanks began closing the gap.

49 A Day at the Museum

With Kelpie's slip of paper in hand, Gilroy and the boys made their way to the watchtower and stood assessing it from the outside. It loomed over them, looking oddly out of place among the much more modern structures on the city block.

"I think I've been here before," said Trey. "Yes! I came here with my parents once." He turned to the conductor. "Why would blotters take over a museum?"

"They've infiltrated many cultural institutions. Anywhere they can counter the influence of Ink, they will." Gilroy squinted up at the building. "And I'm sure they've narrowed their search for Elspet's well. This place must be strategically close."

Everett was dying to get to his family. "Let's go." He moved toward the museum entrance, but Gilroy stopped him.

"Look."

The conductor directed Everett's gaze to the squattish-looking man dressed as a medieval prison guard, opening the door for visitors as they entered and exited the museum. His nose twitched as he sniffed at unsuspecting tourists, and when he turned to the side, the hump on his back shifted under his costume.

"They already know we're in town," said Gilroy. "They'll be expecting us."

It was torture for Everett, knowing his dad and sister were just a few yards away. He watched the steam rising from the storm drains in front of the building. It added to the sinister atmosphere. But it also sparked something for him.

"I have an idea."

Gilroy pointed at a coffee shop across the street. "Not here," he said in a low voice. "Let's discuss it inside."

The three of them found a table near the window, ordered tea, and sat down.

Everett's suggestion was simple. "What if we climb down in the sewer system?"

Trey made a face. "I've had enough time underground."

"Hear me out. If we go below the street, no one will be watching. Gilroy can make one of his tunnels straight through a basement wall."

Gilroy sipped his tea. His mustache twitched from side to side as he considered the possibility. "It would take some time, but it might work. The trouble remains the same: We'd be going in blind. If we had a blueprint or diagram that showed the layout of the building, the story would be different."

Everett's face brightened. "It's a museum, right? Don't most museums have printed maps for visitors?"

"Of course!" said Gilroy. "The clerk at the post office said they give guided tours here daily. But we can't risk going inside."

"Maybe not all three of us," Trey said. "But I could go alone. I remember where the information desk is."

Everett started to protest, but Trey stopped him. "Listen. They have your dad and your sister, which means they're probably waiting for you too." He looked at the conductor. "And you're probably on their most wanted list."

"That's true," Gilroy conceded. "Even my disguises cannae get me in the front door."

"See what I mean? But me—I'm just a kid who got in their way. I'm betting the blotters here don't care about me. They might even think I'm dead."

The conductor scratched his head. "I don't know about that. You said you recalled being in danger at the train station here."

The three of them discussed the merits and risks of Trey's offer. And they tried to devise alternatives. They considered asking an exiting visitor for their map or paying a stranger to go in and get one for them. But that would require waiting for just the right cooperative person.

In the end, they all agreed that the simpler the plan, the better.

"What if you're caught?" asked Everett. "Do we have a backup plan?"

Trey felt confident. "It won't happen. But if it does, the strategy is the same. Gilroy tunnels without a map." He smiled. "And I'll just count on you to rescue me along with your family."

Trey waited by the steps to the museum until he saw a young mother trying to corral three small boys up the stairs while carrying a baby.

"Here, let me help you."

Without waiting for a reply, he scooped up the smallest toddler and walked up the steps next to the grateful mother. When they reached the blotter guard, the baby gave a loud wail. The guard winced and waved them through without a second glance.

He was in.

And then the waiting began. Gilroy and Everett sat in silence. As the seconds ticked by, Everett's hand felt clammy next to the magnet pen in his pocket. The more he thought about what he had done, the worse he felt. He wanted to confess. He wasn't a thief! Why had he pocketed it? What if the magnet interfered with the rescue? He couldn't bear that.

The words were there, but it felt as if the magnet was pulling them back. Just as he finally opened his mouth to speak, Gilroy looked at his watch and frowned. "He's been in there too long."

He rose. "We cannot delay any longer. I need to start

tunneling, even if we don't know the precise location for where we want to end up."

Everett felt torn. "We can't just leave him."

"No. I agree. You stay here and wait for Trey, then join me below ground. I will leave an Ink trail for you to find me."

The conductor flew out the door swiftly and Everett waited uneasily. As he watched the entrance of the museum, time moved at an agonizingly slow pace. He wished he had a watch. The one line from Dot's rhyme kept echoing in his brain: *Whene'er the pounce pot hath been spilled, the hands of time shall soon be stilled.*

Everett crossed the street just as a green-and-cream-colored double-decker bus rattled up in front of the museum. The door creaked open and students disembarked, heading inside for a tour.

It would be hard to find a more perfect cover than a class outing for him to sneak in and find Trey.

Merging behind three other boys his age, Everett kept his eyes down and tried to blend in. The swarthy little blotter at the door scowled at the group, one hand on the hilt of his sword.

"No roughhousing!" he barked. "Single file, single file."

Everett held his breath as he passed by. The guard didn't pay the slightest bit of attention to him. He wondered if it was because he posed no threat. Maybe the blotters didn't care about him because the Ink wanted nothing to do with him. Regardless of the reason, he was grateful to pass unseen.

Once through the front doors, Everett peeled away from the group. His heart beat so fast he thought he might faint. Concentrating on his surroundings, instead of the blotters, calmed him. The lobby featured multiple displays explaining the history of medieval jails in Scotland. Placards described life for the prisoners, and actors milled about in period costumes.

He caught a quick whiff of a strange smell. A strong, chemical kind of scent. What was it—a cleaning solution? Vinegar? Ammonia?

Then he spotted Trey. He was seated on a bench, reading a pamphlet, oblivious to the world around him. Everett walked toward him as fast as he could without attracting attention, winding his way through the crowd that was meandering around the lobby.

"What are you doing?" he whispered. "We've been waiting forever."

Trey looked up, dazed. He didn't seem to recognize Everett. "Do I . . . know you?"

Everett was in no mood to joke. "There's no time for this! We've got to get out of here."

"I guess I forgot." There was a dreamlike quality to Trey's speech and his eyes seemed unfocused.

Everett tried to voice his frustration, but for some reason he couldn't form his thoughts into sentences. "We were about to . . . that is, we were waiting to . . ." His words trailed off into silence.

Unbeknownst to the boys, Mind Murk was pumping through the air in the museum lobby. This strain of it smelled like cleaning solution because that's what it was—a mental eraser. It wiped out any memory of Ink.

Dazed and befuddled, the boys stared at each other, unable to recall why they were there. The lull in the conversation stretched into awkwardness. Struggling for something to talk about, Everett looked at the brochure in Trey's hands. "What's that about?"

"The lady at the desk gave it to me. It's a visitor's guide." Trey held it up for Everett to take but accidentally let go before Everett grabbed it. The brochure dropped to the floor.

Trey bent down to pick it up, and as he did, the notebook Gilroy gave him fell out of his shirt pocket.

Everett and Trey studied the handwriting on the front cover. In large block letters, Trey had written: *The Ink and Me*. Something about those words sounded important and called to mind thoughts just out of reach. Trey picked up the notebook and flipped it open. He stood beside Everett and the two of them read the words together.

I got thrown down a well by blotters. I survived because my new friends found me and made a big X on my head with Ink. I was hurt pretty bad but I forget that part.

The Ink is magic or something. It made me better. I am starting to remember my life and my mum and dad. I know I like music and something bad happened with the blotters and

They read the unfinished story several times. Each time, more clarity returned. And then Everett remembered everything—his father, Bea, their mission. "We have to leave right now," he whispered.

They were nearly to the exit when they heard a woman's voice behind them.

"You there!"

They kept walking.

"You lads by the door!"

Everett glanced back. One of the museum employees was striding in their direction, her heels echoing loudly across the marble floor. Everett's heart began to race. Should they make a break for the door?

With a piercing gaze, the young woman steamed toward them. "You dropped this." She handed Trey the visitor's guide. "Watch your littering."

Trey broke into a smile. "Thanks so much. It won't happen again."

The woman click-clacked huffily away across the lobby.

The boys scurried through the front door and down the steps.

As soon as the fresh air from outside hit their faces, their minds and memories returned to normal.

"I don't know how long I would have stayed if you hadn't come," admitted Trey. "There was something off about the air in there. Did you smell it?"

"I'm just glad you had written out your story. We might have been trapped there forever."

Trey held up the visitor's guide. "At least now we have a map."

Five minutes later, they were standing in the complete darkness of a sewer tunnel. The stench made Everett pull his shirt up over his nose. Their footsteps echoed off the walls as they splashed into the dank waters. Trey flicked on Dot's flashlight.

Gilroy was nowhere to be seen. But there was a faint glowing blue mark a few feet down the wall. The boys trudged over to it. The mark was dripping off the slimy wall. The boys could barely make out an even fainter mark farther away.

"It's not sticking very well," said Everett. "We better hurry."

By around the seventh mark, they came to a fork where the tunnel split into two. Trey shined his flashlight down both. No sign of any more Ink in either direction.

"Which one?" Trey asked. "You make the call."

Everett peered into the dark. His eyes may have been

playing tricks on him, but he thought he could maybe see the tiniest shimmer coming from one of the tunnels. "I say we go right."

The boys forged their way ahead into the blackness.

Ten minutes later, they were completely lost.

Houdini Would Be Proud

50

Bea did not normally sleep with a night-light. She'd never been afraid of the dark. Until now.

She pulled out the little tin and helped herself to two more Cheering Up Pills. That was the end of them. But she reasoned that a little girl in a dungeon can take all the cheering up she needs.

As she savored the sweetness, her thoughts turned from her brother to her father, and how much she wished she was back sitting beside him in church, sharing a hymnal and listening to his rich baritone. She loved his singing. She closed her eyes, remembering a verse from the last hymn they had sung together during a service:

> *God will take care of you all thro' the night,*
> *Holding thy hand, He so tenderly keeps;*
> *Darkness to Him is the same as the light;*
> *He never slumbers and He never sleeps.*

Bea hummed the tune softly in the dark, the comforting refrain boosting her spirits and her courage. She felt along the inside of her sweater sleeve for the secret pocket where she had hidden her pen lid. She hadn't exactly lied to that blotter lady—she did lose things a lot. Just not the cap.

Number three of Bea's Rules for Escape on surviving captivity: Take stock of what tools you can use to break free.

In her time exploring the mysteries of her pen, Bea had uncovered one of the "secrets" Gilroy had promised, and it was in the cap. When you twisted the pocket clip, it unfolded to reveal a thin lock-picking tool known as a hook pick.

She removed it from the cap. It was just the thing for the kind of scrape she was in now. The thought of attempting a genuine prison break with her very own lock-picking tool helped distract Bea from being afraid.

With no light to speak of, finding the door lock was a challenge. She had to feel for it with her hand, her fingertips sensing each variation in the surface of the cold, rusted metal. When she reached the keyhole, her face lit up. The lock had to be at least a century old. That meant the mechanism inside was a standard pin and tumbler type, which Bea was sure she could conquer. Houdini had taught her well.

But her confidence wavered shortly after she inserted the hook pick into the lock. It was so old and corroded, the pins barely responded to the pick. She couldn't exert enough pressure to force them into place.

Frustrated and discouraged, she extracted the pick from the lock and slumped to the floor. If she still had her pen, she would ask the Ink for help. That had worked well for her. But it didn't matter now because her pen was gone.

Even though she no longer had her pen, Bea thought she could hear the Ink whispering. *Second secret*, it seemed to say. *Press and hold*.

Second secret? What else could the cap contain? She felt around the edges of the cap. Instinctively, she pressed and held the very tip. When she let go, it sprung open. There, hidden within the top end of the cap, was a tiny reserve of extra Ink.

She could tell it was Ink because it cast a faint blue glow that reminded her of the lights in the tunnel. If you've ever been in a very dark place, you know the comfort the smallest amount of light can bring. Although nothing had changed, Bea felt much better.

She wondered what would happen if she put some of the Ink in the keyhole. It had healed Trey. Maybe it could fix a rusty lock. She dipped the end of the hook pick into the Ink reservoir, coating it.

When she shoved the hook pick back in the lock, she heard an encouraging creak. It may have been her imagination, but she thought she felt one of the pins shift. Then nothing. The rest of the lock remained unmoving.

Bea shook out her hand, which was cramping up from the tight grip. She inserted the pick one more time and twisted with all her might. There was a loud snap. To her horror, Bea realized the pick had broken and was now stuck down inside the lock.

It was devastating. She was so close.

Maybe if she was very careful, she could tip up the end of the cap and drain the rest of the reservoir into the keyhole all at once. Maybe that would loosen things enough so she could fish the pick out and try again. But she would only have one shot. If it didn't work, there would be no more Ink.

Gingerly, she raised the open lid with both hands.

As she was about to pour it into the keyhole, a single, shrill puppy sneeze echoed off the walls from down the hall, startling Bea and making her jump.

The last of the Ink leaped out of the small chamber, spilling down over her fingers.

Desperately, she shoved her hands against the lock, willing some of the Ink to make it into the keyhole. The only thing that accomplished was to create a smeary mess on the lock.

"Oh, no! Please, no!" Bea sank to the ground in sobs, burying her face in her Ink-stained hands.

Normally, she was the one who could find the bright spot on a cloudy day, but this was too much. Nobody knew where she was. She had wasted the Ink. It was dark and cold and she missed her dad. And Ev.

When she ran out of tears, she rested her head on her knees and sighed a deep sigh. At least her brother was out there somewhere. Along with Gilroy and Trey. They would be searching for her.

The room was getting noticeably brighter. As Bea wiped her tears, she heard a soft whirring and clacking noise behind her.

The noise was coming from the door. More precisely, it was coming from the lock, which was regenerating before her eyes. The tumblers inside were now moving freely. After a few moments, they stopped with a satisfying click.

Bea tugged on the door.

She could hardly believe it. The Ink she wiped on the surface had redrawn and opened the lock. She was free! At least free of the cell.

Her Rules of Escape didn't include instructions for what to do once you have extracted yourself from confinement. Normally, that was when she made sure Everett took notice.

One of the puppies sat outside the door, apparently keeping guard. It looked up at her, confused. Bea put a finger to her lips.

"Shh," she whispered. "Stay."

She looked to the left and right down the long corridor. Just as she decided to head right, the puppy scurried to the left, barking wildly. Loud footsteps immediately started heading toward the cell.

And they were picking up speed.

51 Careful What You Look For

Disoriented by the maze of turns in the sewer, the boys now had no idea where they were. Gilroy was still nowhere to be found.

Everett shone his light all around, at a loss for what to do next. "What about your pen? Does it have any secret powers that might help?"

"Not that I can tell. Unless you want to hear me play 'Danny Boy.' That's the only other song I know."

Desperation was setting in. Everett reached around to scratch his back and brushed against the sticks that were still in his back pocket.

Everett grabbed them and held them in front of himself with both hands. "These might know how to find Gilroy," he said, touching them together. "They pulled me toward him on our way to the post office. And when I got lost, they took me to the park where we found each other."

At first, nothing happened. Then a faint buzz made its

way through Everett's fingers. The sticks vibrated and moved forward. They definitely had an idea of where they wanted to go.

"Come on!"

Everett and Trey had to run to keep up, turning here, doubling back there. Everett's spirits began to lift.

At one point the tunnels shifted and sloped downward. They left the ordinary sewer and followed a narrow passageway further into the earth.

The boys rounded a corner and were met by a chain-link fence. A large sign said: No Trespassing. Peering through the mesh, they saw a body of water on the other side. The sticks had led them all that way to end in a large cave with an underground lake. It was eerily still. Dim daylight trickled down from an unseen opening far above.

There was no sign of Gilroy. Nowhere to go except back the way they came.

Everett dropped his arms. The sticks had let him down, wasting precious time and leaving them more lost than ever.

"I don't know what happened. They worked before."

Trey took the sticks from Everett and examined them under the flashlight beam. "Do they work like a compass? Maybe the blotters have something around here that's interfering with them. I know with a compass, an energy source or a powerful magnet can change the polarity and confuse it."

The magnet! Everett hadn't even considered that the magnet pen might interfere with the sticks. Stealing it might have just ruined everything. Feeling sick, he grabbed the sticks from Trey and shoved them in his back pocket.

If Gilroy wasn't here, he wanted to get away from this creepy lake. He would take the sewage smell over the stale air in the cave any day. "Come on," he said. "Let's get back to the main tunnels. I say we find a manhole and climb up to the street. It will be easier to get our bearings aboveground."

As Everett headed back the way they came, Trey shone his flashlight through the fence one last time. "Look! Over there!"

Everett pressed his face up against the cold chain-link. On the far side of the lake, he could barely make out a faint glowing line that started about halfway up the cave wall and dropped off at the water line.

"Do you think that's from Gilroy?" Trey's voice was full of concern. "What if he fell in the water?"

It did look like the other lines the conductor had drawn. But this one was shaky and did not seem intentional. It reminded him of crayon marks he had made as a toddler, walking along his bedroom wall.

Everett wondered how deep the lake was and how long the conductor could hold his breath. An object bobbing on the surface of the water caught his eye. "Shine the light over there."

When the beam hit it, both boys gasped.

Although darker than normal because it was wet, there was no mistaking the shape of an upside-down conductor's hat.

Stay Out of the Water

Everett began climbing the fence.

"What are you doing?"

"I'm going in there!"

"It's too dark to even see anything."

Perched atop the fence, Everett stared at Trey. "He's our friend! We have to try!"

"If he's down there, you'll never be able to find him."

Everett could not believe what he was hearing. He jumped down on the other side. "What are you saying? Give up on him?"

"I didn't mean it like that." Trey thought for a moment. "Wait a minute."

He scrambled up and over the fence. "Maybe your sticks did lead you here. Do you think they would work underwater? They could be your eyes."

Everett touched them together again and immediately they pointed toward the lake. "That's it. I'm doing this." Kicking off his shoes, he moved toward the water.

"Stop!" yelled Trey.

"I'm not arguing about this."

"DON'T TAKE ANOTHER STEP!"

Everett froze with his right foot in midair. He looked where the beam from Trey's flashlight was pointing. Directly in front of him, he could barely make out the thin line of a tripwire.

Holding his breath, he set his right foot down on the far side of the wire and lifted his left foot high to clear it. He exhaled.

"Thanks," he said. "That was close."

Trey joined him at the edge of the water. "Someone really doesn't want us to be here." His face was gray, but a look of relief crossed it. "Since you're the only one who can use the sticks, I'll stay here and hold the light."

Everett waded in, then felt the pens in his pocket. He turned back and handed his father's pen to Trey. He paused a moment, then handed over the magnet pen.

Trey eyed it with a frown. "Where did you get this?"

"Where do you think?"

Trey said nothing, and Everett didn't wait around for more questions. He stomped back into the icy water.

Four feet from the shore, the bottom of the lake dropped off sharply. Everett barely had time to grab a breath before the sticks pulled him out into the deep water.

Down, down, down into the depths he went. He had to release more air than he wanted in order to depressurize his ears. He still couldn't see anything. He was about to give up when the sticks rammed into the bottom of the lake.

Holding them in one hand, he reached with his other and felt along the slimy pond floor, praying he'd find the conductor alive. But his fingers found nothing but rocks and more slime. Everett didn't know how long he had been down there, but he knew he couldn't hold his breath much longer. Then his hand brushed against smooth metal. Gilroy's pen!

So it was true. The conductor must have drowned in here. Everett went numb the way he had that day the police officers had come to the front door with the sad news of his dad.

He grabbed the pen. The moment he did, his sticks broke loose from the floor of the pond. It was as if they knew that Gilroy wasn't alive anymore.

With nothing left in his lungs, Everett kicked for the surface. He burst out of the water and gulped in the air.

"Catch!" he said, throwing Gilroy's pen to Trey.

It was a wild toss, but Trey instinctively leaped and caught it.

"Hey! I just remembered something else! I was on the cricket team at school. I—"

He stopped mid-sentence, staring past Everett, terror filling his eyes.

Everett turned to look.

Fifty feet away, something was slithering through the

water. In the dim light he could make out the dark, sinuous form of an enormous eel-like creature. Its body was glossy black and segmented like an earthworm's.

Even from a distance, Everett knew it had to be another monster created by that cursed bishop. As quietly as he could, he paddled backward toward Trey.

The eel rose in the air, corkscrewing its way upward toward a large metal crate suspended over the lake. Everett could see a spiked collar wrapped around the eel's neck just behind its head. The collar matched those worn by the dye hounds, except this one glowed a fiery red.

The eel's snout reached the crate and pressed against a button. It was a feed box. At the creature's touch, doors opened and a torrent of fish cascaded from the metal enclosure into the lake below.

The eel dropped back into the water, creating a lasso around the confused fish. Round and round it went, like a dog chasing its tail, its long body stretching into a complete circle.

The tail touched the glowing collar behind its head.

The water within the circle flashed red.

Dozens of fish floated to the surface, stunned by the electric shock.

The eel opened its mouth wide, revealing rows of razor-sharp teeth. With a single move, it devoured the paralyzed fish, tipping back its head to let them slide down its throat.

Horrified, Everett paddled faster to get away. But his

arm slapped the water, creating a loud splash. The eel turned and stared directly at him.

With a shrill hiss, it shot his way like a rocket. Before he knew what was happening, Everett found himself surrounded by the eel. It slithered around him, brushing against him with its scaly, slimy skin. Once again, the long body formed a loop, gathering speed to generate another charge.

The collar behind its head began to glow brighter.

The tail made contact with the neck.

Searing pain coursed through Everett's body, immobilizing him. He lay there on his back, gasping for air, unable to move a muscle, his fingers in a frozen grip around the sticks.

This was how it was going to end.

The eel rose up out of the water like an angry cobra, baring its teeth for the strike.

"I'm sorry, Dad," Everett whispered, feeling teary. "Sorry for not saying good-bye. For Bea. For not finding you."

He closed his eyes, preparing to die. But instead of hearing that unbearable hiss, he heard music. Angelic music. It echoed off the cavern walls.

He thought perhaps the heavenly hosts were there to welcome him home.

But the song was "Danny Boy."

He cautiously opened his eyes. The giant animal was still poised in midair, but it was no longer interested in him. It was gazing at the shore, swaying slightly as if hypnotized by the music.

Trey was playing his pen the way a snake charmer plays a pungi. Whether it was the power of the Ink or the song itself, the animal was completely entranced. Even Everett found himself strangely relaxed.

In fact, he found he could move his limbs again. Though his body felt like lead, the paralysis had worn off.

The creature was between Everett and Trey, blocking his path. Despite the calming music, Everett felt panic rising. Trey's music wouldn't keep the monster preoccupied forever—

As if reading his mind, the eel hissed at Trey. It bared its teeth and hissed again.

And then it whirled on Everett and began swimming back toward him.

He could not endure a second shock like the first. He was certain of that.

Only one idea came into Everett's mind.

He knew his sticks generated energy. So did that monster's glowing collar. If he could somehow overload the circuit . . .

Everett threw himself through the water directly at the beast. He wrapped his arms and legs around the slimy body just below the head. The eel writhed and shook to free itself, thrashing and whipping him back and forth violently.

Hanging on for dear life, Everett brought both arms

around the animal's underside and touched the ends of the sticks together. He could feel the current building. Pulsing up and down his forearms, then coursing back into the metal rods.

With all his might, he shoved the sticks up against the red electrified collar.

There was a loud sizzle. The eel shuddered uncontrollably beneath him, then *BOOM!*

With a brilliant flash of light, it exploded into a million pieces, throwing Everett backward across the water.

He floated on his back, blinded by the explosion, head vibrating.

"Everett!" Trey's concerned voice sounded faint through the ringing in his ears. Everett raised an arm and signaled that he was all right.

"Get out of the water! What if there are more of those things?"

He blinked several times until his vision began to clear.

And he nearly passed out.

From the ceiling, a pair of eyes stared down at him.

53 Back Together

Revived by a new surge of adrenaline, Everett thrashed his way back to shore as fast as he could. "Trey! Shine that light up there!"

Trey complied, and both boys yelled in surprise.

It was Gilroy's face, peering down at them through a small window in a second feed box. He was mouthing something, but the thick metal and glass container prevented any sound from coming out.

"Hang on, Gilroy!" Everett shouted. "We'll get you down!"

But how? Even if they had a ladder, the water made it impossible to reach him from below. They couldn't scale the walls because there were no handholds in the stone surface.

"What about his pen?" Trey asked. "Now that you found it, maybe we could draw a staircase like he did."

He removed the cap. Trey did a good job of mimicking

the conductor's arm waves, but it produced nothing. No matter what he tried, he could not make it write in the air.

"Maybe only Fomentori can do that," said Everett.

For good measure, Trey made another attempt with the pen from Everett's dad.

Nothing.

"You would think we could get one of them to write."

He lobbed both of them back to Everett.

"Oh—I almost forgot."

He reached in his pocket and pulled out the magnet pen. He tossed it back the same way, but it veered off and attached itself to the chain link fence.

Trey went to pull it down and it wouldn't budge. "Gilroy wasn't joking. This is powerful. What's the secret to making it let go?"

"Try clicking it," said Everett.

Trey clicked the top anyway and pulled. "I think that made it worse. The magnet feels even stronger now."

It must have been, because it held fast to the fence, and the metal sticks flew from Everett's back pocket and clung to the side of the pen.

He walked over and both boys tugged with all their might to no avail.

"What happens if you click it again?" asked Trey. Everett did and the magnet released its hold, with the sticks dropping to the ground.

Everett picked them up, thinking. "I want to try something."

He handed the magnet pen to Trey and walked several feet away.

"Give the button a single click."

Trey did, and Everett held out his sticks. They flew to the magnet. Trey clicked it again and they dropped away.

An idea began to take shape in Everett's mind. "You said you played cricket. How's your throwing arm?"

Trey rotated his right arm in a circle. "Pretty fair, I think."

Everett pointed excitedly up toward the conductor. "That metal cage holding Gilroy . . . Do you think you can hit it with the magnet pen?"

Trey eyeballed the distance. "Easy. What for?"

"You get the pen to Gilroy and I'll get to the pen." He held up his sticks.

Trey started to ask another question, then thought better of it. He raised the pen, clicking it to make sure the magnet was on its highest setting. Then he focused on his windup as if he were playing the biggest match of his life. He let it fly. The pen sailed through the air, striking the doors of the feed box with a clang. The magnet held fast.

Everett jumped and cheered. Something finally went right! The butterflies swarmed into his stomach as he thought about what he was going to attempt next. He explained his plan to Trey. "These sticks are pulled to that magnet, even from a distance. I'm betting they will help me fly. At least for a few seconds."

Trey tried to object. "This is crazy! If it doesn't work—"

"Then I will just fall into the water, and we'll figure something else out."

"What if there's a second water snake?"

Everett smiled. "Another verse of 'Danny Boy' would be good."

With Gilroy's pen in his pocket, Everett backed up several yards to give himself a running start. He held his sticks down at his sides. "This is for you, Bea," he whispered.

He raced to the edge of the water and leaped into the air, bringing the sticks together over his head, stretching out his arms to turn himself into a human arrow. He hung briefly in the air, then the sticks kicked in and propelled him up toward Gilroy.

The next thing he knew, he was hanging in the air over the lake. He made the mistake of looking down. He was much higher than he had thought. He could feel his hands getting slippery, which is not helpful when the only thing holding you aloft is your grip on two smooth metal sticks.

He examined the metal box more closely. Like the other one, it featured two doors controlled by a large red button. Holding both sticks with one hand, Everett stretched to press the button. It was only inches out of reach.

He pulled Gilroy's pen from his pocket and held it sideways with his mouth. With both hands back on the sticks, he kicked his legs in unison, making himself swing back and forth. The sticks held fast, even as they rocked.

Everett gained enough momentum for his feet to reach the button. He just needed greater impact to push it hard enough to release the doors. With one more mighty kick, Everett's foot reached the button and pressed it in.

Several things happened almost at once. The doors swung down and Gilroy dropped out of the box toward the lake. But the doors opened with such force that they broke the sticks loose as well, sending Everett tumbling after the conductor and knocking Gilroy's pen from his mouth.

Seeing his pen falling toward him, Gilroy reached out and grabbed it. He swung it in a furious painting motion. Ink sprayed wildly from its tip, creating a sloppy mesh of color. It wasn't pretty, but it was effective. The Ink hung in the air at a slope, stretching all the way to the shoreline.

When the conductor and Everett touched down on it, the sheet of tiny dots flexed under their weight, like a life net used by firefighters. But it held. The angle of the Ink formed a makeshift ramp, sliding Gilroy and Everett back to where Tray was waiting.

Behind them, the magnet pen made a small splash as it hit the water and disappeared into the murky depths.

Overcome with emotion, Gilroy grabbed Trey and Everett in a fierce bear hug.

"It's so good to see you lads."

"We thought you drowned," said Trey.

"It's truly a miracle you found me. And that overgrown death worm you defeated? That was a Black Vermis," he said. "One of the most odious creatures unleashed with the blotters. Trey, where did you get the idea to charm it like a snake?"

"When that thing rose in the air, I remembered an uncle visiting from India who was a professional snake charmer," Trey admitted. "I thought he was a fraud and it wouldn't really work. But it was all I had, so I tried it."

"And you," said the conductor, turning to Everett. "Using the charge in your sticks to counter the charge in the collar of that beast?" He shook his head in disbelief. "Dead brilliant, boys."

Trey grew sheepish when he realized the conductor must have overheard everything earlier. "I'm sorry I told Everett not to go in the water. I . . . I don't know how to swim."

If there was one thing Everett understood, it was that feeling of being ashamed over what you can't do. Over all the ways you're not as strong and smart as Max Courageous. Or the other boys at school, for that matter.

He took a deep breath. "I'm the one who needs to apologize. I can't use the Ink. Not even to write my own name. I was too embarrassed to say anything before. Then I was jealous of everyone else, so I took the magnet pen." He pointed to the water. "And now it's gone."

Everett hung his head and braced himself for a stern reprimand. He knew he deserved to be punished. He felt ashamed of how he had acted. But he was glad to have it off his conscience, regardless of the consequences.

"Everett."

He looked up. To his surprise, the conductor's eyes were filled with warmth and compassion. "Thank you for telling me, lad. The magnet pen is at the bottom of the lake. Why don't we let the bygones rest down there with it?"

Gilroy put an arm around each boy. "All I see in front of me are two of the bravest, most resourceful lads I know."

Everett didn't know whether to laugh or cry. He hadn't even realized the weight he had been carrying until it was gone.

The conductor filled them in on what had happened to him. "The far side of this lake marks the foundation of the old prison. I should've known the blotters would set traps around their lair. I didn't see that tripwire, and the next thing I knew I was waiting to become that creature's supper."

Everett held up his sticks. "Why did these take me down into the water and not right to you?"

"To me?" Gilroy asked. "Why would they bring you to me?"

"That's what they did before."

The conductor laughed. "They're not for finding me, lad. They follow Ink Waves to find Ink. They took you into the water because that's where my pen was."

"There was Ink in Trey's pen. Why didn't they just take me to him?"

"The sticks are sometimes called divining rods," Gilroy said. "They can divine which Ink the person holding them most needs to find."

Everett turned them over in his hands. "Now I want them to find Bea."

The conductor reached down and picked up his hat, which had bobbed to shore. "I doubt the blotters have let her keep her pen. But the sticks may get us close."

The boys told Gilroy all about their experience in the museum, the strange smell and how they forgot everything when they were inside. Gilroy felt responsible for the close call. "Mind Murk," he said, shaking his head. "I should have anticipated it."

He shook the water from his hat and perched it back atop his head. "I cannae tell you how proud I am of you both. We'll need the same courage you just showed for what we're about to do."

54 The Lock Was the Easy Part

Bea dodged into a storage room and ducked behind some old crates just before two blotters burst around the corner.

"The little brat can't have gotten far. There's no exit this way."

Bea identified the speaker. It was the one that kidnapped her.

The woman sniffed loudly. "She's close. I can smell the Stink on her."

A male blotter answered, "You want I should tell the Commander she got out?"

Bea heard a loud slap. "So we can both be sent to the kennel?"

They entered the storage room and set about examining the rows of shelves and poking around in the corners.

"Here girly, girly!" called the male blotter.

Another slap. "Idiot! She's not a cat."

They were standing next to the crates. If they came much closer, they would see her for sure.

"Why are we keeping a little girl as a prisoner anyway?"

The female was losing patience. "Stop talking. The Commander thinks her brother will try to save her. He has Witching Sticks, and the Commander wants them."

"I thought the Sticks was made up."

"What did I tell you about thinking?"

Bea was not going to stick around to help them catch Everett.

Time for Escape Rule number four: misdirection. Bea pulled the empty candy tin from her pocket. Peeking cautiously around the side of a crate, she threw it as far as she could across the room. It bounced off a shelf and clattered to the floor.

"Over there!"

As the blotters rushed to investigate, Bea slipped around behind them and out the door.

With no idea where she was going, she tore off, letting the twists and turns take her anywhere, as long as it was farther away.

She turned one corner too many. A blotter blocked the corridor ahead of her. She slipped down a smaller hallway branching off to the right. That hall ended in an L-shaped turn.

Bea started to take the turn, then heard boots coming from that direction.

She reversed course. There were no side tunnels to take. She was trapped.

55 Not All Kisses Are Gross

Bea pressed herself against the wall, trying to blend into the stone and make herself invisible somehow.

The rocks behind her pushed back. A thin line of blue light formed a rough rectangle around several stones. It looked like that time . . .

"Gilroy!" whispered Bea.

The door opened, and Gilroy himself stepped through, with Everett and Trey behind him. They were utterly shocked to see Bea standing directly in front of them, looking like she was wearing war paint with the Ink smears on her face.

"Go back!" Bea said frantically, shoving them all through the opening. "Close it up, Gilroy! They're coming!" With furious speed, the conductor waved his pen over the lines, pulling the stone wall back into place.

"Trey! Some light, please! I can't miss a line!" The conductor painstakingly removed every trace of their entrance.

Seconds later, a group of blotters reached the corridor intersection where Bea had last been seen. They could not determine how she had vanished or what the putrid smell was that lingered in the hallway.

Within moments, the two blotters who had been tracking Bea reached the corridor. "Sound the alarm!" the old woman hissed. "The prisoner must have had help, which means that a Fomentori is near. Her brother has Witching Sticks. Find him and we find the well. I want every blotter on the premises scouring the surrounding area. Capture them before the Commander hears of this breach!"

On the other side of the wall, Bea was giddy with relief. "I can't believe you found me!"

Gilroy's eyes flashed with pride as he looked at Everett. "You can thank that brother of yours. We weren't sure where to tunnel through, but he's becoming quite the expert at tracking down Ink."

Bea was confused. "But I don't have any Ink. I used the last of it on the lock."

Everett and Trey looked at each other and burst out laughing.

"What's so funny?" Bea demanded.

"You need a mirror," Trey said. "Your face is covered with Ink!"

Everett was not in the habit of hugging his sister, but he gave her the tightest squeeze. He wanted to say something, to tell her how glad he was she was back. But there was a big knot of emotion lodged in his throat that made talking too difficult.

Instead, he impulsively gave her a kiss on her Ink-stained cheek.

As soon as his lips touched the Ink on Bea's skin, the Ink lifted off her face and floated in the air between them.

Floating isn't the right word; *spinning* is more like it. The Ink whirled in a miniature bright blue tornado, hovering in the air. Everett and Bea pulled apart, watching it in amazement.

Gilroy held the palm of his hand underneath the whirlwind, lightly supporting it. The Ink spun itself into a funnel-shaped cocoon. Before anyone knew what was happening, the most beautiful shimmering butterfly emerged from the top of the funnel.

The colors of its wings kept changing. One minute you would think they were as blue as a summer sky, then after one flap they would look like a fiery sunset or a dazzling emerald. The butterfly illuminated the air as it fluttered back and forth between Bea and Everett. Bea cupped both hands and it landed in them, looking at her. Bea's eyes lit up, and she couldn't stop staring at the wonder she was holding.

"I don't even like bugs," she said.

"That's no bug," Gilroy corrected softly. "If I'm not mistaken, she's a muse."

"You mean amusing?" Bea asked.

"A muse," repeated the conductor. "Pure inspiration. Artists and authors around the world wait for a visit from one of these lovely creatures. They have great power to generate untold creativity. And in exceptionally inspiring moments, they can take on a physical form."

"Does she have a name?" Bea held the muse closer to her face.

The air from her beating wings breezed against Bea's eyelashes.

"Depends on whose muse she is," Gilroy said. "They're highly individual. The muse that inspires one artist might do absolutely nothing for the next."

"That's good," said Trey, "because kissing and butterflies aren't for me."

Bea gave a wistful little sigh. "I wish I could keep her. But I don't think she's mine, either."

Everett looked at the muse. He had been the one who kissed his sister. Did that mean this was his inspiration? Was this the missing piece that would give him some kind of talent with the Ink?

He tried to focus on the muse to see if he felt any burst of energy. But looking into her warm eyes filled him with something closer to sadness than creativity. Like he wished he knew her but didn't.

Gilroy interrupted his thoughts. "I don't think this lovely muse belongs to any of us."

Inspiration no one could use? That seemed like a waste to Everett. "Then why is she here?"

"She's collecting motivation."

"Motivation?"

The conductor smiled. "Who do you think would be the most moved by seeing a brother show such great affection to his sister?"

As the truth dawned on Everett, the muse lifted off of Bea's hands. Her wings glowed brighter and brighter until they gleamed white. Then with a *POP!* she vanished, showering sparks into Bea's still open palms.

"Did she explode?" Bea asked, horrified.

"Oh, no, no," reassured Gilroy. "She's off to tell your father you're here. That will boost his spirits, no doubt."

He gathered the three children closer. "The muse will be a great partner. But from here on out, the mission will be even more dangerous. We no longer have the advantage of surprise."

"Do you still think we can do it?" Trey asked.

Gilroy's forehead creased in a frown. "It would be much easier if we had a good supply of Ink."

"We should have kept the bottle with us," Everett said.

The conductor smiled. "With this many blotters, I fear it would take far more than one bottle."

"We can go to the well!"

Gilroy gave Everett a sympathetic look. "Mind Murk can addle the brain. You might not recall, lad, but no one knows where the well is."

Everett grew more animated. "I never told you. Bea was missing and I was worried and then I forgot."

"Forgot what?" Trey asked.

"About Elspet's well. I'm pretty sure I found it."

56 Road Rage

Dot, Jack, and Ronald had driven for hours with no further sign of their pursuers, so they allowed themselves a brief stop to stretch and refuel.

Dot paid the station attendant and clambered onto the motorcycle once more.

Ronald groaned as he folded himself back into the sidecar. "My legs may never be the same after cramming in here all these hours."

"At least something is keeping you from flying off," muttered Jack. "If I make it to Aberdeen in one piece—"

"Honestly," said Dot, kickstarting the motor, "do you always whinge and moan this much? It's a miracle we won the Great War with you two fighting."

Soon they were on their way again, making excellent time on the open road. They were just past Edinburgh when Dot checked her mirror and saw it: a dark speck, far behind them.

"Ron, can you see what that is?"

Ron craned his neck to see. "Blast! It's them!"

Montbanks and his driver caught up rapidly. This time, Mr. Lugg had no intention of staying at a courteous distance. The Inklings watched with a growing dread as the space between them and their pursuers continued to shrink.

The straight country lane provided very little cover. Seeing a crossroads up ahead, Dot knew this would be her only opportunity to lose their pursuers.

"Hang on!" she yelled.

Without slowing down, she wrenched the bike into a hard left turn, screeching around the corner with the sidecar wheel lifting completely off the ground.

It was a bold attempt, but it did no good. Mr. Lugg made the same turn effortlessly, closing the gap. Now there was nothing but a thin, unswerving ribbon of a road ahead of them, with nowhere to hide.

Suddenly, the car accelerated faster and bore down on them. It drew up parallel to the motorcycle. Mr. Lugg turned the wheel, as if to smash them broadside. Dot squeezed on the brake and steered out of the way just in time. Mr. Lugg slowed his vehicle as well, then raced up on the other side.

Suddenly, the sedan veered into the sidecar with a sickening crunch. The motorcycle shuddered, and Dot lost control. They spun around and landed backward in a ditch. Dot and Jack were thrown clear, with Ronald pinned inside the sidecar. The black car pulled off the road a few yards away.

Dot stood up and raised her goggles. "Jack? Ron? Are you okay?"

"I think so," Ron replied. "But I could use a little help extracting myself."

"I'll live," said Jack, brushing dirt from his arm and rising to his feet.

As Jack and Dot went to help their friend, they did not notice Montbanks walking toward them. They did not see him approach the other side of the motorcycle. And they did not see him remove the briefcase from the back.

"I think I need to uncouple the bike from the sidecar to get you out of there," said Dot. She looked up just as Montbanks was hurrying back to his car, briefcase in hand.

"What do you think you're doing?" fumed Dot, scrambling out of the ditch, ready to throttle Eddie on the spot. But it was too late. Mr. Lugg pulled the sedan back on the road and sped away.

Dot turned to Jack. "We must hurry. Now is our chance to lose Montbanks for good."

"What about the briefcase?"

"It doesn't matter," said Dot. "Remember? I gave Osgood the bottle."

Within a few minutes, the two of them were able to right the motorcycle and rescue Ronald.

They reattached the sidecar and inspected the damage. While somewhat worse for wear, the motorcycle remained in working order.

"Let's go back to the crossroads and take a different route," Jack suggested. "Before Montbanks opens the briefcase."

Which, in fact, is what Eddie had just done. He pulled out the drawings and Marcus's worn Bible. "What's this? Where's the Ink?" He flipped the briefcase upside down and shook it to see if anything else would fall out. He roared in frustration.

Mr. Lugg slammed on the brakes. "You want me to go back?"

Eddie seethed silently for a moment, looking out the window. Then he shook his head. "No. Let them think they've won."

He opened his door and threw the briefcase and its contents to the ground. "They will drop their guard by the time they reach Aberdeen. Then we strike."

57 · Motivation

"Marcus."

It was a beautiful voice, and it brought comfort with his very name. He was lying with his eyelids shut, not really asleep, but trying to recover from the latest round of questioning.

"Wake up, Marcus."

He opened his eyes.

To his astonishment, he could see again. And the first image to greet him was the small fluttering creature hovering directly above his eyes.

It was the muse—his muse—still in physical form. She now looked less like a butterfly and more like a miniature person with wings.

As he took in the sight of her, tears streamed down Marcus's cheeks—not from exhaustion or pain, but a mixture of deep grief and even deeper joy. Though he had never seen his muse before, in a way he had, because she bore the face of his beautiful wife, whom he hadn't laid eyes on in years. When she was alive, she had always been his steady source of inspiration.

If you have ever had someone who knew you best and still loved you completely, you know how Marcus felt. Seeing his wife's likeness again in any form was achingly wonderful.

"It's time. They're here, and it's time to go to them."

Marcus wiped his eyes and stared at her. She stared back, eyes full of warmth and confidence in him.

He took in his surroundings. There was an empty IV bag strapped to his arm. Whatever solution they had been pumping into his veins was now gone. His captors were apparently preoccupied elsewhere. He pulled the needle from his arm and sat up.

The muse spoke again. "Write, Marcus. Write yourself out of this."

"But I don't have any Ink," he said.

"It doesn't matter. Write your escape with your imagination."

He thought for a moment. She was right—writing begins long before you need any external tools or support. Even though he was tired beyond belief, he did feel strangely creative, the way he did when he was brainstorming Max Courageous stories.

He almost laughed out loud when he made that connection. Because he realized he was living the most intense version of a Max Courageous plot. Chased on a train. Kidnapped. Trapped by evil enemies with no way out, his children in danger.

The muse read his thoughts. "Yes, the children, Marcus. Find your way to them."

He would not be bait. There on the gurney, Marcus found his inspiration and began to imagine the most important chapter of his life.

58 An Unpeaceful River

Everett led the group back to street level and across town. Soon they were walking through the secluded section of the park where Gilroy and Trey had found him.

As they approached the river, doubts crept in. All he had seen was a dark patch in the water, and only for a moment. He hadn't been close enough to tell if it was what Elspet found more than a century ago. What if he had only seen a shadow from a cloud passing overhead?

They climbed over the grassy rise and took in the scene below. A wave of relief rolled over Everett as he once more saw the black pool in the current. "There!"

He pointed in the direction of the spot for the rest to see. Gilroy squinted and shaded his eyes with his hand. "Where exactly are you looking?"

"Over there," said Everett, redirecting the conductor's gaze. He glanced at Bea and Trey, who seemed equally blind.

"Are you sure?" Trey asked, biting his lip.

Everett could feel his cheeks flush. He wasn't crazy. How could they not see it?

Gilroy studied Everett's expression. "Tell me what you see."

Now Everett was getting frustrated. "Right there—that black circle in the river. Doesn't anybody else see it?"

Bea shook her head.

Trey tried to give him a gracious way out. "Sometimes the sun makes you see spots."

"I'm not making it up! Why don't you believe me?"

"I believe you see something, lad," Gilroy said. "Tell me. What led you to this particular place?"

Flustered, Everett tried to think back. "I got lost on my way back from the church. That's when I thought the sticks might lead me back to you."

The conductor grabbed him by both arms, speaking with an intensity and excitement in his voice that Everett hadn't heard before.

"Listen to me, lad. Do you know what this means?"

Everett shook his head.

"It means you're a dowser."

"A what?"

"A dowser. A finder. You have a gift for locating Ink sources that the rest of us don't. You just found Elspet's well."

Everett tried to wrap his mind around what he was hearing. He had a gift?

Yet the Ink did them no good in the middle of a river. They had to figure out how to collect enough of it from the well to find a way to save his father.

Gilroy removed his conductor's cap and turned it upside down, giving it a good shake.

The top of the hat stretched down toward the ground like a stovepipe. Then Gilroy reached inside and pulled out a strap, converting his cap into a makeshift pail. He gave a nod of satisfaction.

"Here you go. This should hold enough Ink. And it's watertight."

Everett removed his shoes once more and placed the pen and sticks inside them. With the hat bucket in hand, Everett waded out into the frigid river toward the well.

"Be careful," Bea pleaded, clasping her small hands under her chin.

The current was stronger than it appeared, trying to take his body downstream. And the rocks under his feet were smooth and slippery. Every step took all his concentration.

Soon the water was up to his waist, then his armpits. Everett wondered if it would be too deep for him to make it to the well itself. But the river bed leveled off as he reached the middle. Three large boulders formed a break in the current, creating a pocket of nearly motionless water where he could stand safely.

Everett could see the darker circle just ahead of him. As he got closer, though, he discovered that it wasn't a pool of Ink. And it wasn't a shadow. The Ink on the riverbed was projecting the dark image from below onto the surface of the water, the way a lamp makes a circle of light on a wall. That was why it never floated downstream.

His toes found the lip of the well, circled by wide, flat stones. He took several deep breaths, then dove down into the icy waters.

The crystal-clear water made it easy to find his way. He lowered Gilroy's hat close to the riverbed and a most remarkable thing happened: Ink floated up out of the well through the water and filled the hat. It was as if it wanted to be collected, as if it had been waiting for Everett to arrive.

When it reached the brim, the Ink stopped. Everett lifted the hat by the handle and made for the surface. He held it over his head triumphantly as he broke through the water.

"We've got it! We've—"

His victory cry was cut short as he took in the nightmarish scene unfolding in front of his eyes. Bea, Trey, and Gilroy all had their backs to him.

He followed their gaze to the top of the hill, where a swarm of blotters advanced toward the river. Most were on foot, armor-clad to protect them from touching any Ink. Several winged ones dotted the sky, including the old woman who had abducted Bea. The blotters stopped when they saw the conductor and the children. Then one of them spotted Everett in the water and raised a bone-chilling cry.

Before Everett even knew what was happening, Gilroy was in motion. He streaked up the hill toward the blotters, his pen raised above his head. Halfway there, he took a sharp left and ran in front of the entire line of soldiers, waving his arm in wide arcs, dispersing a fine spray of Ink over the field between them.

All of this took place in less time than it takes to describe. No sooner had Gilroy run past than the swath of grass in his wake shot up, taking on a blue-green hue and crystallizing as it rose skyward. Each blade widened out and reached for the heavens until it was taller than the blotters, a formidable petrified grass forest barricading them from the river.

The flying blotters remained aloft, keeping a wary eye on Gilroy to avoid being Inkased.

A lone dye hound managed to bound across the field before the grass shot up. The black menace charged down the hill directly toward Bea, flecks of saliva flying from its wide-open jaws.

Bea stood alone and exposed. Gilroy was clear across the field, and Trey was breaking a low-hanging branch off a tree to use as a weapon. Everett wanted more than anything to wade to his sister's side, but the current made it impossible to move quickly. He watched helplessly as the beast chewed through the distance between itself and its prey.

Bea turned to run, but her shoe caught the root of a tree, sending her sprawling on the ground.

"Get up!" cried Everett desperately. The dye hound was nearly to her, fangs bared for the kill. Then suddenly it howled and tilted its head to one side, as if experiencing some terrible invisible tormentor.

Everett turned and saw Trey had dropped the broken branch and was playing his pen whistle with all his might, his cheeks puffed out and bright red. But no sound was coming out. At least nothing Everett could hear.

But the dye hound could. The piercing high pitch fueled its anger. As soon as the beast identified Trey's dog whistle as the source, it raced and lunged. The two of them fell to the ground, rolling down the embankment toward the river.

The dye hound clamped onto Trey's throat. Clawing at the beast, Trey attempted to break free. But the hound shook the boy like a rag doll until he went limp in its jaws.

One of Gilroy's mustache hairs whistled through the air and lodged itself deep in the side of the animal. Immediately, the dye hound dropped Trey, immobilized by the electricity coursing through its body.

Everett reached the shore and ran to Gilroy and Trey. Bea joined them too, bursting into tears when she saw Trey, wounded and unconscious.

It was a gruesome sight. Blood poured from his neck. His face was swollen, and deep gashes crisscrossed his cheeks. He was barely breathing.

"Will he be okay?" whispered Everett.

Gilroy looked grim. "I don't know."

Bea wiped her eyes. "Can't the Ink save him like before?"

"In the right hands, and with enough time, maybe," said

Gilroy. "These are not ideal conditions. The grass wall will not delay the blotters much longer."

As if on cue, the first line of soldiers began to emerge from the tall blades. Gilroy gave one mighty toss of his arm and another thin swath of grassy forest grew between them—enough to buy a few minutes more.

"We have to leave," Gilroy said. "I'll carry him."

Before he could scoop the boy up, two winged blotters dropped down to attack them. Everett grabbed the broken branch off the ground and swung it at them.

"Get away!" he yelled. "Leave us alone!"

Both blotters rose to just beyond the reach of the stick. Behind them, the sky darkened as a large shape blocked out the sun.

Everett looked up. "Ermengarde!"

The giant bird dove toward the flying blotters, terrifying them into retreat. Then Ermengarde circled back and landed next to the group. She extended a wing, and Osgood slid down from the basket on her back. Immediately assessing the situation, he went over and removed a feather from Ermengarde's wing.

Without a word, he pressed it into Trey's hand and dipped the end of it into the capful of Ink. The same blue that had Inkased Mrs. Crimp and the dye hounds moved up Trey's arm, transforming him into an indigo statue.

"No!" shouted Everett, reaching to pull away the quill.

Gilroy held him back. "It's all right, lad. This is for the

best. Inkasement is different with humans. This will buy time until more can be done."

The conductor carried the unmoving form of Trey up Ermengarde's wing and into the basket. Bea and Everett quickly followed, with Bea carrying Everett's shoes and Everett doing his best to carry Gilroy's full hat without spilling any Ink.

When everyone was aboard, Ermengarde blasted into the air. It wasn't a moment too soon. The blotters crashed through the last grass defense and charged toward the river. None of them even looked up at the sky.

As the bird wheeled higher and higher into the air, Everett watched the blotters wade in and surround the well. They formed a line and began passing burlap sacks one after another, into the river. The pounce pot was being spilled before his eyes.

"They're going to shut it down, aren't they?"

Gilroy nodded. "I'm afraid so."

Everett felt like he had rocks in his stomach. He couldn't bear to watch. "I led them straight to it."

The conductor put an arm around him. "It's going to be all right, lad."

"But that was the last well!"

"Aye, that it was."

"Then how can you say it's all right?"

Gilroy smiled at him affectionately. "Because the boy sitting beside me is a dowser."

"I'm not sure that matters. I don't think the Ink likes me."

Gilroy looked shocked. "Why on earth would you say that?"

"I told you I can't write with it. But you knew that already, didn't you? You didn't give me a pen."

"Aye, I gave you divining rods instead. Different people, different gifts."

Everett remained unconvinced.

"Let's review," Gilroy said. "At the start, you were only able to draw a dot."

"Exactly."

"A dot that led you to Dot."

"Well, right, but—"

"Then you took the group to Hadrian's Well, where I just happened to be passing and where you just happened to save Trey's life. You went on to rescue me and you just found an Inkwell no one has seen for decades."

Everett was stunned at the conductor's analysis.

Bea interrupted Everett's thoughts. "I want my daddy."

She looked completely forlorn. Her face still had streaks of Ink mixed with tears. Her knees were caked with mud and blood. And her sweater now had a big hole in one elbow. "I want to find him and go home."

"We're headed his way now." Gilroy stretched out his other arm and invited Bea to come sit beside him, which she did.

59 · Bless That Pigeon

As Ermengarde spiraled up and away from Elspet's well, Everett couldn't take his eyes off the statue that was once Trey.

"How long can he stay like that?"

"As long as he needs to," Osgood responded. "I once came across a young lady who had been Inkased for nearly a hundred years. She was none the worse for wear, apart from her clothes being a century out of fashion."

One hundred years! Everett couldn't bear the thought of Trey being trapped like that for so long. He wanted to thank him for saving Bea's life. For saving *his* life.

"Look!" Bea brought Everett's attention back to the moment. She was leaning dangerously far over the side of the gondola.

"Sit back down!" Everett grabbed the back of her sweater and pulled.

"It's Dot's motorcycle!" Bea waved furiously. "Are those the Inklings with her?"

Sure enough, Jack rode behind Dot, and Ronald sat

hunched in the sidecar, grinning from ear to ear behind his goggles. He looked up and raised a hand to return Bea's wave.

"We all left Oxford as soon as I told them what was happening." said Osgood. "Hopefully they managed to lose Montbanks on the way."

Gilroy tapped Osgood's shoulder. "Set her down over there."

He pointed to a collection of greenhouses that made up Aberdeen's famed Winter Gardens. The park was only a short distance from the watchtower.

Everett reached out to keep the statue of Trey from tipping over as they descended. He turned to Gilroy. "What will we do with Trey while we're rescuing our dad? We can't carry him inside with us."

Gilroy mulled over that question. "I'll ask Osgood to look after him. The lad will be in good hands with him."

That triggered a memory for Everett. "You said earlier that Trey might be able to get well if he were in the right hands."

"Aye, that I did."

"Did you mean Osgood?" Everett asked hopefully.

"The Ink might be able to save him, but it would take a true Ink healer to treat his condition. And that's a very rare gift. Not one Osgood has, I'm afraid."

Everett bit his lip. "I think I could find a healer for him."

The conductor shook his head. "Being a dowser only helps you find Ink—not a person."

Everett reached for the small piece of paper buried deep in his pocket, now somewhat waterlogged. "What if I've already met her?" He handed Gilroy the soggy card from Nurse Abbie. "She used my dad's pen on people from the train crash, and every one of them got better."

The conductor's eyes lit up as he studied the card. He showed it to Osgood.

"Well, that does sound encouraging, now, doesn't it?" said Osgood. "We'll get the lad to her straightaway."

When they landed, Gilroy, Bea, and Everett disembarked. A wind was picking up. Ermengarde gave a concerned coo, causing Osgood to scan the rapidly darkening sky. "She's right. It's going to be a bad storm. I better get in the air now if you want me to get this boy to that nurse."

Everyone agreed the courier should leave immediately. Everett watched as Ermengarde shot right back into the sky, the first drops of rain hitting his upturned face.

60 — A Plan Takes Shape

There were hugs all around as Dot, Jack, and Ronald motored up next to them. Gilroy and the children took turns filling them in on all that had happened since their departure.

"So what is our plan?" asked Dot.

Gilroy held his hat filled with Ink. "I'm afraid we're in need of a new one. Our timetable has just been shortened considerably. Now that the blotters have located the well, they will no longer have a use for Marcus."

Bea's mouth began to quiver. "You mean . . . you mean . . ."

Dot scowled at the conductor, then put an arm around Bea. "What Gil meant is that since the blotters are currently preoccupied with the well, they will be less focused on guarding your father. This is our best window. We're going to deliver him from that dungeon."

"He's not there."

Everyone turned to Everett. He held his sticks out in front of him with his eyes closed.

"He's not in the dungeon. He's on the top floor of the

tower. At least that's where a small amount of Ink is doing something."

Gilroy beamed at him. "Good work, lad. Your focus is getting sharper. If you're sensing Ink upstairs, that has to be Marcus."

"How do you know?" asked Bea.

"Because blotters cannae use the Ink," Gilroy answered. "They can only get in its way."

A clap of thunder punctuated the conversation. The wind was picking up as well.

"Let's take cover in here," said Ronald, ducking into the nearest greenhouse. The rest of them followed suit. Under less stressful circumstances, Everett would have liked to explore the entire place. The greenhouse was full of exotic plants from all over the world.

Bea inhaled deeply. "It smells like fancy perfume in here."

Gilroy took charge of the group. "All right, then. Let's hear everyone's best ideas."

"How much Ink do we have?" asked Jack. "What I mean is, how much power? What can be done with one hatful of the stuff?"

Dot held up the bottle. "Don't forget we still have this as well."

"I keep thinking that to fight an army, we need an army," said Ronald, giving a puff on his pipe.

Gilroy objected. "Elspet's Ink is one of the strongest

strains I've seen, but using it to generate life? That's a tricky business. It's only happened a handful of times. And an entire living army would require gallons."

As the grown-ups began to debate the possibilities, Everett found it hard to pay attention and not be distracted by his surroundings. It was a tropical paradise, complete with banana trees and bamboo shoots. So many bright colors and unusual shapes. Right next to him stood a plant that was nothing but a giant green stalk. The small plaque beneath it called it a corpse flower. It only bloomed every seven or eight years. When it did, it smelled like rotten meat.

Everett could not fathom why anyone would want to grow something on purpose that stunk so bad. But it gave him an idea.

"Gilroy, didn't you say blotters can smell the Ink?"

"Aye, they do. They find it most disagreeable."

"Which I find very odd," interjected Ronald. "My nose isn't what it once was, but I can't detect any odor at all when I'm using the Ink."

"It's a lovely scent," added Gilroy, closing his eyes and raising the hat up under his nose. He smiled as he breathed it in. "Imagine a mixture of oranges and gingerbread with a hint of—"

"Gentlemen, please," said Dot. "What were you thinking, Everett?"

"How bad does it stink to them?"

"Very bad," said Gilroy. "They find it hard to breathe

when it is in the air. That's why they turn violent when they detect it."

Ronald leaned in close. "Where are you going with this?"

Everett looked around at the adults. "We do need an army."

Jack shook his head. "We just went round and round about this. We don't have enough Ink."

"Not a proper army with soldiers and weapons and the like," continued Everett. "I'm talking about an army of bugs."

"You mean the not-really-bugs kind of bugs, like the muse. Don't you?" Bea asked hopefully, worry creasing her face.

Everett smiled at her. "Sorry, Bea. Bug bugs. I'm thinking about stink bugs." He turned to the Inklings. "There is such a thing, isn't there?"

Ronald nodded. "*Halyomorpha halys*. One little-known fact about this garden-variety insect is that—"

"Do go on, Everett," said Dot before Ronald could finish.

"Until now, we've been trying to keep the blotters from smelling the Ink so they won't chase us. But what if we made things so smelly, they couldn't stand it? What if we released thousands of Ink stink bugs into the building?"

"An infestation of Ink," Ronald said with a devious grin. "I like it."

The plan began to take shape. If they were able to manufacture the bugs (and that was a big *if*), Dot, Jack, and Ronald would distribute them around the perimeter of the building to drive out the blotters. Meanwhile, Gilroy, Bea, and Everett would go to the roof of a neighboring hotel, where Gilroy would draw a sky bridge to take them to the roof of the watchtower. From there, they would draw a trapdoor through the roof and extract Marcus.

"I don't think I'll be much help when we get there," confessed Bea. "The blotters took my pen. All I have left is the cap."

"Why, that's the very part we need," enthused the conductor. "I'll show you one more of the cap's hidden talents."

He took the lid from Bea and pointed out a tiny hole in the top. "See this? We will insert a mustache filament that will act as a homing device. If your pen is anywhere near, it will return to its cap."

Bea's face lit up at the prospect of getting her pen back. "I knew it had more secrets!"

No one in the group had ever used Ink to make a living stink bug before, let alone thousands of them. There was considerable discussion over how it might be done. Since Ronald had written books about strange, imaginary creatures, he was tasked with writing a description of the stink bugs to use for the "recipe."

And since Bea had been so successful in having conversations with the Ink, she was given the responsibility of reading the bug recipe to the hat.

Ronald reviewed the notes he had jotted down. "I'm not convinced I've made these creatures hideous enough.

Something isn't quite right yet. What do you think, Dorothy?"

He handed the paper to Dot, who read it with a frown. "I think this is far too frightening for a child to read."

Bea grew worried. "Why can't they be nice bugs?"

Jack smiled sympathetically. "I'm afraid we need them to be quite intimidating."

"Are you sure?"

Everett had everyone's attention.

"The blotters themselves are scary. What if they are afraid of what *isn't* scary?"

"I say," said Ronald.

Everett continued. "Gilroy told us the Ink smells like gingerbread and oranges. But to the blotters, it stinks. They smell the opposite of what we smell. Maybe we need to think everything in reverse."

"Brilliant!" Jack said. "So you're suggesting we strive for creatures that look as good as they smell."

Bea sighed wistfully. "I would ask for lovebugs."

The Ink in Gilroy's hat gave a loud *POP!* at her words, as if applauding the idea.

She elaborated. "They could still be stinky, if that means smelling like oranges and gingerbread. They wouldn't be creepy-looking, though. And they wouldn't have fangs or teeth. They would be fluffy and round and blue, so if you saw one, you would want to keep it as a pet and not step on it."

As she warmed up, she began to pace in front of her audience. "These bugs would be guard bugs, so they would do whatever they could to protect you at all times. But they would do it in a kind, friendly way where no one would get hurt. They would be smart and warm and soft. And instead of buzzing like normal bugs, they would hum lullabies."

She was about to continue when Dot interrupted her. "The hat!"

Everyone turned to look. Gilroy had set it on the ground and stepped away in disbelief. The Ink was frothing and foaming wildly. Bubbles rose higher and higher, towering several feet above the brim of the hat. Suddenly, the bubble column collapsed, cascading onto the ground in an ever-expanding stream.

As they moved, the bubbles transformed into thousands upon thousands of furry blue bundles. They didn't move like ordinary bugs—they rolled. But they seemed to roll in rhythm. Then Everett heard it: a faint melody coming from the strange creatures. It was a heartbreakingly sweet sound that made him think of the mother he could barely remember.

They were Bea's lovebugs. However it happened, the Ink heard her instructions and followed them exactly. The Inklings all removed their coats to collect the creatures into three bulging and squirming bundles. The children laughed as they watched Ronald trying to control his lumpy jacket.

Everett leaned over to his sister and said, "He looks like Father Christmas delivering puppies."

Bea gently picked up one ball of fluff and held it in her open hand, her eyes bright with amazement.

"I do like bugs," she whispered.

61 Getting Out

The fog clouding Marcus's thoughts had dissipated completely. What's more, his strength had returned. With a prayer of gratitude, he stood up to explore his cell.

Cell was a strong word. In truth, it looked more like an ordinary business office, except that the window was blacked out. He tried the knob of the wooden door, which was, of course, locked. No surprise there. There was a small pane of wired glass in the door. A convenient way for blotters to check on him as they made their rounds.

He crossed the room to the darkened window. From the sound of the city traffic outside, Marcus deduced he was several stories above the street, which was true. The best chance of escape seemed to be by climbing out that window.

He took stock of the resources at his disposal. It didn't take long, because there wasn't much in the room.

An empty bird cage and a chair. He cringed at the memory of those chair legs scraping across the floor when the blotter would move closer to interrogate him. The squeaking of the seat as he waited for the next round of torture.

Marcus grabbed the chair with both hands and swung it as hard as he could at the window.

It bounced off harmlessly, not even leaving a scratch.

Again and again he swung, giving full vent to his fury and frustration. After more tries than he could count, he dropped the chair to the floor, completely spent.

As he lay back down on the gurney to rest, another psalm floated into his brain. *The Lord sets the prisoners free. The Lord opens the eyes of the blind.*

Marcus opened his own eyes, halfway hoping some miracle would appear. But the only thing in his field of vision was a very ugly ceiling. The cracked plaster looked ancient. Exposed pipes ran along the length of one wall. They disappeared into the ceiling just above an air vent.

A decent-sized air vent.

The muse whispered an idea in his ear.

"That's exactly what I was thinking." Standing on the chair, Marcus could just reach the vent. On impulse he pressed the Ink-soaked handkerchief against one of the rusty screws holding the vent cover in place. Nothing budged. He dropped his hand back down and stared up at the vent.

Fluttering beside him, the muse wore a puzzled expression.

"I just thought . . . I don't know. I was hoping the Ink would magically loosen the screws. Silly of me, I suppose."

Chirping excitedly, the muse pointed at the bird cage. Marcus walked over and examined it. It was a rather ordinary cage with black metal wire and a small door that was open. He ran his finger across the bars. "I don't see how—"

Something caught his eye on the floor of the cage. It was his button. Grip had added it to his collection of small, shiny objects. Sifting through the pile, Marcus found a slender piece of tin. He grabbed it and went back to the vent. The small piece of metal was just thin enough to serve as a make-shift screwdriver. The rusty screws resisted at first, but soon all four were in his hand.

There was a loud crash as the cover broke loose, glanced off his head, and clattered to the floor. Bits of dirt and paint showered down around him in a cloud of dust.

He brushed off the debris and looked up to see an opening to the air duct.

An opening just wide enough to escape through.

The muse was back at his ear.

"I'm already ahead of you." Marcus grabbed one of the straps the blotters had used to restrain him and looped it around the sturdiest-looking pipe next to the vent. Then hand over hand, he gripped the strap and climbed up the wall and into the vent.

He had done it! He lay there in the dark for a moment, catching his breath. It was too soon to revel in the accomplishment. He needed to distance himself from that room.

Marcus began to army-crawl forward, painfully aware of how the sound of his movement reverberated off his metal surroundings. He'd made steady progress for about five minutes when his shredded sleeve caught on a seam in the vent wall.

"Of all the rotten luck," he muttered, tugging to free himself. His efforts only served to lodge the sleeve farther in the seam.

Backing up proved impossible.

There was no room to reach it with his hand, either.

He was completely stuck.

Stormy Interference

Gilroy, Everett, and Bea found their way to a hotel directly across the street from the watchtower. A disgruntled guest had the full attention of the lone front desk clerk, allowing the three of them to slip by unnoticed.

Once they were inside the elevator, the conductor pressed the button for the top floor and turned to the children. "It won't take long for someone to look up and notice what we're doing. When I give the word, you'll need to move without hesitation. Understood?"

Everett and Bea nodded. They exited the elevator and found the stairs to the roof. Now they were several stories above the watchtower. On the ground, they could see Dot, Jack, and Ronald approaching the building from different sides. Carrying the lovebugs, the Inklings struggled against the wind and the rain, which was now coming down in sheets.

Dot reached her side of the building first. "All right, my darlings," she said over the thunder as she poured the miniature living pom-poms around the foundation. "Do your loving best." They streamed into every nook and cranny of the building, even climbing up the sides like blue ivy. Then as quickly as they appeared, they were gone, making their way inside the prison.

Moments later, blotters streamed from the building, clutching their chests and gasping for breath.

The conductor wasted no time. "Follow me!" He waved his pen, and the beginnings of a bridge took shape, sloping downward toward the watchtower roof.

The children paused. The bridge was steep. Gilroy stepped onto to it as he drew it, walking as fast as there was a new place to step. "Come on!" he urged. "We must hurry!"

Bea took two or three steps down. Everett followed her. The storm blew the bridge back and forth. The whole thing jerked to the right, causing Bea to lose her footing. She let out a scream as she began sliding toward Gilroy several feet below.

Everett dove and caught Bea's arm, but he could not stop his forward momentum. Together they slid down the bridge, out of control. Everett watched helplessly as they rammed into Gilroy.

The conductor's eyes widened with surprise as his large form plummeted over the edge. Bea shrieked in terror as she followed him off the end of the unfinished bridge, with Everett directly behind.

Clutching wildly, Everett managed to hang on to Bea and catch a jagged corner of the bridge with his other hand.

The sharp Ink cut into his fingers as Bea dangled at a breath-taking height over the street below.

His shoulder felt like it was being ripped out of its socket. He knew he couldn't last more than another second before one of his hands gave out.

When he was sure his arms could endure no more, Gilroy's face appeared in front of him. "You can let go, lad."

Everett looked down and could not believe his eyes. The conductor stood on a platform made entirely of love-bugs, swaying like a blue fluffy smokestack rising from the museum roof.

Everett had no choice in the matter. He let go of Bea and the bridge at the same time.

Landing on the lovebugs, Bea erupted into a fit of relieved laughter, rolling around on a sea of fur. Sitting beside her, Everett was stunned at the miraculous rescue. "How . . ."

Gilroy alighted next to him, smiling a wide smile. "As I recall, Bea asked the Ink to make these creatures to be guardians, didn't she?" The blue platform descended and the three of them were left standing in a puddle on the roof. Gilroy looked up through the downpour at the broken bridge. It was now swinging wildly in the storm and looked like it might break free from the hotel.

"There's no time to finish it right now, but I need to secure it, so we have a way to leave." Pulling his pen back over his shoulder, he cast it forward like a fishing pole, sending a line of Ink toward the bridge. It wrapped itself tightly around one of the supports.

The conductor gave a tug and pulled the line tight, staking his pen firmly into the surface of the roof. He checked the tension.

"That should hold until—"

At that moment, a bolt of lightning tore open the sky and struck the bridge.

An electric charge raced down the line of Ink to Gilroy, who still had his hand on it.

The voltage threw the big man sprawling across the roof.

"Gilroy!" Everett ran to his side, with Bea right behind him. The conductor lay still as stone. There were burn marks on his hand and cheeks. The hairs of his mustache stuck straight out from his face as if the electrical components in them had been fried.

"Wake up, Gilroy!" Bea pleaded, shaking his shoulder. In a panic, she turned to her brother. "What are we going to do?"

Friends in an Air Vent

63

Marcus heard a loud thud over his head, followed by running footsteps. He could also hear rain pinging off the ventilation shaft. From the way things sounded, he deduced he must be close to the roof.

Then another noise caught his ear.

A rumbling through the vent.

A soft padding sound from both directions.

And was that music?

Before he knew what was happening, he was swarmed by miniature furry creatures. In the glow cast by the muse, he tried to take in what they were. He had never seen anything like them. Yet for some reason, he couldn't help but smile as he watched them.

The lovebugs went to work chewing through the snag on the vent that had caught him. He could feel the last threads break free. At last! He could finally move again.

64 Pen Calling

Everett held his ear to the conductor's chest and listened. The rhythm was faint, but it was definitely a heartbeat. "He's alive!"

Gilroy coughed weakly and opened his eyes.

Bea kept patting her hands on both sides of his face as if to reassure herself that he was truly not dead. "You were struck by lightning," she told him.

He smiled weakly. "Joy of . . . being a conductor." His eyes closed again. "Just need . . ." With that, he drifted back into unconsciousness.

Another thunderclap.

More rain.

Drenched and shivering, Everett knew the scent of the lovebugs in the building would be fading soon. They had to get their father and get away. Gilroy would be no help—at least not anytime soon.

"Bea—did you say the Ink from your cap unlocked a door? Maybe it could unlock a roof."

Bea handed the cap to her brother. "It did. But I used it all."

"That's okay." Everett went over and carefully removed a singed hair from the conductor's mustache. "Maybe we can get your pen back. Remember what Gilroy said about a homing device?"

He placed the thin filament in the top of the pen like an antenna. He handed it back to Bea.

"Let's hope the pen knows its owner."

While they waited, Everett took his sticks from his pockets and began pacing. They pulled him to a large, hooded metal vent shaft protruding from the roof.

"It's him!" shouted Bea, running over. She knelt down and yelled into the metal grill covering the opening to the vent. "Daddy! We're here! We're here!"

Everett tried to pry the grill off with his fingers, but it wouldn't budge. He pounded his fists on the metal.

"Dad! Dad!" They were so close.

From the ground at the base of the watchtower, one of the blotters looked up between coughs and pointed at the swaying sky bridge.

"Commander! Someone's on the roof!"

65 So Close

M arcus heard Bea's voice. Could his children actually be on the roof above him?

"Bea! Everett! I'm here!"

A mechanical noise echoed up from the ductwork.

Tap. Tap. Clang. Tap.

It grew louder, and quickly. Whatever it was, it was on the move, banging off the metal walls of the vent and ricocheting in his direction at great speed.

When the source of the sound reached the blue creatures, they began to jostle each other as the object pushed through their ranks. The object scraped against his leg and tried to shoot past his shoulder, but Marcus reached out and grabbed it.

It was, of course, Bea's pen, although it felt more like a fish fighting for its life. Marcus fought back, with the energy of the pen reverberating up to his shoulder. It took both hands to restrain it.

At that moment, the lovebugs began rolling, keeping up with Marcus as he let the flying pen pull him toward the roof.

66 · Showdown

The grappling hook sailed over the top of the building, dragging across the roof until it caught fast on the edge of the wall.

Bea gripped Everett's arm in terror. "They're coming up!"

Lifting with all his might, Everett dislodged the hook and hoisted it back over the ledge. It tumbled to the ground below, eliciting curses from blotters on the ground.

Just then the entire building shook as if in an earthquake.

It was the vent, rattling violently. Suddenly, the hood blew completely off the top and landed with a crash. A furry moving column of Bea's lovebugs rose up from inside the building.

The bug tower rocked back and forth, humming louder than ever. Then the tower grew a pair of arms. Very human arms—arms the children knew well. Bea and Everett each grabbed one of their father's hands and pulled him out of his pillar of helpers. The three of them collapsed in a heaping embrace on the roof.

Marcus was free.

He held his children close. "I can't believe you're here."

Everett returned his father's pen. "You'd better take this, Dad. We may need it to get out of here."

A voice bellowed at them from the sky. "What a touching family reunion."

They spun around to see the Commander hovering in midair, his wings stretched wide. Grip flapped behind him like a bad omen in the sky.

The blotter twirled the grappling hook. Marcus instinctively moved in front of Everett and Bea. "Back as far away as you can, children."

The Commander laughed maniacally as he looked down on them. "Yes, back yourselves into a corner. There's nowhere to go."

Marcus clenched his teeth. "You cannot win."

"Oh, but we already have. Didn't your son tell you?"

Marcus glanced at Everett.

"That's right," the Commander continued, flying closer. "It turns out he *is* a Stink Witch. The boy led us directly to the last well on earth, and we shut it down. A new Blank Age has begun!"

He feigned a sad expression. "So sorry about your young friend. Trey, was it?"

Everett's face burned with anger. A small movement on the roof behind the Commander caught his attention. Gilroy sat up. He looked at Everett and put a finger to his lips.

Bea retreated to the safety of the lovebugs, who formed a barrier between her and the blotter.

The Commander alighted on the roof. Marcus lunged to block him, but the blotter swiftly brought his stone foot up and shoved it into the vicar's chest, sending him hurtling to the far side of the roof.

"You no longer interest me, Reverend."

He advanced toward Everett, who had inched himself closer and closer to the Ink line Gilroy had drawn to fasten the bridge to the roof. The grappling hook whistled as the Commander threw it at his head. Everett ducked, and the claws smacked into the roof, chipping the surface.

The blotter pulled the rope to retrieve his weapon, his eyes spinning. "It's over. You can die knowing you helped rid the world of the scourge of its very last well. Now, give me your Witching Sticks."

A clap of thunder roared overhead as the Commander flung the hook again. Everett rolled to the side, and the hook wrapped itself around the Ink line to the sky bridge. When the Commander moved to retrieve it, Marcus threw his pen from the other side of the roof. It was a solid throw, hitting the blotter squarely in the back. But it simply glanced off.

The Commander turned and laughed mockingly at Marcus. "Did you really think that would stop me?" He stepped on the pen, which gave a sickening crunch under his leaden boot.

While the Commander had his back to him, Everett spied Gilroy's pen, still holding the sky bridge in place. He quickly reached down and dislodged it, snapping it free of the Ink line and releasing the grappling hook. Holding the pen out in front of him, he grabbed the hook with his other hand. "Get away."

The Commander whirled back around and howled in derision. "You dare to threaten me?"

He dove, hands ready to grab Everett's throat. Everett flung the grappling hook in his face, causing the Commander to jump and retreat to the air again.

Lightning illuminated the sky behind him as the raven landed on his shoulder.

"Leave him alone!" yelled Bea. She got up to run to Everett's side, but before she could reach him, the Commander swooped down and grabbed her with one arm.

"Bea!" shouted Marcus. He pleaded with the blotter. "Let her go. I beg you!"

"The girl for the sticks!" said the blotter. "Hand them over and she lives."

"They will do you no good."

It was Gilroy speaking. The Commander turned and glared down at him. "No, Fomentori. It's *you* who do me no good! It's you who cost me my foot. And it is you who will pay first when I restore it."

Gilroy gave him a confused look. The blotter grinned

in smug satisfaction. "Oh, yes. I know the sticks reverse Inkasement."

"Not true," said the conductor.

"Silence! The sticks will be mine, and there will be no question: All will bow to my greatness! Now give them to me!"

"Over my dead body," Gilroy seethed.

"No," said the Commander. "Over hers." He lifted Bea high over his head and prepared to hurl her off the edge of the building

"Wait!" shouted Everett.

The blotter paused with Bea raised above him.

"You can have the sticks."

"Steady, lad," Gilroy said softly

Everett stared resolutely up at the Commander. "Give us Bea, and I'll give you the sticks. Do whatever you want with them. Find a well. Fix your foot. I don't care. Just give me my sister."

Grip flapped up and away as the Commander flew lower, contemplating the offer. "Hand them over."

Everett still had Gilroy's pen in hand, which he aimed at the blotter like a weapon. "Set her down first if you want them."

"You do not give the orders."

"I'm warning you," Everett shouted. "Set her down or else."

"Or else what?" the Commander sneered. "Don't take me for a fool, boy. That pen is worthless in your hands. I know all about your limits. You're pathetic. You can't even write with that Stink."

In that instant, Everett had a moment of crystal clarity. The blotter's words, which would have cut so deeply days earlier, now didn't matter, because he knew who he was. And he didn't care anymore about what he couldn't do.

"You're right. I can't use this." Everett looked the Commander in the eye. "But he can."

He threw the pen to Gilroy, who caught it without even standing up.

The conductor whipped the pen through the air.

A burst of miniscule Ink droplets sailed into the sky. It looked like they would shower down on the Commander's head, but at the last minute, he darted out of the way. Dropping Bea from his grasp (into the waiting arms of her father), the blotter dove with ferocity on the conductor.

Gilroy was too weak to fight back against the Commander's pent-up rage and fell back flat on the roof. The blotter locked his fingers in a choke hold around the conductor's throat, pinning Gilroy's arms under his knees.

"It's over! Do you hear me? Over!" he screamed.

Marcus ran to help. One of the Commander's powerful wings came down hard and pinned him to the roof.

Everett searched the scene desperately. He saw his

father's crushed pen. The tip was still attached to the reservoir of Ink.

Scooping it up, he ran and jumped on the Commander's back. As he brought the pen down on the blotter's neck, he had a flashback of the first time he had tried to use his father's pen. Once again, a single dot of Ink emerged. It reached the skin just as the Commander craned his neck around. He stared directly into Everett's eyes, his swirling pupils filled with intense hate. "NO!" he shrieked, recognizing with horror what was happening to him.

At first, Everett feared the speck of Ink had not been enough. But then the blotter's eyes became fixed and unseeing as a thin blue film stretched out from that single dot on his neck and swallowed him whole.

The Inkasement was complete.

"I guess I *did* know how to use that pen," Everett said to the statue.

Marcus freed himself from the now-stony wing and, with great effort, heaved the gargoyle off of the conductor. Gilroy coughed, gulping in air. "That was a mite too close."

Rising stiffly and straightening his legs, he massaged his neck as he sized up the new statue. "Well, he said he wanted to be reunited with his foot."

"Caw!"

Grip flapped his wings above them and descended on the statue. "It's over," he said, an eerie echo of the Commander's last words. He looked confused, tapping tentatively on his former master's head with his beak.

Gilroy gently reached a hand toward the bird. "There, there."

The raven remained still, allowing the conductor to remove the collar from his neck.

"Isn't he one of the bishop's creatures too?" asked Everett.

"Oh, no," said Gilroy. "He's been a prisoner of that blotter as well."

He shooed the bird away. "Off you go."

Grip took to the sky, looping once above them, then turning to the south and disappearing. As everyone watched him go, a loud clanging brought their sights back to the rooftop.

"Look out!" shouted Everett

Three more grappling hooks sailed up over the lip of the wall and pulled tight.

Gilroy limped away from them toward the far side of the roof. He took his pen, and with a few flicks of his wrist, he drew a rope ladder up to the unfinished bridge. Everyone except Bea moved toward it to climb up.

She looked at her lovebug fighting force. "We need one more thing from you. Can you slow down those blotters?"

"Bea," prodded Marcus, tugging her hand. "We have to go now."

As everyone hurried up the ladder, they saw Bea's final request being granted. A million blue pom-poms rolled to the edge of the building and over the side toward the climbers. Shrieks of fear and disgust rose from below as blotters dropped back to the ground, incapable of resisting the tidal wave of still-somewhat-pungent love bombs rushing down upon them.

67 Out on a Limb

Everyone regrouped inside the greenhouse to dry out. Marcus received enthusiastic handshakes and pats on the back from Jack, Dot, and Ronald.

"Do we need to get farther away from the blotters?" Everett asked Gilroy apprehensively.

The conductor smiled. "They got what they wanted. Besides—they don't know we're out of those wee little blue rascals."

"Well, we're not entirely out of them," Bea said, holding out her hand with the one lovebug she had claimed as her new pet.

Dot handed Marcus the bottle of Ink that had started it all. "I believe this belongs to you."

Marcus took it from her and looked at his children. "How on earth did you ever find me?"

Starting from the beginning, Everett and Bea took turns recounting every detail, from the arrival of Osgood and Ermengarde, to the dye hounds, to the train ride, to Kelpie.

"Oh! And the Cheering Up Pills!" said Bea. "You have to try them. I would give you one, but I ate them all."

Marcus smiled and squeezed his daughter. "Well, I feel pretty cheered up already, just being back with you." He held up the bottle. "Is it really true? Is the Ink all but gone?"

"There are no more wells in operation that we know of," said Jack. "I might have another pen or two tucked in a bureau drawer or wardrobe around the house. We will need to stretch this supply as far as we can."

"All isn't lost," said Gilroy, giving Everett a quick wink. "I wouldn't be surprised if we hear of more Ink being discovered in the near future."

"Dad, watch this. My sticks know how to find Ink." He took the bottle from Marcus and went to the door. He was about to set it down and walk across the greenhouse for a demonstration, when two men in dark suits appeared.

"Well, well."

It was Montbanks, with Mr. Lugg on his heels. Everett backed up a step, holding the Ink close. The men ignored him, focusing their intensity on Dot.

"We had an agreement, Sayers," said Eddie. "It seems you had no intention of keeping it."

Dot fell silent.

"Nothing to say? What about you, Jack? You accused me of being dishonest. Is breaking a promise your idea of honesty?"

Ronald jumped in to defend his friend. "Now, hang on a minute. Our motivation was nothing like yours. You—"

Eddie held up his hand. "Stop talking. It's time for you to learn that lies have consequences."

He snapped his fingers. Mr. Lugg stepped forward and cracked his knuckles while Eddie continued his speech. "My associate finds this part of his job extremely satisfying. I will give him five minutes with each of you until you hand over what is mine."

Eddie grabbed Dot by the arm. "All right, Sayers— ladies first."

"Wait."

Jack walked over and looked Eddie in the eye. "I will always find you despicable. But I will not become like you to fight you."

Jack turned to Everett, his shoulders slumped in resignation. "Give this man the bottle."

Everett could not believe his ears. After everything that had been done to keep the Ink away from this evil man, were they really going to hand it to him?

"We cannot abandon the right in the name of what's right," said Jack. "We gave him our word. A promise is a promise."

Eddie nodded his head and Mr. Lugg shifted his intimidating frame toward Everett.

Everett looked from one Inkling to the next. "You may have made a promise," he said, "but I didn't. "

With that, he slipped under the bodyguard's arm and out the door. The move caught everyone by surprise. Mr. Lugg recovered and darted out after him.

Everett ran blindly, with no plan. He could hear Mr. Lugg's boots punishing the ground behind him as the big man tried to catch up.

Everett rounded a bend in the path, and an ancient maple tree loomed in front of him. He tucked the Ink bottle under one arm, which made climbing a challenge. But he managed to scramble up from one limb to the next until he was high above the ground.

Mr. Lugg entered the clearing and looked around. Winded from the exertion, he placed his hands on his hips and inhaled rapidly.

His eyes followed the tree upward until he spotted Everett.

Mr. Lugg sighed and cursed under his breath. He removed his jacket, folded it neatly, and set it on a park bench. Then he rolled up his sleeves and began scaling the tree.

The abnormally large man moved swiftly upward, branches creaking in agony under his weight. Everett scurried farther up, hoping a man who was the size of a tree himself might think it unwise to climb the thinner branches.

Attempting to sound braver than he felt, he shouted down at the man, "I'll never give it to you."

"Then I guess I'll just have to take it."

Snapping limbs as if they were matchsticks, Mr. Lugg soon reached the branch where Everett was perched.

Everett crept out on the limb until it was dangerously slender beneath him, bowing under the strain. He made the mistake of looking down and instantly regretted it. The ground was a dizzying distance below him now.

The bodyguard was already sliding slowly along the branch toward him. He stretched out and caught Everett's shoe.

"Let go of me!" shouted Everett, wrapping his free arm around the branch and kicking his foot furiously.

"Give me that bottle!"

There was a loud crack as the branch broke. Mr. Lugg kept a crushing grip on his foot, suspending Everett upside down in the air.

"Hand me the Ink," he seethed, "or I swear I'll drop you!"

Everett didn't want to die. But after all that had happened, he wasn't about to let Eddie Montbanks have the last of the Ink.

He held the bottle tightly in his left hand. Then he strained upward and reached his right hand toward Mr. Lugg. "Help me up."

The bodyguard took Everett's hand and released his foot so Everett was hanging right side up below him. "I'm not lifting you any farther until you hand over that bottle," he growled.

Everett could read from the man's expression what was about to happen. He was going to drop him to his death regardless, once he had the Ink in his possession. Everett felt the stopper with his left hand.

Eddie arrived on the scene below and took in the drama unfolding in the canopy above. "Hurry up! The others are right behind me!"

Taking a deep breath, Everett lifted the bottle. He brought it to his mouth and bit the stopper, pulling it free with his teeth.

Eddie practically squealed in horrified shock. "What are you doing?"

Everett spit the stopper to the ground defiantly. Then in one motion, he raised the bottle to his lips. He tipped back his head.

And Everett drank all the Ink.

The veins on Mr. Lugg's neck bulged out as if they might burst right through his skin. He let out a war cry and flung Everett from the tree like a sack of potatoes.

As he sailed through the air, Everett had no time to panic. The only moment in his journey he remembered was the point at which he stopped flying upward and began plunging toward the ground.

68 Ink on the Inside

Being catapulted from a three-story tree is not conducive to a long life. And no safety expert would recommend swallowing a bottle of Ink as a way to survive.

Everett hadn't really been thinking that far ahead. All he knew was that the Ink was powerful, and he knew he didn't want the man in the tree to have it. So he drank it.

And then he was flung through the air toward certain death, crash-landing in a patch of heather. His body made a sickening crunch on impact, with all the air instantly forced from his lungs.

Over the past summer, Everett had gone swimming several times in the public pool near the vicarage. While he enjoyed jumping in and splashing around with his friends, his favorite thing to do was to lift his feet from the bottom of the pool, lean forward, hold his breath, and let his body go completely limp. There was something so peaceful about it. With only the water supporting him, he felt weightless and calm in the silence below the surface of the pool.

That was the closest comparison he could come up with to how he felt after drinking the Ink. When he hit the ground, it was as if he landed in a sea of liquid light. The Ink formed an invisible pool of pure relaxation where he felt weightless and unafraid.

At the same time, he could feel the Ink at work on his injuries. It wasn't exactly painful, but there was a sort of pressure, as if the Ink were pushing and stitching pieces of broken bones back together. At one point the skin on his chest and back became intensely warm, followed by a stab of freezing cold.

None of this was visible to Eddie Montbanks, who ran to where Everett landed, sure he must be dead.

Mr. Lugg climbed down from the tree and caught up to his employer, waiting to see what would happen.

"Sorry for killing him, boss."

Eddie didn't care about a possible murder. He was too upset that Everett drank the Ink. He had not anticipated that move. All his fortunes were disintegrating because of one stupid boy.

Everett's body lay completely still in the heather, clutching the cracked bottle in his lifeless grip. Through the glass, Eddie could see small traces of fluid still in the bottle.

He knelt and pried it from Everett's unresponsive fingers. "All right, kid. You're not gonna need this. You can let go now."

Just then, Everett sat up. Eddie fell backward in terror,

retreating like a crab with the bottle. Mr. Lugg stepped back too, disbelief registering on his face.

Anyone would have done the same had they seen Everett's eyes in that moment. They were now a glowing cobalt blue with an electrical storm brewing in the center.

Everett intended to yell at his attackers. What came out of his mouth was a deafening roar that was part thunder, part raging river.

Eddie scrambled to his feet and fled, with Mr. Lugg right behind him.

Everett wanted to chase them to get the bottle back, but his vocal display of power had taken everything out of his traumatized body. He sat on the ground, unable to move. Turning his head, he saw the somewhat hazy sight of his father, Bea, and the others all racing through the park toward him. And then he passed out.

Hospitals Aren't So Bad

69

Everett woke up to warm, peaceful sunlight streaming through an open window. He rolled over and took in his surroundings. He was dressed in his pajamas, lying in a clean, soft bed. But it wasn't his own bed; from the looks of things, he was in a very sterile hospital room.

"He's awake!"

Everett turned to see Trey sitting up in a bed next to his, grinning and looking back to his normal self.

Everett smiled back at him. "You're not blue!"

Marcus and Bea came bounding into the room, followed by Nurse Abbie. Bea threw herself on top of her brother, wrapping her arms around him and holding on tight.

"Easy now," said Nurse Abbie, picking up Everett's chart from the end of the bed. "He's still recuperating." She placed a hand on his forehead, her eyes full of concern.

"How long was I out?" Everett asked with a yawn.

"Three entire days!" said Bea.

Everett filled everyone in on the details he could remember before and after being thrown out of the tree. Marcus could barely contain his emotions as he listened to the story. He kept patting Everett's arm and squeezing his hand, unable to say anything.

"I never would have thought of drinking the Ink," said Trey. "That was brilliant."

"I don't know," said Everett. "Eddie Montbanks ended up with the bottle. There was still a little Ink left in it."

He shifted his attention to Trey. "Enough about me. I want to hear what happened to you."

Trey told Everett how Osgood had brought him back to London. It was no small feat to sneak a blue statue of a boy onto a military base without being questioned.

Convincing Nurse Abbie to get involved was another matter. But she had seen enough incredible results from using the pen to know there was more to the story.

Once Osgood had reversed the Inkasement surrounding Trey, Nurse Abbie set about using a combination of Ink and conventional medicine to treat his wounds. Trey's memory had returned almost immediately.

"It turns out I don't live in Newcastle anymore. I live in Aberdeen."

"That makes sense," said Everett. "You seemed to remember being there."

Trey continued. "A few weeks ago, my parents got nervous seeing so many blotters coming to town. For my own safety, they sent me back to Newcastle to visit my gran. I was angry at the blotters, which is why I went snooping around Hadrian's Well and got caught."

He shook his head. "I don't know what I was thinking."

"At least we got to meet you this way," said Bea.

Just then, a face peeked around the door. "I hear someone's awake."

"Gilroy!" Bea hopped off Everett's bed and ran to the conductor.

He gave her a big hug, beaming at Everett over her shoulder. "Welcome back, lad."

Then he said to Trey, "I've brought you some visitors."

An Indian man and redheaded woman came into the room, their faces a mixture of concern and excitement. They rushed to Trey and wrapped themselves over their son. There wasn't a dry eye in the room during the reunion.

Marcus studied the couple intently. "My mind is still a blur, but you look incredibly familiar."

Trey's father smiled. "We met only recently, sahib. The spice shop." He extended a hand. "Now we can exchange names. I'm Purushottam Thomachan. This is my wife, Margaret."

"I don't believe it!" Marcus turned to the others excitedly. "Trey's parents are the people who gave me the bottle of Ink."

Everett was stunned. He turned to Trey. "I thought you said they were musicians."

Margaret spoke up. "We are. The spice shop paid the bills and provided a cover."

She sighed sadly, looking at Marcus. "I fear we set off a terrible chain of events by giving you that bottle."

Gilroy shook his head. "We cannae go down that path. Besides, it was that bottle of Ink that saved your boy from a tragic end."

"And then Trey saved me," said Everett.

"And me!" Bea shouted.

Trey grinned broadly and wrapped an arm around each parent. "I'm just glad we're all here."

Nurse Abbie lifted Everett's wrist to check his pulse. "I hate to break up the party, but this young man is not quite as far along as his friend. He's going to need some rest."

"Can I go home soon?" Everett asked hopefully, looking at his father.

Marcus and Gilroy exchanged a look Everett couldn't quite read. Marcus took a deep breath. "Home is a little complicated right now . . ."

Back Home

The congregation of St. Francis had suffered through a great ordeal, and while they were elated to learn that their beloved vicar was alive, they were gravely concerned that the church and vicarage were in ruins with no funds to pay for their rebuilding after the arson.

There was also some confusion about the blue statue of Mrs. Crimp, although there was remarkably little curiosity shown as to where the real Isadora had gone.

Then an anonymous donor stepped forward to fund the entire reconstruction. What really happened was this: Gilroy called in a favor from Sir M., his builder-class Fomentori friend.

Sir M. replicated the original church and the vicarage entirely out of Ink, all in far less time than it would have taken to rebuild via conventional construction methods. Only an experienced eye could tell the difference from the original materials.

"No offense," Bea told Gilroy as she inspected the new

turret, "but his stairs look much better than the ones you drew."

"None taken," chuckled Gilroy. "And you'll be happy to know he used indelible Ink. No worries about it washing away in the rain!"

Nurse Abbie, Trey, and the Inklings all attended the official dedication ceremony for the new sanctuary and marveled at the construction. Afterward, the children gave Trey a guided tour of the vicarage. Bea repeated her trunk escape, which Trey appreciated with just the right amount of amazement.

Everett introduced Trey to his Max Courageous collection.

"These are incredible!" said Trey, turning the pages. He was immediately captivated by the daring exploits.

It made Everett happy to have a friend who shared his love of MC. He handed Trey a stack of comics. "You can borrow them if you want. I have them memorized."

There were hugs and tears all around as they said their goodbyes. Everyone agreed that one of the best uses of all their pens would be regular correspondence with one another.

"Aberdeen's not so far," said Bea. "Especially now that we know who works on the train!"

No words can describe how happy Bea and Everett were to have their family back together again. As the three of them sat down to breakfast each morning, Marcus would have the children retell different parts of their extraordinary adventure, never tiring of hearing how incredibly courageous and creative they had been. If you ever run across certain issues of Max Courageous, you might find a few of his exploits sounding vaguely familiar.

As for Mrs. Crimp, the children were dreading the day Osgood reversed her Inkasement. But they needn't have worried. Her time enveloped in the sheer goodness of Ink worked wonders for her personality. She emerged from her frozen state a softer woman, full of genuine affection for the entire Drake family. What's more, she seemed to be rather smitten with Osgood, much to the children's amusement.

"I wonder when that nice messenger will be back," she would say, pulling open the front curtain and staring wistfully out the window. It was all Bea and Everett could do to not laugh out loud at the thought of Osgood courting The Cramps.

Everett hoped Osgood *would* be back. He was ready for another adventure. At first he thought it was drinking the Ink that had changed him. But it was the entire experience that had made him feel like a new person.

One morning he woke with the realization that it had been weeks since he told himself there was something he *couldn't* do. He felt more confident, and at the same time less focused on himself. The world was bigger, and he found he was keenly interestED in whatever was coming next.

It occurred to him that maybe he didn't need to wait

for an adventure to come his way. Maybe couriers and conductors weren't necessary to start his own search for the next Inkwell. After all, he still had the sticks Gilroy had given him.

One day, sitting next to Bea up in the turret, Everett held the sticks and stared at them, reliving the most exciting moments from those few eventful days. He tapped them together and once again felt the surge of current shooting toward his shoulders.

As he stood up, they began to pull him forward, then down the stairs.

"Ev!" Bea popped up from her seat and ran to the top of the stairs. "Where are you going?"

"Out," was all he managed to reply. He barely heard her, his attention consumed by the movement of the sticks. She watched him descend the staircase, then raced back across the room. Moments later she bounded down the steps behind him, pulling a second arm through her sweater.

"Wait," called Bea, eyes shining as she raced down the stairs. "I'm coming with you."

Acknowledgments

It's been a joy to write this book, from start to finish. And that's saying something, because it has been a long process with multiple rounds of rewrites. Many, many people have had a direct influence on the final shape of it.

I'll start by giving a nod to all the industry professionals who ultimately declined to represent the book. Several of you took the time to give meaningful feedback that helped it eventually find a home. That was generous and gracious on your part. Special thanks goes to Sally Apokedak for seeing enough potential in an early draft to tell me plainly where it needed to be better.

I'm deeply indebted to my agent, Curtis Russell of P.S. Literary. Your brilliant editing and unflagging belief in this book deserve all the credit for it becoming a reality. Thanks for your steady hand on the wheel through the endlessly bumpy route to publication.

Thank you also to my editor Melinda Rathjen, along with Catherine Hoort, Kaitlin Mays, and everyone at Hachette/Worthy Kids, as well as my publicist, Nicole Banholzer. I can't tell you how humbling it has been to have such an incredible team love these characters as much as I do. What an honor to work with you all.

I must thank my posse of young test readers, many of whom are no longer that young. You're all Inklings in my book, and your enthusiasm for each iteration made it a delight to keep revisiting it.

Lastly, thank you to my entire family: I feel so rich and grateful for you and your encouragement all along the way. Kids, you're my joy. And Karin—what can I begin to say? This book is as much yours as it is mine. I love you. Thanks for celebrating every step of this journey with me and making my life immeasurably better.

Here's to the next adventure!

About the Author

J. D. Peabody has always loved stories, and his career has been spent improving his ability to write and tell them. *The Inkwell Chronicles: The Ink of Elspet* marks his first venture into children's literature. J.D. is a native of the Pacific Northwest, where he lives with his wife, who offsets the perpetually gray skies. Learn more about J.D. and his books at www.jdpeabody.com.